T0304996

Frankie

Frankie

Graham Norton

CORONET

First published in Great Britain in 2024 by Coronet
An imprint of Hodder & Stoughton Limited
An Hachette UK company

4

Copyright © Graham Norton 2024

A CIP catalogue record for this title is available from the British Library

Hardback ISBN 9781529391442
Trade Paperback ISBN 9781529391459
ebook ISBN 9781529391466

Typeset in Sabon MT by Palimpsest Book Production Ltd, Falkirk, Stirlingshire

Printed and bound in Great Britain by Clays Ltd, Elcograf S.p.A.

Hodder & Stoughton policy is to use papers that are natural, renewable and recyclable
products and made from wood grown in sustainable forests. The logging and manufacturing
processes are expected to conform to the environmental regulations of the country of origin.

Hodder & Stoughton Limited
Carmelite House
50 Victoria Embankment
London EC4Y 0DZ

The authorised representative in the EEA is Hachette Ireland, 8 Castlecourt Centre,
Castleknock Road, Castleknock, Dublin 15, D15 YF6A, Ireland

www.hodder.co.uk

For Bailey, Madge and Douglas – the best.

Life . . . [is] a lament in one ear, maybe, but always a song in the other.

Seán O'Casey

Everyone cared. Damian understood that. Everyone aspired to, or at the very least pretended to care, but he was different. He was an actual carer. It was his job and he knew that he was good at it. He still bristled when people asked him what he really wanted to do, or his mother on the phone wondered if he'd like to go back to college – *Maureen Collins didn't do as well as you in the Leaving Cert and she got into law.* True, it had never been his dream job, but if he enjoyed it and it paid his bills then what more was there? It turned out that looking after wealthy old people in their large west London homes suited him. In his mind all the houses and flats blended together into a faded autumnal blur of thick carpets and gilt-framed paintings. The work itself was relatively easy, especially as he normally chose the creaking floors of night shifts. Some pill-giving and pillow-wrangling and then he could just read or watch films on his laptop. Come morning, if he had the time – and he usually did – he liked to head home on the bus and watch the city coming to life. So many people with things to do and places they needed to be. He imagined the cramped flats they had left, and would go back to, compared to the high-ceilinged spacious rooms he had spent the last twelve hours in. It wasn't fair, of course it wasn't, but equally he doubted anyone taking the tube escalator two steps at a time would envy the people he cared for, their skin like veined wax, the pain of night cramps making them scream out, crusty deposits in the corners of their mouths. At least they had Damian. To not feel abandoned and alone in the dark of the night seemed like such a simple human need, but the elderly people Damian cared for had to pay Hamilton Homecare handsomely for the privilege.

The bus shuddered and jolted its way slowly across London, heading back to the small terraced house in Shadwell that he shared with two permanently out-of-work actors. Damian leaned his head against the window, wondering if there'd be enough milk when he got home. A large poster on Tottenham Court Road reminded him that he wanted to upgrade his phone, and then, as the bus idled in traffic near Aldgate, he thought about work. There was something unusual about his new client. Even after nearly two years, that word still felt so awkward to Damian – a *client* always seemed to suggest someone looking for advice on the most tax-efficient way to transfer foreign currency, not someone slumped on a toilet waiting to be rescued. His manager, Nadine, had sounded brighter than usual when she had called.

'You live east, right?'

'Yes,' Damian replied warily.

'Well Wapping is east, isn't it?'

'Yeah, it's just below me. Why?'

'New client. She lives in Wapping. Frances Howe, eighty-four. Lives alone. Broken ankle. I'll text you the address.'

'How do I get in?'

'Her friend will be there. Seven p.m. Don't be late, Damian.' A warning. There had been complaints in the past.

'Why doesn't her friend—'

'Do you want to work, Damian? And she's Irish so that'll be nice for you. Seven o'clock.' Nadine hung up without waiting for a response.

Damian was intrigued but also slightly irked. It annoyed him when Irish people were just lumped together. It reminded him of the way straight friends proudly announced the existence of their other gay friend. 'You've got to meet him. You'll love him.' As if their sexuality reduced them to dogs on a playdate in the park. He failed to see how any amount of Irishness would give him something in common with an incapacitated eighty-four-year-old woman. What interested him more was that she lived in Wapping. He didn't know the area well but it seemed unlikely that anyone of the age and means to use Hamilton Homecare would choose to live there.

Shadwell, where Damian and the actors lived in a tiny worker's cottage, was only separated from Wapping by the Highway, a wide road that was constantly busy with traffic heading out to Canary Wharf and the mysteries of whatever was to the east of that. Damian had not been very adventurous in his eight years of London life. His first two decades on Earth had been spent surrounded by the fields of West Cork, and he couldn't say that he had missed them very much, if at all, since he'd left Ireland. His life now was a strictly zones one and two affair.

Damian had never felt much inclination to explore Wapping. He'd made occasional forays into its little cobbled streets to have a drink in one of the ancient pubs that still managed to cling to the river despite the gentrification. The old brick warehouses were now all homes for wealthy young bankers and lawyers. If he ventured west, taking the scenic route to Tower Hill tube station, he'd pass through St Katharine Docks with its yachts and cafés, dwarfed by the drama of Tower Bridge. Damian had imagined that Frances Howe might live at that end of Wapping, where the trees were leafier and the cars shinier, but Google Maps disagreed. It led him to the edge of a plain little park about halfway between the Highway and the Thames. Damian stopped and looked up. 'Cleaver Buildings 1864' was engraved on a weather-worn stone plaque. Four storeys high, the building stood awkward and alone. Clearly it was a survivor, its neighbours having been demolished or perhaps bombed during the war. The whole place had an air of neglected romance. Sash windows, large and bright, sat in the yellow brick walls that surrounded stairwells and walk-ways painted in a dark red, but what made the building really appealing were the ornate railings that ran along each floor. It was what Damian imagined New Orleans might look like. There seemed to be two front doors on each landing. Some had bikes leaning outside, while others had planters of flowers. It was too old to be a council block, so Damian assumed it belonged to a housing trust. It remained unclear to him how an old lady who lived here could afford private homecare.

The evening felt mild, a premature hint of spring in the air. From the nearby park came a cheerful cacophony of dogs and children. Damian pushed open the metal gate and headed to the stairs; number four was at the far end of the landing on the second floor and had neither bike nor flowers. The windows were clean and the door looked recently painted. No bell. He knocked and the door opened immediately – clearly, he was expected. Damian was greeted by an elderly lady with short, suspiciously dark hair. She was tall and stylish in a slightly bohemian way. Strings of multicoloured beads cascaded down her mannish white shirt, which she wore over a pair of brightly patterned loose trousers. Her mouth was a smear of red lipstick.

'Damian?' She smiled and extended a hand for a brisk, firm handshake, setting off a jangle of bangles.

'Yes. Nice to meet you.'

'Nor. Nor Forrester. I'm Frankie's friend.' As she spoke, she turned and walked into the gloomy interior. Damian followed, closing the door behind him. 'Here she is!' Nor was standing in what had once been a spacious room but was now completely filled with oversized pieces of furniture. Damian stepped forward. A dark wooden dining table was pushed against the wall under the window opposite a faded velvet chesterfield sofa, so large that Damian couldn't help wondering how it had been brought into the room. Perched on a high-backed wing chair beside a cabinet of glassware was the person Nor had pointed to.

'This is Frankie!' Her voice seemed too loud, her cheerfulness forced. 'Frankie, this is Damian.'

The old lady in the chair looked at him. She did not seem to be overly impressed. She nodded.

'Nice to meet you,' Damian said as he took off his light backpack, then the three of them all waited for each other to speak.

Frankie looked older than Nor. Her hair was grey and swept to one side with a black clasp. Her face was drawn and make-up free. On a small stool she rested her left foot encased in plaster.

'Frankie had a bad fall.'

Frankie's pale grey eyes darted to her friend.

'I didn't have a fall. I fell. I tripped. The end. Stop saying I "had a fall".' Her voice was a light rasp, as if she needed a drink of water.

'Well, we don't want you to have another one and that's why young Damian is here.' Nor turned to him. 'I have to run, but let me show you around.' She pushed past him into the cramped square hallway. 'Kitchen in there, bathroom . . .' She pointed at the doors to the right. 'And this is your room.' She opened a door to a small narrow space containing a single bed. Damian peered in and saw the walls were hung with mismatched paintings and photographs. Most of the dark carpet was covered with cardboard boxes.

'More of a storeroom really, but you can keep your bag in here and I suppose lie down?' She seemed uncertain of how Damian might spend his night.

'Perfect.' He put his backpack on the bed.

Nor grabbed his arm and lowered her voice to a whisper. 'Apologies in advance. She's not herself. Very cranky after the fall. I don't blame her, of course, but she needs help – not that she'd admit it. She has crutches, but this flat is like an assault course. If you make her tea and toast in the morning, I'll pop in to check on her before lunch.' Without really pausing, she raised her voice again. 'Well, that's me for the off. Be good, Frankie. I'll see you tomorrow.' All of this was announced from the hall. At the door she retrieved a large Daunt Books tote bag that was on the floor. Plunging her hand into it, she pulled out a set of keys.

'For you.' She handed them to Damian. 'Good luck.' She raised her eyebrows to suggest that he might need it. Then, with a rattle of beads and a clank of the knocker, she was gone.

This was always the awkward bit. That strange beginning when patient and carer tried to assess who they were dealing with, while also attempting to assert their specific role in the arrangement. Damian took a deep breath and dived in.

'Now, Frankie, would you have a cup of tea?'

The suggestion seemed to make her sadder than she already was.

'I would.' Her voice was quieter now, barely even a whisper.

'Milk? Sugar?' Damian paused by the door to the kitchen.

Frankie squinted as if she didn't quite understand, but then came the soft reply. 'Black. Half a teaspoon of honey. It's just by the kettle.'

The kitchen was small but very well stocked and organised. Uniform bottles of dried herbs and spices filled some open shelves by the cooker, while fresh herbs flourished in pots on the window-sill. Woks and pans hung from hooks in the ceiling and a wide selection of what looked like expensive oils and vinegars were pressed together on the countertop.

'You're a cook, Frankie?' Damian called through the open door. The old woman didn't reply at once but then, in a voice that was surprisingly loud and firm, she announced, 'Yes, I cook.' Her tone suggested she did not want this to be the start of a conversation.

Damian rolled his eyes. This was going to be a long night. He hoped she went to bed early.

He turned on the kettle and found two clean mugs. He noticed the honey was French and the label handwritten.

'Where do you keep the tea bags, Frankie?' He kept his voice bright and positive.

'There aren't any. Loose tea is in the green caddy.'

Damian wished he had never suggested tea. Who didn't use tea bags? Even his granny had moved on and she still made her own soda bread.

'It's there.' Frankie's voice was so loud in his ear, Damian let out a small shriek. The old woman was in the doorway, swaying on her crutches.

'Away and sit down, Frankie. I'm here so you can rest.' He gestured back towards the living room and her chair.

Ignoring him, Frankie continued, 'Be sure to warm the pot. Then three teaspoons will be enough. One for each of us and one for the pot. It's quite strong, Assam. Do you like Assam?'

Damian stared blankly at her. He liked tea. Did that count?

'I'm sure it'll be lovely.'

'I used to get it from a little shop in Covent Garden but of course that's closed down now. Nor picks it up for me from Harrods.' She nodded towards the branded metal caddy. 'Please don't think I'm throwing my money away in that place.'

Damian wondered if it was Nor Forrester who was paying his wages.

'You go away in and sit down. I've got this.'

Her expression was unnerving. Her pale eyes suggested she doubted that he had *got this*, or indeed got anything at all. Nevertheless, she did as she was told and slowly hopped back into the living room. 'Use the tray,' she barked.

Once the tea was brewed, Damian sat at the dining table with his mug. Frankie sipped hers without comment, which Damian took to mean she approved.

'It smells so lovely in here.'

'Peach oil.'

'Oh.' Damian was no wiser.

'You dab it on the lightbulbs. You never heard of that?'

He shook his head. 'No, no, that's a new one on me.'

A moment of silence as they both enjoyed their tea and then Damian tried again.

'You still have the accent. Light like, but you can hear it all the same. Whereabouts are you from?'

'Originally just west of Ballytoor in County Cork.' She delivered this information as if replying to an enquiry from a policeman.

Damian had met this type before and felt quietly confident he could crack her. He pounced.

'Ballytoor? Sure, I know it well. I'm only from Mallow. My sister married a fellow from Stranach just beyond Ballytoor. Do you know it?'

Frankie's head snapped towards Damian. Apparently she did.

'Mmm, I do. Yes. I do.' Her eyes drifted to the window for a moment and then she raised herself in the chair. 'Would you put on the television there? The news channel. The BBC one, I can't stand that Sky lot – and make sure the subtitles are on. They mumble. The whole lot of them.'

Damian did as he was told and then cleared away the tea. When he had washed and dried the mugs, he stepped back into the living room.

'I'll be in my room if you need me, Frankie.'

'Right. Thank you.' The old woman waved him away and then her hand went to her face. Was she wiping away tears? Damian wasn't sure.

About an hour later, Instagram stories were beginning to repeat themselves when Damian heard Frankie moving around. He went to the door to check on her.

'Do you need anything?'

'No. No. I'm just going to get ready for bed. It'll take me a while,' she told him as she worked her crutches in the direction of the bathroom.

'Let me help you.'

'No,' her voice sharp. 'No, thank you.' A milder tone. 'I can do everything myself. Except my sock. I'll need you to get that off.'

'OK.' He waited, ready to assist.

'I'll shout when I need you.' The bathroom door shut.

Damian wandered into the living room and watched some reporter standing by the side of the road talking about floods. His eyes moved around the room. Paperbacks were stacked in haphazard piles on the floor and the walls were covered in a similar patchwork to the one he had found in his room. He didn't know much about art, but these didn't look like the pictures he normally saw in the homes of old people. These seemed too modern. Abstract and messy, some bright and geometric, others more like pale scribbles, they didn't seem to fit with the old heavy furniture or indeed the small neat woman who was currently in the bathroom. Maybe a dead husband had collected them. Damian was fairly certain these pictures were not all by the same artist. Had she inherited them from a relative? He stored his questions away as kindling for the chat he was determined to have. He saw it as a matter of professional pride to get this old lady to allow him into her life.

Frankie's bedroom was unexpected. If anything, it was even smaller than the one Damian had been given and what should have been the window was completely blocked up with precarious towers of books. The only light came from the bedside lamp, which shared its plinth with more books and an array of pill bottles. Frankie sat on the bed wearing a long-sleeved baby blue nightdress. The thin shiny ribbon around the neck made Damian guess it had been a gift. He very much doubted Frankie had gone into a shop and chosen it. He looked up at his charge from where he was crouched on his knees peeling off her one sock. He rolled it into a ball, then, examining Frankie's feet, asked, 'Would you like to me to cut your toenails for you?'

'No!' She sounded shocked by the very suggestion and quickly pulled her legs up and under the covers.

'OK. Well, if you change your mind . . .' A smile; his same calm, even tone.

Frankie reached for a book and then, as if remembering there was someone else in the room, said, 'Watch the television if you want. It won't bother me in here.'

'Right.' He stood to leave her. 'And what time would you like your tea and toast in the morning?'

Her brow creased. 'Sure, I can do that. Don't worry.'

'Frankie, come on, I'm being paid. Let me do something for you.'

A sigh. She opened her book without looking at him. 'Around seven thirty. And use the unsalted butter. Just a smear of marmalade.'

'Will do. Good night. Sleep well.' He began to slowly close her door.

'Please.'

He stepped forward. 'What was that?'

'Please. For the toast. I forgot to say please.'

'You're very welcome.' He made sure the door was closed before he allowed the smile to spread across his face.

Ireland, 1950

Happiness was not to be trusted. This was a lesson that Frances Howe had learned at a very young age. Eleven, in fact. No, she was ten, about to turn eleven, because she had been at Catherine Woodworth's birthday party and Catherine was the first in her class to leave the childish ways of ten behind. For the girls, the idea of turning eleven had become confused with how wealthy Catherine's father was. This was a party unlike any they had attended before. The function room of Langton's Hotel had been hired for the occasion. There had been little pastry pots stuffed with chicken in a sauce, and on the way out each child had been handed a party bag with a pencil and a bag of sherbet. Eleven seemed to be a world of untold sophistication.

When the party had finished at six, Frances gathered in the lobby with her friend Norah Dean, along with three other girls that Norah Dean's father had agreed to give a lift home. While the others chattered excitedly to Mr Dean about the fizzy drinks that had been served by actual waiters, Frances had sat quietly in the back seat, her head leaning against the window. This was what happy felt like. The whole afternoon it had seemed like she was finally in time with the music. She was looking forward to telling her parents what a good girl she had been; it seemed that being nearly eleven was having an effect on her. She hadn't just rammed her mouth with the sweet little butterfly buns, but had made sure to eat two boring sandwiches first. A napkin had been picked up and used. Remembering what her mother had told her, Frances hadn't been overly physical in her desire to win at musical chairs, and, despite knowing that there was a snow globe lurking under all the layers of gift wrapping, she hadn't held on to the parcel for too long as it was being passed around. In her mind's eye, she could see her parents smiling at her and telling her what a fine young lady she was growing up to be.

When Mr Dean pulled the car into her home's short driveway, hidden from the road by heavy pine trees, they found the Howes' house in darkness.

'Are your mammy and daddy here, Frances?'

She hesitated. It didn't seem as if they were. Her father's car wasn't in its usual place. At the same time she knew it would be wrong to inconvenience Mr Dean.

'They'll be around the back, in the kitchen.'

Mr Dean was opening the back door of the car. 'Are you sure?'

'Yes, thank you Mr Dean.' She smiled, pleased that she had remembered to thank the grown-up, and jumped from her seat. 'Bye,' she said with a wave to her friend Norah and headed towards the back door. The headlights of the car swung past her, and suddenly it seemed very dark and quiet.

The door was unlocked as Frances knew it would be, but the house was empty.

'Hello,' she called into the hallway. The only reply came from the clock that continued to tick and tock on the wall by the cooker. Her footsteps sounded oddly amplified as she crossed the room and switched on the light. The brightness made everything seem better, or at least closer to normal. Her parents would be home soon. The wire cooling rack was still on the table, from when Frances and her mammy had been baking that very morning. She'd been allowed to stir the cake mixture and then lick the spoon. It was strange to be in the kitchen without the heat of the oven, the warmth of her mother; Frances pulled a chair out from the kitchen table and sat down to wait.

Later, when people told her story for her, she learned that she had waited for over two hours. She had no idea afterwards what she had done during that time. She hadn't got a book, or used her colouring pencils. She hadn't even climbed up to open the biscuit tin. Frances assumed she had just sat still like a good little girl because bad things didn't happen to good little girls.

She remembered hearing the car engine and seeing the headlights fill the hallway through the glass panels of the front door. She had tried to feel happy her parents were home but she knew that something didn't feel right. Cars all sounded like cars but this one did not sound like her daddy's. Then the dull thud of the door knocker echoing through the house. How could that sound ever augur good news?

Frances walked slowly down the hall as if she knew that, once she reached the door, nothing would be the same again. The violent banging of the knocker came once more. 'Hello?' The muffled sound of a man's voice.

'Hello,' Frances replied.

'Hello.' The man's voice had changed. It was soft and lilting, the way lots of grown-up men talked to little girls. 'Can you open the door for me there, love?'

Frances looked up at the lock.

'I can't reach it.'

'Right. Right.' A pause. 'Is there a door you can open?'

Frances thought about the back door and suddenly panicked. This man could just walk in.

'Who are you?'

'It's the guards, pet. We need to talk to you.'

Frances considered this. The man did sound like a policeman.

'The back door.'

'Great. Great.' She heard footsteps on the gravel and the man's voice repeating 'back door' to an unknown companion.

The comforting familiarity of the kitchen was abruptly overwhelmed by the appearance of two Gardaí. All Frances could see were dark suits and caps. They seemed to fill the whole room so she waited by the door. The older guard with a wide red face spotted her.

'Hello, pet. Will you come and have a sit-down?' It was the voice from behind the door. He patted a chair by the table.

'Where are my mammy and daddy?' The answer to this question had to be why these men were standing in the kitchen.

The policemen looked at each other. They had perhaps not been expecting Frances to be so direct. The younger guard took a great interest in the floor, while the senior officer licked his lips.

'Is your name Frances?' he asked.

'Yes. What's happened to Mammy and Daddy?' Her voice sounded strangled, as if squeezed from her by the invisible grip that was holding her little body rigid.

'There's been an accident, Frances, so we don't want you to be here by yourself.' He paused to assess how this news was being received.

'Are they all right? Where are they?' Frances could feel everything falling away. This was beyond her worst nightmares. What was there in the world if her parents had ceased to be?

'They're in the hospital, pet. The doctors are looking after them.' The guard knelt on one knee, his hand resting on the table. 'Now is there anyone who can mind you for a little bit? A granny maybe, a neighbour?' His face was too close to hers. She saw the dark hairs in his nostrils, the yellow of his teeth. Frances tried to speak but found she couldn't. Her whole body had seized up and begun to vibrate. All she wanted was her parents but she had no idea how she could reach them. She squeezed her eyes shut. They would come to her. She would open her eyes and they would appear. But they didn't. There was just the guard staring at her, and then looking back at his colleague.

'I want my mammy and daddy,' she managed to say in a series of gasps and then, as if the singular and profound truth of this statement had released her, Frances Howe sank to the floor and began to sob.

Her parents were dead. They might have been heading to the hospital, but only to its morgue. A coroner would confirm what the guards at the Howes' house already knew: Frances's parents had drowned. It had been a freak accident. Their car on a pier, late afternoon. They had been enjoying the view, or perhaps they had been waiting to buy fish from a returning trawler. What had happened next was unclear. It could have been that the brakes had failed, or had Frances's father thought the car was in reverse when he pressed the accelerator? Whatever the cause, witnesses had seen the car shoot off the end of the pier and disappear almost at once beneath the surface of the water. A couple of lads had run down from the road and dived in, but it was useless. The water too deep, the visibility too poor; the men dived and dived again until they knew it was too late to help, then they climbed the metal ladder on the side of the pier to be comforted by the small crowd that always seems to gather from nowhere at such times.

It hadn't taken long for rumours to start. It had been a bad death. Money problems. The poor little girl. How could they leave her? people had asked. At least they didn't bring her with them, others had replied. True, true enough. A tiny sliver of silver in the darkest of linings. Later, much later, Frances would hear these rumours. Girls at school testing her, trying to give themselves some currency in the vicious classroom jungle they were all trying to survive. She refused to believe them. Her parents had loved her too much to ever choose to leave. The whole thing had been the Lord's doing and, as people never seemed to tire of reminding her, He worked in mysterious ways.

The Gardaí had taken their sobbing charge to the rectory. Frances's mother had a sister, who was married to a Church of Ireland minister, the Reverend Derek Roper. However, despite living in the same town, Frances hardly knew her aunt and uncle. When her mammy and daddy talked about them, her Aunt Mona was usually referred to as 'Poor Mona', and if they were all in a room together Frances noticed that, while the sisters chatted, the men had very little to say. Her aunt whisked her away from the policemen, wrapped her in a blanket and held her while the two of them wept. Crying with someone else had been a strange sort of comfort, especially because that person looked so like the mother she had lost, the same brown hair framing her soft features, the same warm bosom to cradle her head. Frances had only been vaguely aware of her uncle standing to one side of the fireplace, saying prayers. Derek Roper did not resemble her father. His skin seemed too tight, forcing his knuckles, ears and chin to protrude like knots on a tree. His faith appeared to be sincere but sharing it with others had never been his strong suit. He performed his pastoral duties the way he had been taught at ecclesiastical college, but there was never an ease or a humanity about him. Being a spiritual shepherd would have suited him much better had there not been an actual flock involved.

For the first few weeks after her parents' funeral, Frances felt as if she was something to be watched, like a pot on the stove that might boil over, or a bath being filled. Her Aunt Mona slept in her room and there was no talk of her returning to school.

Her aunt and uncle took it in turns to teach her various subjects at the large pine table in the kitchen of the rectory.

Months passed and little by little Frances knew that her emotions had shifted. Things weren't better, that was impossible, but she didn't cry as much. A new normal had been established. Her aunt left her to sleep alone and her days were filled with helping around the house or doing her lessons. It was made clear to Frances that raising the subject of her parents was not to be encouraged. When she had asked if she could bake a cake like her mammy had shown her, her aunt had patted her hand and urged her 'not to upset yourself'. At the rectory, food was not something that provided comfort or even pleasure. Aunt Mona believed the only good potato was a boiled one; not for the Ropers the indulgence of buttery mash or a cheesy gratin, like Frances's mother had made. Baking was not about chocolatey treats, just scones or a dry sponge cake for a church sale.

The first time they had driven past her old house, she had cried out with shock and surprise. The tall, dark pine trees were gone and the house looked smaller. Frances didn't like it. The cosy home of her memory was no more. This one seemed bare and anaemic; vulnerable, somehow.

'Now, Frances, that's not your home any more. Another family lives there, because you have a lovely new home with us.' Her uncle, behind the steering wheel, began to speak using his church voice. 'For every house is builded by some man; but he that built all things is God.'

Frances wondered if she would ever return to school. Over one of her kitchen table lessons, she asked her aunt and Mona explained, 'Your uncle doesn't think you're quite ready. Maybe some of your friends could come and visit?'

Frances liked this idea. She remembered girls from her class coming to play at her old house. Her mammy would bake treats and let them try on her clothes. It wasn't like that with Aunt Mona.

'Norah is here to play with you,' would be announced from the bottom of the stairs and the girls would be dispatched to Frances's room where they sat awkwardly, trying to remember what they had ever talked about. Frances tried and failed to think of questions she could ask about their teacher or other girls in their class. Time did not fly.

'Thank you, Mrs Roper,' the girls chorused as they almost ran from the front door to a waiting parent, not even attempting to disguise their relief at making an escape.

One Friday evening before dinner, Frances was summoned to her uncle's study. Friday afternoon was when he wrote his sermons and his desk was piled with thick, uninviting books. Her aunt sat on a small velvet chair to one side. Outside, the sun was still shining, but all three of them sat in dusty gloom.

'Frances,' the reverend Roper pressed his hands together as if to pray. 'Your aunt and I have spoken and prayed, and the Lord in his wisdom and mercy has chosen us to be your guardians.' He paused. He always spoke in slow and steady bursts, as if he was preaching to slightly simple sinners. 'Do you understand what that means?'

Frances swallowed. 'I think so.'

Reverend Roper glanced at his wife. Mona gave an uncertain smile. 'You will live here with us,' he continued, 'and we will care for you as if you were our own. Our heavenly Father has sent you to us and we must do our Christian duty.' He nodded as if agreeing with himself. Clearing his throat, he looked at his niece. 'Do you have anything you'd like to say, Frances?' He cocked his head to one side. It seemed he was expecting her to speak.

She had so much she wanted to ask, things she longed to know. Why had the heavenly Father sent her here? Why had he *gathered in* her mammy and daddy?

'Thank you,' she said quietly.

Her uncle smiled and slowly closed his eyes. 'Let us pray.'

Frances bowed her head and listened to her uncle asking the merciful Lord to bless the house and those that lived in it. What she couldn't understand was why Uncle Derek was still asking this man for anything. Merciful? It had been made very clear to her that this Father in Heaven was anything but. Why should she ever expect anything good from him again when he had chosen to do something so catastrophically cruel? She dug her nails into the palms of her hands.

'Amen.'

'Amen,' Frances and her Aunt Mona repeated.

Amongst the parishioners of St Ann's there was a general consensus that granting the Ropers a child of their own must have been one of the *mysterious ways* the great Redeemer had in mind when he had plucked the Howes from the pier. To many, having a childless rector felt like there was a thin veil of sadness draped over the whole parish. Hard to rejoice when the Lord had not blessed his minister with the greatest gift he could bestow. Little Frances Howe holding her aunt's hand as they made their way to their pew at the front of the church on a Sunday morning gladdened the hearts of the congregation. Barren no more.

At the end of their first summer together, it was decided that Frances would not return to primary school. Instead, she would start secondary school a year early. Ballytoor had a grammar school that catered for the Church of Ireland community from the surrounding area and, since the reverend Roper was on the board of governors and an occasional teacher at the school, it made sense for Frances to attend. He spoke to the headmaster and everything was arranged. When the news was delivered to Frances, it was just another dark shadow cast across her new life. While it might have been a relief not to be hidden away all day with her Aunt Mona, the thought of entering a classroom where she knew no one was terrifying. How welcome then was the news that her friend Norah Dean was skipping her last year at primary school too?

What had been mere friendship became something more. They literally clung to one another in the unfamiliar world of the grammar school. The two girls held hands as they tried to navigate their way from one classroom to the next. They sat beside each other and either walked home together or shared the back seat of the car when Norah's father happened to give them a lift. Mr Dean was especially kind to Frances. He had always felt guilty for being the one who had left the little girl alone outside the darkened house that day. Lifts to and from school with Reverend Roper were a very rare occurrence, and that was perfectly fine with Frances. She dreaded sitting with Norah while her uncle asked pointless questions about the Old Testament or quizzed them on Bible verses. She didn't want her friend to be exposed to the full dreariness of her life at the rectory.

It soon became apparent that Norah was more suited to secondary school. She found the lessons easier than Frances and she quickly established herself as a superior hockey player, while Frances lurked on the sidelines with her stick, hoping the ball never made its way anywhere near her. Other girls sought out Norah in the lunch queue and after school they sometimes walked home with the two younger girls. Frances reluctantly prepared herself for losing her only friend. In the dining hall she glanced across at the table she feared she would be relegated to, containing a group of girls with greasy hair who wore hand-knitted school jumpers.

She felt herself about to land on the bottom rung of the social ladder. But that wasn't what happened.

Norah and her parents, perhaps sensing that the rectory was not the easiest place for a young girl, began to include Frances in their lives. She was often invited to stay over, and at weekends, when the family went on trips or excursions, Frances was often with them. Norah had two brothers, but they were older, so Frances became like the unofficial sister Norah had always craved. The Ropers were happy to encourage this new development; the Deans were churchgoers and it was assumed these invitations were made out of pity or a sense of charity. At first Frances had thought the same, but it never felt like that. Being with the Dean family was easy and fun, in contrast to the way things at the rectory were stiff and awkward. Besides, it wasn't as if Frances was holding Norah back. She was on every sports team and socialised with other more popular girls. Frances didn't mind because she always came back to her.

It was Norah's mother who guided Frances through puberty and showed her how to use pads and the thin belt.

'Now, when you get home, explain to your aunt that you've started . . . that you're a woman now, and she'll make sure you've everything you need.'

Frances must have looked stricken because Mrs Dean just laughed and stroked her hair in a way that suggested she was still very much a little girl and not a woman at all.

That evening, when Norah's mother had dropped Frances back at the rectory, she had stepped into the kitchen to have a whispered conversation with Aunt Mona. After that, boxes of pads would just appear in her bedroom.

Norah had developed faster than Frances and the two of them studied Norah's breasts, wondering how big they might become. With Norah's encouragement Frances would squeeze them and then the two girls would roll on the floor laughing. Before long, Frances began to develop too, and this time her Aunt Mona was the one who suggested they go shopping for undergarments. Standing at the sink with her back to Frances, she explained, 'Your Uncle Derek thinks you look obscene and I have to agree. It's not nice, so it's time to get you fitted for a brassiere.'

Frances didn't think she was capable of being more embarrassed, but then that afternoon old Mrs Lane had pushed her into a dressing room at the back of A La Mode on Weir Street, practically torn the school blouse off her and began cupping her breasts. 'I was mortified,' she exclaimed to Norah later. 'All I could do was look at the hairy mole beside her lip. I thought I was going to be sick.'

Frances had scanned the headless mannequins hopefully. They were all wearing bras edged with pretty pieces of lace, like the ones Norah wore, but Frances had walked out of A La Mode with a paper bag containing two sturdy bras the colour of tinned rice pudding. Frances would have struggled to define precisely what *sexy* meant, but she was certain that her new underwear was not it.

Boys changed, or maybe it was just the way that she and Norah thought about them. Up until that point in her life, Frances had either feared or ignored them, but, as they began to look at her differently, so her own gaze was altered. They were still frightening, with their loud voices and sudden scuffles, but some of them, the boys in sixth year mostly, were also . . . interesting? Appealing? Frances wasn't sure. All she knew was that it gave her a delicious thrill when she thought that one of them noticed her. She became more aware of the way she parted her hair; she made sure her knee-socks never ended up pooled above her ankles. She took little dabs from Mrs Dean's bottle of Shalimar.

Of course, Norah got more attention from the boys. She wore her short hockey skirts around the school more than Frances felt was strictly necessary. Boys would offer to carry Norah's heavy school bag home for her and she let them. Frances would walk behind them, bent over with her own satchel of books. She felt like the drawing of Sancho Panza that was on the cover of *Don Quixote* in the school library. Once more she resigned herself to losing her friend, but yet again Norah proved herself to be fiercely loyal. It was as if Norah only entertained the boys so that the two girls could laugh about them afterwards.

'He thought Heathcliff was a place!'

'The cheek of him trying to hold my hand. Fingers like sweaty sausages!'

They howled at the cluelessness of boys and yet Frances still found herself staring at the dark hair above Roger Bailey's upper lip, wondering what it might feel like to touch his wide back. She never shared these fantasies with Norah because it would have felt disloyal. They had each other, and that was all that mattered.

In their fifth year, some of the girls began to be allowed to attend socials, small dances organised exclusively for Church of Ireland young people. It had never been overtly explained, but Frances presumed the socials were held so that Protestants could meet, marry and produce babies to be used like sandbags against the constant spring tide of Roman Catholic births. The dances were heavily chaperoned and always involved some element of supper with tea and sandwiches. The venues moved around the parishes of West Cork, but at the end of November a church social was to be held in St Ann's parish hall in Ballytoor.

This dance became the focus of the girls' lives. They practised their steps to Norah's only Bill Haley record, laughing and sweating in front of the sofa, even though they were certain it was more likely to be Ruby Murray and Dean Martin songs that the band would play. They discussed outfits, which consisted largely of Norah volunteering what she was willing to lend Frances. All the talk was fun, but deep down it seemed doubtful that her aunt and uncle would ever give permission for Frances to attend. Norah dismissed her fears: 'Of course they'll let you go. It's a church thing. Just ask them,' and Norah's confidence gave Frances courage. She tried her aunt, whose instant response had been, 'Ask your uncle.' Frances doubted that she had even heard the question. She stood in the hall, unsure of what she should do. 'Well, ask him!' Aunt Mona urged her impatiently and directed Frances towards the study door.

'Come in.'

The door creaked open and Frances stepped into the darkness. Her uncle sat behind his desk, peering above his half-glasses.

'Well?' His voice made Frances regret her plan at once.

'I was wondering . . .' She cleared her throat and started again, hoping to sound more confident, 'I was just wondering if I could go to the social next Friday. Aunt Mona said to ask you.'

Her uncle's eyebrows arched with surprise. He had evidently not been expecting this request.

'The dance?' he asked for clarification.

'Yes.' Frances would have liked to hold on to a chair or lean on a table, but there was nothing.

'Well, I really can't think why your aunt thought you should ask me such a question. That is not a good idea. Wholly inappropriate, I would say.'

'But you'll be there,' Frances blurted out.

Reverend Roper removed his glasses. 'I,' he paused for dramatic effect, 'will be saying the grace before supper and thanking the committee. That is hardly the same thing as attending a dance. A dance, I might add, that is intended for adults, not seventeen-year-old schoolgirls.' He tapped his fountain pen on the desk for emphasis.

'Norah Dean is going . . .' Her voice trailed away. She already knew her request was hopeless.

'Oh, oh,' his voice grew louder, 'and I suppose if Norah Dean stuck her hand in a fire, you would too?' Not waiting for an answer, he continued, 'I don't care what the Deans consider appropriate behaviour but I can tell you nobody from this house is going to parade themselves like . . . like . . .' He struggled to find a comparison, but then alighted on 'a backsliding heifer being brought to market! "The works of the flesh are manifest!"' Reverend Roper shook his head with disgust and Frances understood that the conversation was over.

On the Saturday afternoon following the social, Norah and Frances raced up the stairs into Norah's bedroom. Pressing herself against the closed door to make sure no one could barge in, Norah announced in a stage whisper, 'I kissed a boy!'

'No.' Frances clutched at imaginary pearls. 'Who? Who did you kiss?'

Norah pulled her friend over to the bed. 'Trevor Sweetnam. Shirley Sweetnam's brother and he's at university in Dublin.'

Frances gave an appropriate gasp of shock and approval.

'How? Where did it happen?'

'At the end.' Norah was laughing now as she remembered it. 'When we were getting our coats. He pushed me behind the rail, and then again afterwards outside, when Daddy had gone to get the car he was still there and he took me behind the statue of Padraic Pearse and we did it some more. I mean, like, lots.'

Frances was hot with envy. 'What was it like?'

Norah thought for a moment. 'I'm not sure. It was weird.' Then she leapt from the bed. 'Wait here!' And she ran from the room, to return a moment later holding something.

'Let me show you!'

Frances didn't understand.

'Here,' Norah was brandishing a tube of her mother's lipstick, 'let me put this on you.'

Frances obediently puckered up and Norah traced her lips. Her work complete, she leaned back. 'Now you're me and I'm him.'

Norah leaned forward and pressed her lips against those of her friend. Her hands spread against Frances's back and pulled her closer. It was soft and warm and for a moment Frances found she was enjoying it but then Norah was edging her tongue forward and the wetness made her pull away.

'I don't like it.'

'That's what he did,' Norah assured her. 'Come on, we'll try again.'

Frances held her arms out to stop her leaning in. 'No. I don't like it. Stop.' If kissing a boy was a sin, and she was fairly certain it was, then what was this?

'All right then.' Norah shrugged. 'You were the one who wanted to know what it was like.'

For the rest of the afternoon it appeared to Frances as if her friend was sulking, and, as for the kissing, neither variety was ever mentioned again.

And then Norah was gone. The thing Frances had dreaded since she had lost her parents. It shouldn't have come as a shock, she knew that their schooldays were drawing to an end, but the nature of her friend's departure was so sudden and seemingly without a backward glance that she had no choice but to feel abandoned.

'My Aunt Christine in London has a place for me in a secretarial school in Wimbledon. You know, where they play the tennis?' Norah's face practically glowed with pleasure and excitement. Frances tried to share the joy but couldn't help wondering why her friend didn't show any reluctance at all to leave their special bond behind. It was as if Norah's suitcase had been packed and waiting all along, her friendship with Frances just a way of killing time.

'My aunt has paid for me to fly! Aer Lingus to London. I'm going to wear my church coat, you know the blue one? I mean, I don't even know what people wear in London.' It sounded to Frances as if Norah was already trying to affect an English accent.

'Clothes like the rest of us, I imagine,' Frances said, hoping she didn't sound as resentful as she felt.

Norah paused and looked at her friend. 'You must come and visit me.'

'Of course!' Frances said without conviction.

The walk back to the rectory didn't feel like going home. Norah, the Deans' house and all that had given her comfort since the death of her parents was behind her now. When she went through the gates of the rectory she hid behind the small stone shed to the side of the house and allowed herself to cry. She had no idea what her future might hold but she knew she was going to have to face it alone. She blew her nose on the hem of her skirt and went inside.

Very soon Frances had more to think about than the absence of Norah. Her aunt and uncle wanted to know what she was going to do after school. Frances had no idea. Some other girls, like Norah, were off to secretarial courses, two had got into the bank, some had gone back to help on farms or with the family business. Avril Harper was engaged already, while clever clogs Fiona Wilson was studying English at UCC. Frances looked at herself in the mirror. What might she be? She had scarcely come to terms with the idea of herself being a schoolgirl, and now she had to transform into something or someone else. The only subject she excelled at was home economics, so her teacher

Mrs Lovell had encouraged her to try Cathal Brugha, the catering college in Dublin, but her Uncle Derek would not hear of it.

'The whole place is run by papists for papists, and besides, Dublin is no place for a girl of your age and lack of experience.'

Frances wondered how she might ever accumulate experiences if all her uncle did was forbid her from having any.

Mrs Lovell told Frances not to be downhearted and promised to have a think about other ways her flair for the culinary arts might be developed. Frances thanked her but assumed that it was just something teachers said so that hopeless cases would move along and not dawdle around their desk.

Mrs Lovell, however, was true to her word. One evening, just as it was getting dark, the rectory doorbell rang. It was her former teacher bearing a small glossy pamphlet. It seemed a Mrs Hurley had opened an 'Ecole Gastronomique' on Oliver Plunkett Street in Cork city. The courses ran for six months and the idea was to teach young women the techniques of traditional French cuisine. Frances listened intently as Mrs Lovell described the school and the high regard she had for Mrs Hurley. Apparently she had worked in Paris as well as London and had only come home to Cork to raise her children near to their grandparents. It was hard to gauge the reaction of Reverend Roper but he seemed to be doing more nodding than shaking of his head.

'Well, thank you, Mrs Lovell. We'll certainly consider it as an option,' he said as he showed her to the door.

As they sat at the dining-room table a little later, he asked Frances, 'And this course up in Cork, do you think it's something you'd like to do?'

'Yes,' she replied without hesitation.

'And you'd stick at it? You'd persevere? Because I imagine it might be very difficult.'

'I-I'd like to try. I think I could do it.' She wasn't sure how confident to be. She didn't want to provoke her uncle into repeating 'Pride goeth before destruction,' which she knew was one of his favourites. But then her Aunt Mona had chimed in with 'In fairness, Derek, Frances does have a knack for the kitchen. She has a real flair for it. Takes after her mother.' Her aunt smiled at her and Frances felt an unaccustomed warmth towards her. If she hadn't known it would immediately sour the moment, she might have hugged her.

The next day it was decided that Frances Howe would be the newest pupil of Mrs Hurley's Ecole Gastronomique. Frances allowed herself to imagine a future where she worked in restaurants. She would travel to Paris and bake cakes so ornate and delicious that they would cause people to burst into spontaneous rounds of applause. Norah would come and visit her, begging to be her friend again. A dark-haired French chef would fall in love with her – but then the thought of having children reminded her of her own parents, and she was brought back down to earth. This was Ballytoor and wonderful things didn't happen to people here.

Frances would get the bus to Cork and the train home every day. Her nerves on the first Monday morning quickly melted away. Mrs Hurley wasn't a gorgon throwing pots and pans across the room, she was a tiny woman who patrolled the classroom, pausing behind each student, who were a mix of ages but all women. Sometimes she gave an encouraging smile, or at other times she might take hold of a whisk to demonstrate an improved technique. It quickly became clear that Frances was the star pupil. Her whole face blushed beetroot red when Mrs Hurley made everyone come and taste the hollandaise sauce that Frances had made. Her choux pastry was held up to the light to demonstrate how delicate it should be. Soon Mrs Hurley began asking Frances to assist her in demonstrations, and Frances felt the comforting echo of the times she had spent helping her mother in the kitchen. Finding something that she was good at was like discovering a key, one that could at last unlock the mystery of her future.

The bus journeys became flights of imagination, as Frances conjured up menus and wondered if this might be her life. Already the insecurity of her schooldays seemed so far behind her and, while she hadn't exactly formed close friendships with her new classmates, she found she didn't miss Norah nearly as much as she had feared. The older women on the course asked her to join them for tea at the Pavillion; the younger ones urged her to follow them down to O'Brien's Ice Cream Parlour or over to the Tivoli. Frances was never able to accept these invitations because she had her six o'clock train to catch, but just being included felt like a social revolution.

Back in Ballytoor, even the rectory had taken on a different atmosphere, at times almost playful as Frances tried out recipes for her aunt and uncle. '*Magnifique!*' Reverend Roper had exclaimed with what Frances thought might have been a laugh. Mrs Hurley got a mention when grace was being said. Her aunt fluttered around the table exclaiming with delight at the little roses made from tomatoes that edged the plates. The French for happiness was '*bonheur*' and Frances held that word in her mouth, felt it on her tongue, savouring it as if it was a boiled sweet.

On the first Thursday of the final month of her cookery course, Frances returned to the rectory to find a strange car parked outside. As she removed her coat at the bottom of the stairs, she heard her uncle calling.

'Frances, is that you? Will you join us please?'

His voice was coming from the large front drawing room,

which was rarely used, except for tea after a committee meeting or when the bishop was visiting.

Inside, her aunt and uncle were sitting on either side of the fireplace, and on the longer of the two sofas was perched an older clergyman. When they caught sight of Frances, they all stood.

'This is Canon Frost. Canon, this is Frances.'

The canon smiled and stepped forward to shake her hand.

'We've met before, I think. My late wife was involved with the Girls Friendly Society. If I'm not mistaken, you were a member, no?'

She liked the sound of his voice. Deep. His hand was warm and soft.

'Yes, I was. A long time ago.' She gave a laugh to suggest how far she had come since the girlish pursuits of the GFS.

'Sit. Please sit.' Reverend Roper led by example. Frances chose the shorter sofa opposite the canon.

'Your uncle tells me you are developing quite the prowess as a chef.'

It struck Frances as odd that they had been discussing her at all, though it pleased her to think that the Ropers were proud of her.

'I'm trying my best. I enjoy it.'

'Important skills for life.' The canon smiled at her and she noticed the way his face creased around his dark brown eyes. His high forehead was tanned. He seemed like a man who knew something of life, actual life, not the sanitised make-believe her uncle dealt in.

'Now, Frances, Canon Frost had a request.'

Reverend Roper looked at his guest and the canon looked back at him. Frances wondered what any of this had to do with her.

'The canon would like to take you to tea on Saturday afternoon.'

Frances was not quite sure how to respond. 'Oh?' She noticed her aunt smiling broadly.

'I've booked a table in Langton's for half past three.' He seemed almost nervous. 'If that suits?'

'Yes.' She remembered her manners. 'Yes, thank you. That sounds lovely.'

The tea *was* lovely. Frances wore a high-necked blouse, her dark kilt and the shoes with the small heel that Norah had given her to wear to the social that she hadn't been allowed to attend. Canon Frost – 'Please, call me Alan' – sat opposite her, wearing a grey tweed jacket over his black shirt and white collar. He smelled of pipe smoke and a light citrus that Frances assumed was his soap or a cologne of some sort. He poured her tea and asked her what she thought of the cakes. She lied. The cream didn't taste fresh and the buns weren't cooked evenly. A shame, and easy to remedy. Not telling the truth made her feel worldly.

After an initial awkwardness, conversation flowed quite easily. She liked him. He talked about his parish of Castlekeen, which was about ten miles west of Ballytoor. Frances laughed as he told her stories of visiting farmers in wild, remote places – the old bachelor who shared a bedroom with his sheep, the one who wore a vest made of old fox furs. He seemed relaxed and confident of his own goodness. There was none of her Uncle Derek's self-conscious piety. This man did not feel the need to demonstrate his worth to the Lord.

He asked about her parents and Frances was surprised by how easy it was to speak about her loss. Then Alan described what it had been like to lose his wife. It seemed cancer had rendered her an invalid almost as soon as they were married. Perhaps the most surprising detail he confided was what a comfort her Uncle Derek had been during his period of grief. Who shall comfort the comforter? Frances found it hard to imagine Reverend Roper providing solace to the bereaved – he certainly hadn't when she was a little girl – but then maybe Alan was talking of prayers intoned while he wept. That, her uncle had done.

The tea ended when Canon Frost excused himself – Saturday night was when he needed his rest most. They stood in the lobby. It hadn't changed much since that afternoon when she had been ten years old and blissfully unaware of how her world was about to be turned upside down.

'Well, it's been very nice getting to know you, Frances.' He shook her hand and then bent to kiss her on the cheek. She felt the damp warmth of his lips against her skin.

'Nice to meet you too,' she replied and she meant it, though she was still mystified about why they had met for tea. On her way home the only thing she could think of was that perhaps he wanted to employ her as a housekeeper, or some sort of secretary, but if that was the case, why wouldn't he or her uncle have mentioned it?

The next day had been an even busier Sunday than normal. It was the harvest festival in St Ann's and Frances and her aunt had been at the church early, taking delivery of fruits and vegetables and arranging them around the altar and on the steps leading up to the stone porch. Afterwards there had been refreshments in the parish hall. Because they had been kept late washing dishes and emptying the tea urns, lunch had just been a bowl of soup, with a roast for dinner. Frances had made a tarte Tatin and her aunt and uncle gave gratifying gasps of appreciation when she brought it to the table There was a mood of quiet contentment. They were all tired, but the day had gone well with many compliments for the decorations and no cross words between the ladies of the parish. After the pots and pans were scrubbed and put away, Frances imagined she would go to her room and maybe listen to the radio for a little while before bed. The bus to Cork meant early starts.

She was just heading upstairs when she heard her aunt's heels scuttling across the tiles of the hallway.

'Frances!'

She turned around.

'Frances, dear, your uncle has something to tell you.' Mona's head was swaying from side to side and her eyes had an almost manic glint in them. If Frances hadn't known better, she might have thought her aunt was inebriated.

Obediently she came down the stairs and followed Mona into the study. Uncle Derek was standing in a slightly posed manner by the fireplace.

'Ah, Frances, there you are. Please sit down.' He indicated the chair where he usually sat to read his *Irish Times*. Frances could sense an odd atmosphere. She glanced at her aunt, who was now fidgeting anxiously by the doorway. It didn't seem as if they had bad news to impart, so when Frances sat she was more intrigued than nervous or frightened.

'Canon Frost enjoyed meeting with you yesterday and he feels you also had a pleasant time.' He paused and peered at his niece to see if she concurred.

'I did, yes.' Was this when she would learn of the job offer?

'Well,' her uncle flashed a rare smile, 'Canon Frost has asked me for your hand in holy matrimony and I have agreed.'

Unable to contain her excitement, Aunt Mona emitted a little yelp.

Frances found herself blinking as she continued to look at her uncle. She thought she had understood what he had said but, no . . . she must have misheard.

'Marry me? Become my husband? But I . . .' There was no end to the sentence that could fully convey everything she was feeling.

35

She had liked Canon Frost, even found him slightly attractive, so maybe she could . . . but then what about the rest of her life, all the things she had imagined for herself? The dark-haired French chef? It felt like heavy velvet drapes were closing all around her, obscuring the light of possibility. She became aware that her uncle was still speaking.

'. . . and to lose his wife in the way he did, so sad. He's still a relatively young man, forty-five at the most, he deserves a second chance at happiness.'

Frances couldn't believe what she was hearing. Her mouth was dry, and every word she thought of was lost before she could utter it. She twisted in her chair to seek out Aunt Mona. Was she going to allow this union to happen?

'Isn't it marvellous, dear? So distinguished. A canon, a home of your own. I'm so very happy for you.'

She leaned in to kiss her niece's cheek and then pulled away. 'Oh dear. Are you not happy?'

Frances bowed her head to hide her tears.

'Derek?' Mona appealed to her husband with a quiver in her voice.

The reverend Roper cleared his throat.

'Now, Frances, perhaps this has come as a shock. I understand it is a great deal to take in, but it is as you heard only this morning in the Gospel according to St John. Were you listening? Remember, verse sixteen, "*Ye have not chosen me, but I have chosen you, and ordained you, that ye should go and bring forth fruit, and that your fruit should remain: that whatsoever ye shall ask of the Father in my name, He may give it to you.*"'

Frances listened to her uncle's voice. He sounded so calm and certain. The Lord had spoken.

Wapping, 2024

'You're still here?' Nor sounded surprised to find Damian sitting beside Frankie's bed.

'I'm just going. Sorry. I'll leave you to it.' He stood up from the low wooden chair he had been using and grabbed his backpack.

Nor stepped to one side to allow him to pass.

'And we're seeing you this evening?'

'Yes.' He nodded. 'Seven again, right?'

'Correct. I won't be here, but I'll leave something for her dinner. You can just heat it up.'

'Her!' Frankie squawked from the bed. 'Hello to you too. I'm not a her and I'm still capable of deciding what I want for my dinner.'

Nor looked contrite.

'Of course you are, darling. Now. Are you getting up or staying in bed a bit longer?'

Frankie sighed. 'I don't know. My head is all over the place. Look what the boy found.'

She held up a small black and white photograph. Nor peered at it. 'Oh my God! The state of us.'

Damian was still at the door. 'I wasn't snooping, like. It was just stuck into a frame next door. I thought I spotted Frankie.'

'Ha!' Nor gave a laugh that was more like a bark. 'Me, not so much.'

'Well,' he said with a nervous giggle. She was correct. He had not realised that the fresh-faced girl with a pale silk headband in her hair was the mannish old lady he had met the night before.

'You really haven't changed, Frankie – I mean even your hair is the same.'

'Grey!' her friend objected.

'But the side parting, the short bob.'

'I know, I know. I swear it must be subconscious. I'm not trying to recapture my youth. It just seems manageable, low-maintenance.'

'Well, I don't think I'll be embracing the Alice band again any time soon. Now. . .' Nor turned her attention to Frankie's carer. 'Damian, wasn't it?' He nodded. 'You must be off. Go and talk to young people. Live, young man, live!' She threw open the front door with a dramatic flourish. Damian shrugged his bag onto his shoulder and left with an awkward wave.

Nor returned to the bedroom and leaned against the wall.

'Well, you're in a better mood today. I'm guessing it wasn't as bad as you expected?'

A shrug and a sniff. 'He's a nice lad,' Frankie conceded. 'You know he's from West Cork?'

'I thought I heard the accent.'

'The accent you couldn't wait to lose!'

Nor laughed, throwing her navy-blue wrap across a chair. 'I wanted to fit in. Hiding in plain sight has always worked for me, hasn't it?'

Frankie raised an eyebrow. 'Well, something worked, that's sure and certain.'

'Frankie!' Mock outrage. 'I've always been good to you. I'd like to do more, if only you'd let me.'

'I'm joking.'

'So am I.'

The two women smiled at each other.

'I've got the driver today, so if you can manage the stairs we could go out for lunch. Fancy it?'

The old woman in the bed shook her head. 'I don't think I can face it. I'm sorry. That young lad, I don't know how he set me off. I must have bored him to tears. Maybe it was his voice, you know, that he knew the world I was talking about, but I haven't told those stories for years, maybe ever. It made me feel ancient, mind you, thinking about the old days. Ballytoor. Your mother. She saved me, Nor, she really did. After Mammy and Daddy, I mean. There was no love to be had in that rectory.'

Frankie pulled herself up in the bed, then continued, 'You know, when I was telling Damian about going to live with the Ropers, I remembered that everyone thought a child was a gift from God for them, but I don't think that's true.'

Nor sat down on the end of the bed with a slight groan. 'No?'

'No. I don't think they ever wanted children. I'd say they saw me as God's way of testing them. And I'm inclined to say they failed.' She gave a wry smile.

'Your Aunt Mona wasn't the worst. I don't suppose she had an easy time of it either, being married to him.' Mona patted her friend's leg through the covers. 'People were different with children back then. You forget. We all forget. A good parent was one who managed to keep their child alive. Nobody wondered what their child was feeling. You were told how you felt.'

'I know. I know it was different. It's not Mona I blame so much, it's Uncle Derek. Constantly quoting his Bible, but not an ounce of kindness in him. To treat a child like that . . . even then.'

Nor tipped her head back. 'He was a little stiff, I'll grant you that.' She gave a chuckle. 'Daddy couldn't stand him.'

Frances pushed a strand of hair behind her ear and confessed, 'You know, I started to tell Damian about marrying Alan, and then I realised I couldn't. I didn't have the words. How could I explain to anyone why I went along with that?' A slow shake of the head.

Nor took her friend's hand. 'You didn't have a choice.'

Frankie thought about this for a moment. 'Well, that's certainly how I felt at the time. If I'd disobeyed my uncle, where would I have ended up? I had nowhere to go.' She looked at Nor, remembering something. 'You know your mother came to talk to me?'

'Did she? I don't think I knew that.'

'Yes. Came to the rectory and we sat in my room. She asked me if I was sure, told me I didn't have to go through with it, but of course I thought it was too late then. Everything had been arranged. I'm sure she knew I was lying when I told her it was what I wanted. I mean, I was crying when I told her. Oh, the tears! All I did was cry.' She laughed quietly.

Nor smiled too but then her face hardened. 'Canon Alan Frost. Another award-winning Christian.'

'I know, I know,' Frankie agreed enthusiastically. 'And what was he thinking, marrying a child?'

'It was a different time – and besides, he was the canon, he could do what he liked.'

Frankie snorted. 'And he did.'

Ireland, 1957

I

'Are these all the clothes you have?'

Frances didn't feel a reply was necessary. She had arrived at Castlekeen rectory with one suitcase, which Miss Nagle, Canon Frost's housekeeper, was peering into with a mixture of pity and disdain. The housekeeper was a short, squat woman of indeterminate age, her long hair gathered up in a hairnet. It reminded Frances of a dead fish caught in its net.

Miss Nagle picked up one of the dresses, a white-trimmed lemon summer dress with short sleeves. It was one of Frances's favourites. The housekeeper shook her head at the obvious inadequacy of the garment.

'No. I'm sorry, pet, but these won't do. They're not right at all.'

Frances sat with her hands in her lap, still wearing her coat. She was perched on a low chair beside an empty dressing table. Her husband had informed her that this was 'the lady's sitting room'. Just off the first landing at the top of the stairs, it contained two large mahogany wardrobes and a low chaise longue that Frances doubted could bear the weight of even the smallest of humans. A single window overlooked the wide gravel crescent that fanned out at the front of the rather imposing

41

rectory of Castlekeen. It felt far further away from Ballytoor than the ten miles it actually was.

Miss Nagle was now holding a skirt and tutting with disapproval.

'He was in such a rush to get rid of Mrs Frost's wardrobe. The first Mrs Frost.' A small smile of apology. 'Lovely things,' she added wistfully. 'But then, she was very thin.' Frances's face must have betrayed a flicker of offence because Miss Nagle hurriedly continued, 'You have a lovely figure, lovely, but Mrs Frost – well, she was dying.' Miss Nagle tipped her head to suggest that this fact had clearly given the first Mrs Frost an unfair advantage. 'I'll have a word with the canon. I'm sure we can find you things more in keeping.'

Frances raised a questioning eyebrow.

'In keeping with your new position.' Miss Nagle bent forward and rubbed Frances's knee. 'Don't worry yourself. We'll have it all sorted in no time.' A wide smile as she opened the door to leave. 'Well, you're very welcome and, you know, just make yourself at home. Because you are. At home, I mean.' Miss Nagle seemed to be amused by herself. 'Oh, and the canon is out tonight so it'll just be a kitchen supper at six.'

Frances opened her mouth to ask a question, but Miss Nagle had gone. Surely on their first night as a married couple in their new home, Alan would have mentioned if he was leaving her alone. It was her third day as the new Mrs Frost and, contrary to what her Aunt Mona had assured her, it seemed to be getting more difficult, not less.

Their marriage ceremony had been conducted on Wednesday afternoon in St Ann's. Reverend Roper had been the celebrant in front of a very small congregation consisting of Frances's Aunt Mona and a couple from Castlekeen – the Thorntons, who were good friends of the canon.

Frances had worn a flared knee-length dress in cream brocade, which she and her aunt had made from a Butterick pattern, and in her hair was a short veil held in place by a diamante comb that they had bought on a special shopping trip to Cash's in Cork city.

'You look beautiful, Frances,' her aunt had whispered with tears in her eyes. Looking in the mirror, Frances was surprised to find that she agreed. She did look pretty. Her eyes seemed brighter, her lips fuller. For a moment she wondered who she was reminded of, but then she realised it was her mother in the photograph of her own wedding day. She had allowed herself a pang of regret. Maybe she should have invited some of her schoolfriends to see her in her wedding finery? She resolved to send a photograph, once she had one, to Norah in London. Standing in the church, however, faced with her groom dressed in his standard white collar and jacket, listening to the sound of dry coughs echoing around the transept, any hint of excitement quickly faded away. She spoke her name and repeated the vows, but none of it made sense to her, nothing seemed real. Frances had never been one of those girls who fantasised about their dream wedding day, but she was very aware that it wasn't this. The canon's deep voice filled the church as he intoned the familiar phrases about sickness and health. How was it possible he was referring to her? When he slipped the gold band onto her finger she felt as if she was looking at the hand of a stranger. Then it was all over and Mr and Mrs Thornton were congratulating her as if she really was a wife. Her aunt kissed her on the cheek and said, 'I hope you'll both be very happy.' Frances supposed that if everyone said something was true, then it must be. At eighteen, she was a married woman.

Canon Frost had opened the passenger door of his large black car. Frances knew it was a Ford Prefect because her uncle had admired it. No *Just Married* sign adorned the back of the car, nor were there trails of tin cans tied to the bumper. Frances, in her cream dress, was the only clue that a wedding had taken place. As the car edged forward she managed to smile and wave to the small group standing on the steps of the church, who did the same. Frances knew for a fact that her aunt had a packet of confetti in her handbag, but for whatever reason that was where it remained.

The honeymoon. They were heading to the Ring of Kerry and two nights at the Parknasilla Hotel, overlooking Kenmare Bay. When Frances had told her aunt where they were going, Mona had repeated the word Parknasilla as though it were another name for the kingdom of Heaven.

'Two nights?' She was incredulous. Evidently this seemed excessive.

'Yes,' Frances confirmed, secretly thrilled that her aunt was so impressed. Frances knew the hotel must be grand because Carol Woodworth's elder sister, Mabel, had had her wedding reception there, but she now suspected it was even more glamorous than she had imagined.

Mona's eyes began to dart around the room in a panic.

'You'll need evening clothes. Two dresses! You can't be seen in the dining room both nights in the same dress. I mean, you can borrow my green satin, but the blue taffeta is very fitted.' She looked at her niece's body doubtfully.

'No. I only need one. The first night we arrive too late for the dining room so Canon Frost, Alan, has arranged for a plate of sandwiches in the room.' As she referenced the sleeping arrangements she could feel herself redden, but her aunt didn't seem to notice.

'Well, that is very sensible. I shudder to think what an evening meal might cost at Parknasilla. Now come with me and we can try the satin on.'

* * *

It was after dark when Alan took a sharp left and steered the car down the long driveway to the hotel.

'And here we are,' he said as he parked alongside cars even larger than his. Frances did enjoy his voice. Its depth and confidence eased her nerves and made her feel as if her marriage wasn't such a terrible idea after all. Alan came around the car to open her door and offered her his hand to step down onto the gravel. She could hear and smell the sea. A light breeze tugged at the veil she was still wearing.

'In the morning, the view is quite staggering. Little islands, the sea, mountains . . . really the best I've seen. Hopefully we get a fine day.' He flashed her a tight smile. All Frances heard was the word *we*. She was part of a *we* now. Alan picked up their cases and began to walk towards the hotel. Frances studied it as she drew closer: large and slightly institutional-looking, it appeared to be an overgrown country house that aspired to be a castle. She could make out the dark outline of various turrets against the night sky.

Frances had convinced herself that the mere act of stepping inside the hotel would make her feel as though she belonged. Immediately, she realised what a foolish notion that had been. Two porters swooped down on them and took the cases from Alan, while an oily-looking man in a dark suit rushed from behind the small reception desk to greet them.

'Welcome, Mrs Frost. And on behalf of us all at Parknasilla, may I offer you our congratulations.' He shook her hand as if he was trying to draw water from a pump.

Frances mumbled her thanks and looked for Alan to guide her through this ordeal.

An English voice rang out.

'It's a bride!' His words sounded loud and sharp to Frances's ear, unaccustomed as she was to hearing British voices in real life.

Then a small group of people came and gathered by what she assumed was the entrance to the bar, and began to applaud.

'Congratulations!'

'Who's the lucky chap?'

Frances smiled and bowed her head as she scuttled over to the reception desk to rejoin Alan.

The oily man, presumably a manager of some sort, was clutching a key attached to a large brass tag.

'If you'd care to follow me, Mr and Mrs Frost. Your room is on the second floor.'

As the couple went up the stairs, the group by the bar called after them.

'Good night!'

'Sleep well!'

Their words were followed by raucous laughter and then the sound of a woman's voice: 'Oh, darling, leave them be.'

Glancing to her side, Frances could see the grim fury in her husband's face.

'Here we are.' The manager opened the door, switched on the light and then handed the key to Alan with a little bow. 'Breakfast is served in the dining room until ten in the morning. Will there be anything else I can help you with?'

'No, thank you,' Alan said before shutting the door with some force.

'Such boorish behaviour. I would have expected more of an establishment of this calibre. Apologies.'

Frances shrugged. The people downstairs hadn't made her feel any more uncomfortable than anything else that had occurred during the day.

She looked around. Dark furniture and heavy fabrics filled the room. The bed had a half-canopy and in the small bay window area there was a table with a plate of sandwiches half covered with a white napkin. The foil neck of what Frances assumed was champagne protruded from an ice bucket. Catching sight of herself in a gilt-framed mirror, she reached up and took off her veil. She placed it on the end of the bed. It felt as if they were waiting for someone else to join them. Alan cleared his throat.

'Are you hungry?'

Frances nodded. The bright tomatoes and frayed edges of meat she could see peeking from the bread looked delicious.

Alan pulled two chairs up to the table and they sat.

'I didn't order this.' He tapped the bottle and Frances wasn't sure what he meant. Was he saying there had been a mistake, or was he worried that she might think he was celebrating, or perhaps he was trying to tell her how esteemed he was in the eyes of the hotel management? Unsure of how to respond, she sat very still.

'Would you care for a glass?' He sounded hesitant.

'Would you?' Frances had never tasted champagne, so couldn't be certain if she wanted it or not.

Alan considered the bottle for a moment.

'Why not?' he said as he pulled the bottle from the silver bucket.

It helped. Frances found that getting ready for bed wasn't nearly as embarrassing as she had feared. Alan had used the bathroom first, emerging in a pair of tan striped pyjamas, the jacket buttoned all the way to his throat. He looked odd but fully dressed at least. Frances noticed that he was still wearing his black socks. Then it was her turn. Her nightdress was new. Another purchase she had made with her Aunt Mona. She had barely been able to concentrate in the shop because she was so concerned her aunt would use this opportunity to give her *the talk*. Once she'd agreed to marry Alan, Frances had lived in fear that either her aunt or her uncle would attempt to give her what she had heard referred to as *marital instruction*. As the days passed, however, she began to think that they were as reluctant as she was, and the bone-chilling horror of *the talk* would be avoided. But then the day before the wedding, directly after lunch, her uncle, without even waiting to drink his tea, made a great show of folding his *Irish Times* and placing it on the table.

'Well, I will leave you ladies to it.' He gave Mona an encouraging smile and left the room. Frances immediately tried to get up from the table, but her aunt stopped her. 'I thought I should have a word.' She smiled kindly, and Frances realised there would be no avoiding the inevitable.

'Is there anything you'd like to ask me about your duties as a wife?' Mona said, her voice slow and calm as if she was asking a killer to put down their knife.

Frances pretended to consider the question for a moment before answering, 'No, I don't think so.' The truth was that she had many questions about what her married life might entail, but none of them involved the bedroom. Norah had heard from Avril Harper what went on between men and women, and had spoken about it to a degree that Frances had felt bordered on the unhealthy.

'Well, if you're sure . . .' Mona failed to hide her relief. 'And if you think of anything . . .' But Frances was already clearing the table.

Now, as she brushed her teeth in the hotel bathroom, she tried to imagine kissing Alan. Anything beyond that was a murky mystery. All the things that Norah had described seemed so far removed from the man waiting for Frances in the bedroom. Alan must have a penis, she knew that, but it was impossible to picture him having it out in the open near her, or, even more implausibly, putting it in her. She wiped her mouth with the small towel, took one last look at herself in the mirror and went to face her new husband.

Alan was sitting up against his pillows; all the lights apart from the lamp on her side of the bed had been turned off. Neither of them spoke. She pulled back the heavy blanket and quilt and climbed into the high bed.

'Do you want to turn out your light?' His voice seemed to blend into the thick fabrics swathed around the bed.

Frances understood it wasn't really a question and extinguished her lamp. She sensed Alan shift beneath the covers.

'You must be tired – I know I am.'

Frances gave a murmur of agreement.

'Probably best to begin our married life tomorrow, in that case.' Alan turned and found the side of her face, which he kissed, before turning away from her. 'Good night.'

'Good night,' Frances said into the darkness and then lay on her back, listening to the breathing of the man next to her, until she fell asleep.

The morning skies were grey, but the day was dry.

'Not the best, not the worst,' Alan declared as they strode out of the hotel and approached the car.

'You were right, the view really is lovely.' Frances felt this was the sort of thing a wife would say. She was agreeing with her husband and showing enthusiasm for the trip he had arranged.

'I told you it was.' Alan seemed more relaxed, happy even. There was a smile on his face as the car growled into reverse and crunched across the gravel. 'We don't have time for the whole Ring of Kerry, we have to be back for dinner, but worry not, we'll see plenty.'

'Wonderful.' Frances took off her headscarf and folded it in her lap. She already felt older.

The day was pleasant. Alan was easy company and Frances quickly understood that it was her job to ask questions so that her husband could answer them at length. The names of islands, the history of houses they passed, where the other cars on the road came from; never once did Canon Frost utter the words, 'I don't know.'

They had eaten the picnic provided by the hotel sitting in the car looking out over Derrynane Beach, Alan happy to share his views on such diverse topics as Daniel O'Connell, the monks on the Skellig Islands, and standing stones. Frances mostly nodded to indicate her continued attention, while trying not to get crumbs on the floor of the car. Whatever Alan was telling her, her main thought throughout the day was that there was no longer any doubt: tonight was the night when Canon Frost was going to do what men did to their wives.

'You look lovely,' Alan said that evening when Frances emerged from the bathroom in her aunt's dress, ready for the dining room. She was very self-conscious that it was a little long and she worried she might trip, but she smiled and said, 'Thank you.'

Dinner was not a relaxing experience. Frances was constantly on edge, afraid that she might get something wrong. They both chose the lamb from the trolley, and Alan ordered a bottle of red wine. All around her, the voices were British, which made her feel even more uneasy. Alan seemed oblivious to it all and spent much of the evening talking about Bishop Charles Graves.

'He originally owned this land. He was the Bishop of Limerick – *our* bishop, you understand.' The canon made strange little sounds as he chewed a mouthful of lamb to indicate he had not finished what he wanted to say. 'You're familiar with the writer Robert Graves?' By now Frances understood such questions didn't require an answer, so she just continued to listen and hoped her face expressed interest. 'Well, he was the grandson of the bishop.' As Alan pursued some errant peas around his plate, he went on to inform his new wife that he been an admirer of Mr Graves but was appalled by his novel about Jesus. 'I trust you haven't read it?'

'No.'

'No, of course not. The very idea of Derek Roper allowing such a book inside the rectory!' He laughed as if he had said something amusing. Frances smiled because she knew she should.

Upstairs, the preparations proceeded in much the same way as they had the night before. Frances pulled up the blankets and turned out her lamp. The newlyweds lay still and silent for what seemed like several minutes, before Alan spoke.

'Do you know what to expect?' His words reassured Frances. He would be her teacher.

'I think so,' she replied, and then, without any further warning, Alan's mouth was on hers. It seemed a little forceful, but not entirely unpleasant. His hands found her breasts and began to rub them both, in a manner not dissimilar to the way she kneaded dough. He shifted his body to be on top of hers. Frances wasn't sure what to do with her arms – should she hug him? She opted for leaving them at her sides. The kissing and rubbing continued and Frances felt the warmth of excitement growing within herself. Suddenly Alan stopped squirming against her body and uttered an 'Oh!' that sounded like mild surprise. In little more than a whisper, he said, 'I do apologise,' before rolling back to his side of the bed.

Frances had no idea what had just happened. Should she ask Alan if he was ill? Had she done something wrong? Perhaps she had been mistaken not to use her arms in some way. As she lay listening to Alan's breathing slowly become less laboured, she felt something wet soaking through her nightdress onto her thigh. She reached down and found a warm, viscous liquid. Frances remembered that Norah had talked about this, though she had got the impression that there should be more of it. The events of the last few minutes would, Frances realised, remain a mystery, because there was nobody in her life to whom she could turn. And besides, even if she had wanted to compose a letter to Norah or confess to Aunt Mona, she didn't have the words to describe so much of what had happened. 'Married life' really didn't seem sufficient.

II

That first night at Castlekeen rectory was to become the norm. Alan would be out at a committee meeting for a charity, or what he would refer to vaguely as 'diocesan business', leaving Frances sitting at the kitchen table with Miss Nagle and whatever the latter had prepared for their supper. Frances worried that perhaps it was the sin of pride, but she had assumed that one of the reasons the canon had wanted to marry her was because of her newly acquired skills in the kitchen. That seemed very far from the case, however. Alan rarely ate in the rectory, and when he did he seemed perfectly content with whatever Miss Nagle placed in front of him. Frances, who had never thought of herself as a fussy eater, found that she was not so easily pleased. It was difficult to decide which dish in Miss Nagle's extremely limited repertoire she disliked most. There was an anaemic sausage casserole, where carrot slices and chunks of pale sausage jostled together in an opaque liquid that was neither sauce nor gravy, more of an unsettling combination of tasteless and flesh-meltingly hot. Or there were her scrambled eggs, perhaps Miss Nagle's signature dish – if she were to sign her name making a cross with the charred end of a stick. What made them even worse, in Frances's opinion, was knowing how very simple it was to scramble an egg. Served on toast that had made barely a nodding acquaintance with the grill, little piles of scrambled eggs reared up like jaundiced Skellig Islands surrounded by a mysteriously yellow Atlantic Ocean. Where did all the liquid come from? Was it possible Miss Nagle had got confused between scrambled and poached and inadvertently created a hellish hybrid of them both?

'You know, I'm very happy to cook,' Frances suggested sweetly on more than one occasion, but her offers were always rebuffed by a resolute Miss Nagle.

'Sure isn't that what I'm here for? You'll be busy enough once you get involved in the parish. Do you bake?'

Frances said eagerly that she did.

'Well, that's what you'll do then,' Miss Nagle said, serving Frances a spoonful of mashed potato overcooked to the point of milky mush while still featuring hidden bullets that were completely raw. How did she do it? It was almost a gift.

Baking proved to be the salvation of Frances. Her cakes became the talk of the parish. Whether it was a bring-and-buy sale to raise money for the lepers in India, the cake stall at the fete in Castlekeen, or a supper after a social, organisers soon learned they could charge a premium for something baked by the new Mrs Frost.

'French butter!' Mrs Buttimer, the sexton's wife whose own baking had received rosettes at Ballytoor show, was keen to register her disapproval. 'Can you imagine? French butter. Galvins order it in specially. I've seen them getting it out of the back fridge for her.'

'Well, I don't care if she buys butter from the moon,' her husband replied with his mouth full. 'That is powerful pastry, powerful!'

Slowly, the parishioners, even the sexton's wife, became less suspicious of the very young new wife of the canon. She was unassuming, happy to help with the washing-up or stacking of chairs, and, most importantly, she never failed to appear at every parish function with some freshly baked treat.

Mr and Mrs Thornton, who Frances had first met at her wedding, were regular visitors at the rectory. Whatever their private feelings might have been about their friend the canon marrying someone who was scarcely more than a schoolgirl, they always made an effort to make Frances feel welcome and included. The Thorntons seemed younger than Alan – late thirties, Frances guessed. Bill Thornton was short but trim and energetic. His hair was already receding but what remained was turning an attractive metallic grey. His wife's hair, whatever colour it might have been, was now very blonde. At first Frances had felt intimidated by her glamour, but she soon found her a great help. Rachel was the one who would whisper parishioners' names in Frances's ear as they approached. She explained the politics of the rota for flower-arranging in the church. Bill always seemed happy to make himself available to ferry Frances about in his car, or help with any of the frequent domestic emergencies like leaking ceilings or faulty wiring at the beautiful but neglected rectory.

Bill Thornton was the land agent for Viscount Howorth, whose family were the owners of the castle that gave the village its name. The family seat was empty for most of the year as the viscount preferred to spend most of his time on their estate in Norfolk, so the Thorntons had quite an easy life living out of both sight and mind of their employer. The castle and its formal gardens edged the water to one side of the small harbour. Halfway up the tree-covered hill above it was the handsome rectory with its wide Palladian porch, and at the top of the hill was the church and its graveyard. Frances had never been to England, but this end of the village was what she imagined it would be like there, whereas the west end of Castlekeen, with its long, low street of multicoloured cottages and pubs, seemed much more Irish. The parishioners were also a strange hybrid. Frances noticed the congregation of Christ Church featured far more retired British people than St Ann's had. They occupied the front few pews each Sunday, and, even before Frances heard them speak, she knew they were different from the rest of the congregation. It wasn't so much the expensive fox furs or the waxed moustaches, but more the sense that only people who didn't have to be up to milk cows could have put such care into their appearance.

When Rachel suggested that Frances help with the Sunday school, Alan wasn't sure. Should the canon's wife be seen to be leaving the service? Clearly the first Mrs Frost had not chosen to do it. Rachel dismissed his objections, declaring it a splendid idea, and so Alan agreed. For Frances it was a blessed relief not to have to sit through the whole service but instead to gather in the small side room to read Bible stories and teach the children hymns and prayers. The two other women who ran the Sunday school were mothers of children in the group. They smiled indulgently at the new Mrs Frost.

'Soon you'll have one of your own.'

'Ah, you're great with them. You'll be a natural.'

Frances just smiled awkwardly in response. She was aware that there was a general expectation that she would soon produce a bouncing baby. She supposed that was how many of the parishioners must have made sense of her youth. The canon, everyone assumed, wanted to procreate and, after the barren invalid who had last shared his bed, he was just making sure with this very young filly. Indeed, that had been what Frances herself had suspected when looking for clues to solve the mystery of her marriage, but it transpired that the canon was just as uninterested in her fecund womb as he was in her cordon bleu cooking.

After the strange events at Parknasilla, Frances wondered when her husband might try once more to start their married life. Their first five nights in the rectory had all followed the same pattern. Each evening when the lights were extinguished, he found her face in the darkness and gave her a chaste good-night kiss on the cheek or forehead. On the sixth night, his mouth lingered and then found hers. After that it was the same routine as at the hotel, except this time he had pushed her nightdress up to her waist. Frances braced herself for what was about to happen, making her breath a little louder, hoping that the panting might communicate her excitement and willingness to proceed. Sadly, once more her husband uttered a small whimper that managed to suggest both animal lust and disappointment. He rolled away, leaving Frances to use her nightdress as a napkin.

These attempts were repeated on a weekly basis. Some were more successful than others – once, Frances felt the warmth and hardness of Alan pressing against her upper thigh and he had spread her knees apart, only for it to end once more with a brief shuddering groan and the nightdress scrubbing at the sheets. After two months, Frances had given up on ever being properly introduced to the mysteries of married life. She couldn't understand how she would be able to have a baby of her own, and the reason for Alan Frost deciding to marry her at all remained unknown.

One afternoon she came across Miss Nagle on the landing bearing an armful of her new *appropriate* clothes. The older woman seemed startled, even embarrassed, and gave a nervous laugh.

'Oh, there you are. The canon just asked me to move your things into the blue room, at the top of the house.'

Frances didn't want to give Miss Nagle the satisfaction of seeing that this was news, and unwelcome news at that, so she replied as breezily as she could muster, 'Of course. Thank you very much.'

'A lovely room. The only one in the house with a sea view.'

'Lovely,' Frances repeated. Did Miss Nagle honestly think that a glimpse of the ocean made up for being evicted from your marital bed? Frances waited for the housekeeper to round the corner with her bundle and then raced down the stairs to find her husband.

She knocked at the study door.

'Enter.'

Alan looked up from his desk and seemed perfectly delighted to find his wife standing before him.

'Yes?'

Unused to being direct, Frances twisted her arms into a knot before she blurted out, 'I just saw Miss Nagle moving my things upstairs.'

The smile left Alan's face. 'Oh. Oh dear.'

'Yes. Oh dear.'

'Frances, I'm very sorry. I had intended to speak to you. I . . .' He stood up and moved around the desk. 'Come and sit.' He led her to the small sofa to the side of the fireplace.

'Frances. This is very difficult to speak about, but, well,' he pulled at his collar, 'things, you know, between us, have not been the way I would have wished.' He studied her face. 'Do you understand?'

'Yes.'

'Well, I've been doing some reading,' he gestured vaguely towards his desk, 'and it seems that things might be improved if we don't share a bedroom.'

Frances wasn't following. How could that possibly improve the situation?

'Sorry, I—'

He grasped her hands and spoke quickly. 'Of course, I will visit you, in your new room, and there we can be as husband and wife. But otherwise we'll use our bedrooms for sleeping. Alone.'

This did not sound like married life to Frances. It sounded as if she had failed as a wife.

'Is there anything I should . . . am I doing anything wrong?'

Alan gasped. 'Oh no. No, my dear. This is entirely my concern.' He leaned forward and kissed her forehead. 'Please don't worry. We have only just embarked on this journey. All will be well.' He pulled her into an embrace. Together they lay back against the sofa, and neither of them moved. For the first time since she had walked down the aisle of St Ann's, Frances felt like Mrs Frost.

III

The driving lessons were Alan's idea.

'You could be more involved in the parish. Pastoral visits, even. I can't get everywhere as often as I'd wish.'

The idea did not appeal to Frances. 'Your car? I don't think I could ever drive such a big car.'

Alan waved her objections away with his breakfast fork.

'No, no. I need the car. No, we thought we might get you one of the little Fiats from Italy. Mrs Arnopp has one. Have you seen it? So small, I'm not sure where they put the engine.' He appeared to find this idea so amusing that he had to cover his mouth with his napkin.

'We? Who's we?'

'Oh, Bill of course. He knows a dealer in Cork and he said that he's happy to teach you.'

Frances had assumed Alan would be her teacher. 'Bill? But couldn't you?'

Alan seemed genuinely touched that his wife might want to get driving lessons from him. 'Oh, my dear, no, no, no. I'm far too busy and, besides, Bill has the patience for it. I don't want to snap at you.' He gave her the smile he reserved for special occasions. Frances knew this was no longer up for discussion. It had been decided: she was going to drive a car.

As it turned out, Bill was the best kind of teacher, clear, encouraging and strict without being frightening. Frances surprised herself with her rapid progress. They began their lessons on the wide turning circle outside Castle Keen, and then progressed to short, slightly stressful runs on the long tree-lined avenue. With Bill's even voice constantly reminding her what she should be doing, Frances relaxed into it. The clutch became smoother, the braking less abrupt, the steering didn't drift, and Frances had to admit that she enjoyed it. By the end of the first week, she had gone as far as the lake road and back.

Her suppers with Miss Nagle, which had been stilted at the best of times, became much easier as Frances shared stories of her progress or what she had encountered on the roads. The older woman was happy to fill in any gaps in Frances's local knowledge: who owned the barking sheepdog that always leapt out at cars, where the low road at Ballytoor Cross went; she even knew where had the cheapest petrol, despite arriving at work each day on her heavy black-framed bike.

One afternoon, as Bill and Frances headed back from the lake road, the idea of reversing was raised. Bill felt Frances was ready.

'Really? Do I have to?'

Bill laughed. 'Of course you do.'

'But why? I could always just keep driving until I find a place to turn.'

'Trust me, Frances, there will come a day when you'll need to reverse. Let's drive back to the castle. Nobody can watch you there. You'll be fine.'

Frances did as she was told, indicated as Bill had taught her, and drove down the avenue. Outside the castle there was an unfamiliar car. It was dark green and even larger than Alan's.

'Oh God!' Bill exclaimed.

'What?'

'It's the viscount! He didn't let us know he'd be back. Just stop the car – I must head in.' He looked at Frances. 'Will you be all right heading up to the rectory?'

'Of course. It's just up the hill.'

'Sorry about this – oh, and, if you see Rachel on your travels, can you let her know who's back?'

'Of course, just go!'

Bill jumped from the car and hurried across the gravel. Frances noticed he was heading towards the side of the building and not the double front door that he normally used.

It only took Frances a few minutes to walk to the top of the hill. The rectory seemed quiet. Miss Nagle's bike was missing, which meant she was probably in the village getting provisions. Frances took off her scarf and laid her coat on the old church pew that lined one side of the hallway. She thought Alan might want to know that the viscount was in residence so she headed to the study and gently tapped on the door before opening it.

The first thing that greeted her was a loud yell from Alan. The curtains were drawn and it took Frances's eyes a moment to adjust to the dim light of the desk lamp. Alan was sitting behind his desk and looked very strange. Was he ill? His hair was ruffled and his grey cardigan seemed twisted on his body. It was a moment later before Frances saw Rachel Thornton crouched on the floor by the side of the desk. Her hair, too, looked dishevelled and her lipstick was smeared across her face. The trio froze. No one spoke; the only sound was Rachel trying to catch her breath. Frances had no idea what it was she was looking at, but it was very obvious that she was intruding. As she pieced together the various parts of the scene before her, she felt her heart jolt upward in her chest. Her breath became shallow and uneven. Just then, Rachel moved her head to look up at Alan and the light of the lamp caught a thin thread of saliva that went from her mouth to—

Frances shrieked and ran from the room. She raced up the stairs, already trying to banish the image from her mind. It was too horrible. Alan exposed like that. Despite her best efforts she kept seeing it again. She felt sick. What really struck her was how raw everything had looked, wet and meaty, like some awful uncooked thing.

'Frances!' It was Alan's voice coming from the hallway. 'Frances!' She looked over the bannister.

'The viscount is back. Bill is looking for Rachel.' She spat out the words. Behind her husband she could see Rachel standing in the study doorway, smoothing down her hair. She reacted quickly when she heard Frances's news.

'Oh God, Alan. I must go.'

Her heels clicked across the hall and then she was gone.

Alan was looking up at his wife. 'Frances, I'd like to speak with you please.'

Frances looked at him. His shirt tail was protruding from his trousers; a sheen of sweat bathed his face.

'No!' she shouted and raced up to her room, slamming the door behind her.

Wapping, 2024

There was scarcely room for two people in the tiny kitchen. Damian was at the sink and Frankie was perched on a small stool by the window.

'The secret to kale is to massage it. That's it. Use your fingers. It practically cooks itself.'

Damian wasn't used to this level of engagement with his patients. But after the uncertain start, he was enjoying it. Walking down the gentle slope from the Highway to Frankie's home was a journey he looked forward to every afternoon. He wondered, if he had spoken to all the old people in his care, if he'd listened as much as he did to Frankie, whether they might also have stories like hers, but he doubted it. Damian had even begun to use the kitchen at home for more than microwave meals or heating up pizzas in the oven. The actors didn't complain but were clearly baffled by Damian's growing friendship with a woman in her eighties. Damian didn't really understand it himself, but he knew he enjoyed seeing Frankie blossom in the presence of an audience. The old woman still refused most of his offers of actual care or assistance, but the pleasure she got from his company and his attention was obvious, and that was fine by Damian, so long as Nor continued to pay his bills.

The previous morning, while waiting for Nor to arrive, Frankie had explained some of the mystery surrounding her obvious wealth. Apparently, many years ago, Nor had worked for the theatre impresario Bernard Delfont in the West End and, while there, had met and married a very wealthy American producer. 'He wasn't a particularly successful producer,' Frankie was quick to explain, 'but he was a very rich one. Family money. East Coast. As close to *old money* as you can get in America. So now Nor is a very merry widow – and more importantly, certainly to me, a very generous one. I don't know where I'd be without her. That woman has rescued me so many times! Toast, Damian!' The smell of burning bread filled the air.

'Sorry, sorry. It's your fault.' He rushed back to the kitchen. 'Also, you might ask her to buy you a toaster. Who still makes toast under the grill?'

'I do,' Frankie called from her bed. 'Not all change is progress.'

When Nor made her noisy entrance, she was carrying several green Harrods bags. Perched on Frankie's bed, she proudly produced a package from a food hall carrier.

'Fresh crab from West Cork!' She beamed expectantly at them both.

'Oh Nor, really. How much did you spend on that? You know it won't be fresh, not really.'

Nor rolled her eyes dramatically and waved her package. 'Well, it seems this isn't the only crabby thing from West Cork.'

Damian snorted.

'I don't know what you're laughing at,' Frankie snapped. 'You can't even make toast.'

Damian held his hand in the air.

'I'll leave you to it.' Then, blowing a kiss to Frankie, added, 'Till seven,' before closing the door behind him.

Nor looked at her friend. 'I'd say that boy is a success.'

'Sweet,' Frankie conceded. 'Though he keeps me up half the night talking.'

'He keeps *you* up?'

Frankie shook her head. 'Stop it. It's not that, it's just having him around has reminded me of things I haven't thought about for years. Canon Alan, can you imagine?'

'Oh!' Nor clapped her hands excitedly. 'Speaking of! I came across the most wonderful word.' She paused for effect. 'Parthenophobia!'

'Parthewhat?'

'Parthenophobia! That's what he must have been – parthenophobic.'

'And what on God's green earth is that?'

'Fear of virgins.'

Frankie laughed. 'Well, I was certainly that! It would explain a lot.'

'Yes,' Nor was laughing too, 'it's the age-old thing. Madonna versus whore. You were the madonna and—'

'And,' Frankie interrupted, 'the Thornton woman was, well, not quite a whore, but afterwards I heard stories, plenty of stories.'

'Oh yes, I remember my mother telling tales about Mrs Thornton. Do you think herself and the canon continued their liaison?'

Frankie sucked her teeth. 'I'm sure and certain they did. Marrying me was just a smokescreen, I'd say. That affair, or whatever you'd call it, had no doubt been going on for years. I wonder if he was the same with the first wife? Is there a word for fear of a virgin with cancer?'

'Stop it!' Nor laughed despite herself. 'You're awful.' She folded an empty Harrods bag. 'I wonder what happened to them all. Did you ever hear?'

'I know Alan is gone, finally. It seemed God was in no great rush to meet him. Well into his nineties, he was. The Thorntons, I don't know. So strange to think of those lives continuing after I left. Bill was so kind. How did he stay married to her? I know it was the days before divorce, but still. I think he loved her.'

Nor pursed her lips. 'Poor sap.'

'Love. It's like ordering food you know you're allergic to.'

'Ah, Frankie.' Nor chuckled. 'When did we become so old and cynical?'

Ireland, 1958

I

Three months had passed and Frances felt as if she might be losing her mind. Christmas had come and gone, sermons had been given, a threadbare tree decorated and then dismantled by Miss Nagle, and still no mention was made of what had been witnessed in the study. Frances refused to wear the silk scarf that Alan had given her. He had presented it with a peck on her cheek that had made her flinch. Sleep, something she had never doubted, now came only slowly and was fitful at best. Her mind couldn't stop trying to tally what she had seen with the way life was continuing around her. Frances knew what had been interrupted and yet everyone and everything seemed hell-bent on convincing her that it had never occurred. As she lay waiting for sleep, she sometimes thought that she should go to Alan, begin a conversation, confront things. But how? She wasn't the one who had been caught doing something ungodly. Where was the apology she was clearly owed? Why hadn't Alan tried to explain or excuse? Trust was gone, but not just in her husband; it was as if the world had betrayed her, again, and nothing was what it seemed.

She had tried to write to her friend Norah, to tell her everything, but before she had finished her letter an envelope with a British stamp had arrived for her. It was from Norah. Page after excited page about her life in London. The flat she shared in Pimlico with three other girls, her new job working for theatre producers in the West End. She had met famous actors. True, Frances hadn't heard of them but that didn't matter, they were known in a world where such things were important, not this village in West Cork where people did unspeakable things without any consequence. She ripped up her letter to Norah. Frances couldn't tell her about life in Castlekeen. What life? Going up and then down the stairs for something to do. Listening to Alan's collection of classical records, re-reading the same three E. Nesbit books she had found hidden away in a shelf of theological philosophy. Her friend would think she was an idiot, a hopeless idiot.

How had their lives become so dramatically different? They had been the same, friends with their whole lives ahead of them, and now one of them was having a new adventure in an exciting city, while for Frances everything seemed over already, any sense of a future cut short. Was her life really going to be reduced to accepting compliments on her baking from parishioners who gossiped behind her back about her inability to produce even a single baby? The injustice of it all lay like a heavy weight across her shoulders. She had trained herself to not think about her parents, not spend time imagining the other life she might have had, but now she did. Her mammy and daddy would never have let this happen to her; this could not have been the life they wanted for her, their daughter who they loved above everything else.

Briefly, she had considered escaping. Surely what Alan had done gave her the right to undo her wedding bonds. She had gone as far as trying to speak to her Aunt Mona about the situation, but it had just added to her frustrations. When she began

to describe the scene from the study, she found that she didn't
have the words to really tell her aunt what had occurred. It didn't
help that she only had a half-formed idea herself of what Rachel
and Alan had actually been doing. Her aunt had ended the
meeting abruptly.

'I'm not going to sit here and listen to this, Frances. If what
you're trying to tell me is that Alan Frost is an unfit husband for
you then I'm sorry to say you are still a very silly girl. He is a
man of the cloth and you should be on bended knee in gratitude
that such a man chose you to be his wife.'

Frances fumed. What about Rachel Thornton and what she'd
been doing on her knees?

'I don't want you to mention this to your uncle. Is that clear?
He is not to be upset.'

Frances had agreed and driven slowly back to Castlekeen in her
new Fiat. Doubtless, something else she should be grateful for.

Since the study incident all visits to Frances's bedroom had
ceased and for the most part Alan communicated only through
Miss Nagle. If this made the older woman feel awkward or
uncomfortable she certainly didn't show it. Frances wondered if
she knew about Rachel and the canon. Was that why she had
vacated the rectory that afternoon? Frances had tried to casually
drop into conversation questions about Rachel Thornton, but
Miss Nagle invariably replied saying she hadn't seen Mrs
Thornton for weeks. The lie of an accomplice or a sign that the
affair had ended? Who could tell? Frances felt entirely alone.
Even the afternoons she had enjoyed with Bill Thornton had
come to an end since he had decided she was capable of driving
by herself.

The pastoral visits that Alan had mentioned turned out to be
a glorified delivery service. There were small parcels of books
or sometimes donated foodstuffs to be brought to the poorer

families or the more isolated elderly parishioners. Miss Nagle
would arrange the packages in order of delivery on the pew in
the hallway, and give Frances detailed, albeit sometimes confusing
directions before waving her off.

It was one of those days when the rain is more of a greasy
mist. Not enough to leave the windscreen wipers on but too
wet not to use them at all. Frances blamed this for getting lost.
She had been heading to an old fisherman who lived up the
mountain above the pier at Stranach and who was to receive a
small basket of fresh eggs. It was the last stop on her rounds
and, as Frances drove, she found herself wondering why all he
needed was eggs. If the fisherman had everything else – say,
bread, potatoes, milk – then why not eggs? Even more perplexing
was where exactly he lived. Miss Nagle had said there was a
road after the long blue cottage, but it didn't seem to exist.
After abandoning her first pass, she turned the little car in an
open gateway and headed back towards the pier. She noticed
then that there was a road on the other side of the blue cottage
so turned into it. Quickly the narrow lane became a dirt track
with a mohawk of grass running down the centre. At the top
of the ridge the track came to a sudden end where it met what
appeared to be a bare, uneven farmyard edged with a few
outbuildings and a stone house that looked like it had been dug
out of the hill. Frances decided this must be the place she was
looking for.

She took her basket of eggs and crossed the deserted yard.
The door wasn't even as tall as she was. She knocked and somewhere in the distance a dog barked its reply. She heard movement
from within and prepared her best canon's wife smile for this
needy parishioner.

The door opened and, instead of the ancient fisherman she
had expected, a tall broad-shouldered man stepped out,

stooping so as not to hit his head on the lintel. When he stood up, she had to tilt her head back to look at his face as he loomed above her. There was the trace of a smile lingering on his handsome features, as if Frances had interrupted a joke he had been sharing with someone inside. Was that why he was making her nervous, or was it his eyes? They were very pale, closer to grey than blue, and matched the streaks of silver in his dark hair.

A small collie nudging against her leg made her realise that she hadn't yet spoken.

'Hello. I'm Mrs Frost, the canon's wife.'

'Away in, Biddy.' The man wasn't listening. Instead, he had grabbed the dog by the scruff of the neck and was pushing her back into the house. 'Sorry about that. She's just being friendly like.' He finished his short speech with a tentative smile. Frances had not expected his voice to be so quiet.

'Please, no need. I like dogs.' Frances paused. 'Are you Mr Sullivan?'

'I am.'

'Well, these are for you.' She held out her basket.

The man looked puzzled. 'Eggs? Who is after getting me eggs?'

Frances tried to repeat her canon's wife smile. 'They're from the parish.' She was going to say more but then remembered that she had no idea why the parish thought he might want or need this gift.

'Oh!' He nodded his head as though he had solved a problem. 'These are Protestant eggs, aren't they?' His smile was broad.

Frances wondered if it was some sort of trick question but answered, 'I suppose they are, yes.'

'It's not me you want, then. It's the souper Sullivan down the hill you're after.'

'Souper?'

'You know. Swapped sides for the soup during the famine. I'm O'Sullivan – you want Jim Sullivan. You passed his gate coming up the lane.' He pointed down the hill.

Frances suddenly understood her mistake. She had heard of soupers. There had been a few families at school where the 'O' was missing from their names: the Briens, the Mahonys, former Catholics who had accepted help during the famine. People had long memories.

'I'm so sorry to have bothered you.' She knew that she should turn away and go back to her car, but instead she continued to smile up at the handsome stranger.

'Don't be sorry at all. We have few enough callers up here. Can I . . . I don't know now . . . I can offer you a cup of tea? Milk? I have fresh milk?' Now he seemed nervous.

Frances considered his offer. Milk. A glass of milk was quick. Where was the harm in that? It wasn't like sitting down and waiting for a kettle to boil.

'A little milk, that would be lovely. Thank you.'

His face lit up. 'Grand. Milk. Come in, so. Come in.' He stepped aside, allowing Frances to make her way into the house. 'The place isn't the way I'd like it to be for a visitor. Sorry now for any mess.'

'Don't be silly. It's very kind of you to ask me in.' Frances peered around her, waiting for her eyes to become accustomed to the dark. She could see the fire at the far end of the room, and the glow from the window, and little else. Gradually she made out a table covered in a worn oilcloth. Behind that there was a bench against the wall. She noticed a couple of small religious pictures, the Virgin Mary in one and a saint whom Frances couldn't identify in the other. Just the act of being in this room seemed transgressive. The dark floor was just hardened earth and the fireplace was clearly where all the cooking took place. Frances had never been in such a home before. It was like stepping back in time.

'You're welcome. Very welcome. Are you all right with Biddy there?'

The collie was weaving around Frances's legs.

'Yes. Yes. She's a lovely girl.' She bent and stroked her fur. It felt greasy to the touch. 'I'm Frances, by the way. Frances Frost.' She held out her hand.

'Frances Frost. That's a great name altogether. I'm just plain John. John O'Sullivan.' His hand was rough and warm in hers.

He went to the table and lit an oil lamp.

'Sorry about the dark. My mother didn't trust the electric when they came around with it. I'll get it next time, I suppose.'

Frances just smiled. She had no idea that having electricity was a choice.

'Your milk.' John lifted a cloth off a large bowl on the table and ladled some milk into an enamel mug. He handed it to Frances.

'Sláinte.'

'Sláinte,' she replied awkwardly. She never felt confident speaking Irish.

She put the cup to her lips and was shocked to find the milk was warm.

'Oh!'

'What? Is it not good?'

'No. I mean, I was just expecting it to be cold.'

John laughed. 'Not a bit of it. This is fresh milk.'

'Fresh. Yes.' She still didn't understand.

'Fresh from the cow like. I just brought it in.'

Suddenly Frances knew what he meant and she could feel herself blushing. She wasn't sure why but the idea of drinking something still warm from the body of an animal seemed obscene, almost carnal. In an attempt to hide her embarrassment, she forced herself to take another gulp of the milk.

'Lovely. It's so creamy.'

'It is that.' John laughed. 'You're after giving yourself a fierce moustache there.' He reached forward and without warning wiped his finger gently across her upper lip.

It was as if all the electricity John's mother had rejected was suddenly being channelled into Frances. She had never felt an emotion like it. The smell of his skin like freshly cut grass and wet earth. The heat of his body so close to hers. The breath from his laughter touching her face. Her desire frightened her. All she wanted was for this John O'Sullivan to take her in his arms and do whatever it was to her that Alan hadn't. It alarmed her how strong the urge was to throw herself against this stranger. John had stopped laughing and was staring into her face as though he could read her mind. Her heart raced with the excitement of the moment. Something was about to happen. But no, it couldn't. What was she thinking? Her fear triumphed and she was stumbling backwards towards the door.

'I must, I must go. Late, I'm late, but thank you, thank you.' She was speaking to the floor because she didn't dare look at his face again. She had managed to open the door when she realised that she was still holding the mug. She held it out. 'Sorry. Thank you again.'

John took the mug and followed her out of the house.

'What about the eggs?' He was holding her basket.

Frances didn't pause in her dash to the car. 'Keep them. Give them to someone?'

'I'll run them down to Jimmy later,' John called across the yard.

Despite her best intentions, Frances turned back.

'Thank you so much.'

The smile on John's face, the sheen of the misty rain on his skin, made Frances long to run back to him but instead she clambered into her car.

'If you're passing, call again!' Was he laughing at her? Frances smiled and waved as her car bounced and jolted across the yard to the lane. Of one thing she was certain: she could never come back here.

That night sleep again refused to come for Frances but not because of her customary imagined rages at Alan and Rachel. On this evening she stared up into the darkness of her room and all she could see was John O'Sullivan. She felt again the touch of his finger on her face, the way he had looked at her before she had fled his cottage like a madwoman. She imagined what might have happened if she had stayed. His hands on her body, the taste of him kissing her. Sliding downwards together till they were intertwined, writhing on the wet ground. As her fantasy unfolded, she began to touch herself, and the pleasure of it made her gasp. Overwhelmed, she began to weep. Silent tears traced the sides of her face and soaked into the pillow. Why was she crying? Had she found love or lost her mind?

After her afternoon in Stranach, Frances felt like a different person. She no longer spent her days fretting about Mrs Thornton, Miss Nagle or even Alan. John O'Sullivan consumed every ounce of her being. Suddenly all the love songs she heard on Miss Nagle's radio in the kitchen spoke to her. Frank Sinatra's 'I've Got You Under My Skin' made her want to shout, 'Yes! That's me, that's how I feel!'

If anybody noticed anything different about Frances, they didn't mention it. Life continued unaffected, apart from the obsessive thoughts wound tight as yarn in Frances's mind. She saw John walking down the main street of Castlekeen until the man came into focus and she saw she was mistaken. Was that him driving the car heading towards her? It was! It wasn't. Her car made detours along the coast road, getting as close to Stranach as she dared. The steering strained against her grasp. The furtive touches under the covers at night became less tentative and more frequent. Of course she knew that, despite not having acted on her desires, this new inner life was born out of impure thoughts. She was a married woman, but then she reminded herself that Alan was a married man. Surely she was like Lear had been in her English class, 'more sinned against than sinning'?

It was six days before Frances did actually see John O'Sullivan again. She had just delivered a parcel of books to the Clarke sisters who lived up behind the co-op creamery and was walking back to her car when she thought she saw John driving towards her. She prepared herself for the disappointment of realising that it wasn't, but the closer the old black car got the more certain she became. Without thinking, she waved, frantically. It was less a casual greeting and more of an appeal for roadside assistance. Blushing, she yanked her arm back down, but the job had been done. The car slowed and John was leaning out of the window.

'Frances Frost.' His smile was wide. Frances suspected that he was still somehow laughing at her or playing a game she was unaware of, but she didn't care. She felt elated.

'Hello.' Desperate to prolong this encounter, she attempted to think of something to say, but her mind flapped uselessly like a bird against a window pane.

'I have your basket.'

Truthfully, Frances had not thought about the eggs nor their basket since she had left them with John, but now she felt a convenient conviction that she must return the basket to its rightful owner. It was the right thing to do.

'With you now?' she asked.

'No. I'll drop it down to you sometime, or . . .'

'Yes?' She leaned forward expectantly.

'Is that the easiest?' He hesitated.

'Or I could come and get it now.' Frances was winded by her own forwardness.

If John was surprised by her suggestion, he hid it well, merely raising an eyebrow. 'If you've the time . . .'

'If it suits you, of course.' Frances was now flustered by the reality of her suggestion. She would be alone with John O'Sullivan. The possibility of her fantasies played in her mind like a flip book. She knew she was blushing.

'Not a worry. Follow on there in your car.' He waved in the direction of the coast road and she scuttled back to her Fiat.

The journey back to Stranach became increasingly tense. Frances's knuckles turned white as she gripped the steering wheel. Partly this was due to the prospect of being alone with John, but it was also because of the amount of tea she had consumed with the Clarke sisters. Her need for the toilet was becoming urgent. By the time her car bounced its way across John's farm-yard, her desperation outweighed her embarrassment.

'I'm so sorry, but I wonder if I could use your toilet?' she announced, as soon as her feet were on the ground.

John looked uncertain. 'Are you sure? It's nothing fancy like.' He pointed to the side of the house.

Frances understood that he must be referring to an outhouse of some kind but was beyond caring. 'Thank you,' she called as she made her way as quickly as she dared in the direction John had pointed.

The toilet wasn't as primitive as she had feared. Its whitewashed stone walls and slatted wooden door were clean and there was real toilet paper, not just strips of newspaper. It was only after she had relieved herself that she became aware of having to face John. The toilet seat felt warm against her bare flesh. John had sat here. She jumped up – it all felt too intimate. She smoothed down her skirt and came outside but she couldn't see John.

She approached the door of the cottage; Biddy the collie was lying close by, slapping her tail against the ground in a half-hearted greeting. Frances knocked on the door. John opened it and she stepped inside.

'There's some water for you there,' he said, indicating a bowl that sat in the stone sink beneath the window. Since there were no taps it wasn't clear where the water had come from. 'And a towel.'

'Thank you,' Frances said.

As she rinsed her hands and dried them she could hear John moving around the room. Neither of them spoke. When she turned, she was startled to find John standing directly behind her.

'Your basket.' It looked like a doll's toy in his hands. 'Jimmy had the eggs.'

'That's kind of you. Thank you.' She touched the basket but John did not immediately release it.

'I was glad to see you today,' he said, sounding unconfident.

'I was too. I mean, to see you.' Frances didn't want to move, afraid she might break a spell.

John twisted his neck as if his collar was too tight. 'You were on my mind there like.'

It took a moment for Frances to respond. 'Me too. You too. The same, I mean.'

He smiled and then she smiled and then it was as if someone had fired a staring pistol. They were on each other. His mouth found hers, and as one they cast the basket aside. She gripped her hands around his back, feeling his muscles beneath the rough wool of his jumper. He made a low moaning sound as his tongue explored the inside of her mouth. Then his hands were on her hips and he was rubbing the fabric of her skirt up and down. She felt it catch her knickers and tug at them. Her knees buckled and John had to stop her from falling. As he held her, he pulled his face away.

'This is mad. We must stop this.' His jaw jutted forward, his breathing shallow.

'We will,' Frances said and then began to kiss him again, but something had changed. She could feel him resisting her, not yielding to her touch. She looked up at him.

'What?'

'I'm sorry.'

He ran his hand through his hair and exhaled. 'This is too dangerous. For you. And for me. We can't.'

'But . . .' But Frances knew that the moment was over. She wanted to plead with him but of course he was right. This liaison could only exist as a fantasy.

'I'll go,' she said quietly.

'Right so.' His voice also a whisper.

He opened the door, allowing the afternoon light and sea breeze to flood in. It seemed to sober them both up.

'I'd better take the basket.' Frances sounded business-like.

John stooped to retrieve it from the floor and handed it to her.

Outside, Biddy was standing, her tail a hairy banner.

'I hope . . .' John began but then his voice trailed away.

'Yes,' Frances said, because she somehow did understand. They had shared something and it would never be repeated. She felt like an escaped convict being returned to their cell.

Her car door open, she threw the basket over onto the passenger seat. Turning back, she held her wind-tossed hair away from her face.

'Goodbye then.'

John stood above her, his face tensed. A slight twitch in his jaw.

'Right, right.' And then very gently he leaned forward and pressed his lips against hers.

He stepped back, their eyes met and then he was leaning forward to kiss her again. This time it was more insistent. Frances returned his kisses. The mouth, the hands she thought she would never feel again. John's arms pulled their bodies close and he ground himself against Frances. She could feel his hardness. Biddy began to circle them, scratching against their legs, whimpering with confusion. Frances didn't care. She felt a hand on her breast and gave her own small whimper.

Suddenly John wasn't pulling her towards him. He was pushing her away, angling her towards the open car door. His face was red and contorted.

'John? What? What is it?' She tried to push against him but she was no match for him.

'This . . . this . . . it can't be,' he said as he put her in the car and slammed her door. 'I'm sorry. Go! Just go!' he shouted through the closed window. Was he angry? Was he crying? The shock and force of what was happening meant she couldn't tell. Before Frances had a chance to ask for some sort of explanation, John had marched back to the house followed by his dog and shut the door with a slam.

Frances could still taste his kisses, her body still pulsed with desire, but it was as if her lover had been a phantom. There was no sign of him. Just the cottage pushed into the hill, and the old farm machinery rusting quietly. A chicken high-stepped its way around the side of the house, confirming that there was nothing to see.

Frances did the only thing she could think of. She drove home.

II

Four days passed. Frances had no idea how she endured them and certainly had no clue how she could face the coming weeks and months. She spent most of the time in her room feigning illness. Miss Nagle kept her supplied with cups of tea and toast.

'Would you not see Dr Michaels? I'm sure he'd come out this afternoon, if you'd like.'

Frances shook her head.

'Are you sure now?' Miss Nagle raised her eyebrows and flicked her tongue against her upper lip. 'You never know, it might be good news. Glad tidings, if you get my meaning.'

For a second Frances didn't but then she realised the old woman was talking about pregnancy. Clearly Miss Nagle wasn't so knowledgeable about what went on in the rectory.

'No.' Frances tried to sound firm. 'No doctor. I'll be down later.'

She watched the weather through the window. The clouds were almost purple with the promise of heavy rain. She would have to face the world. Missing more parish events might make others jump to Miss Nagle's baby conclusion. She shuddered.

John. John O'Sullivan. Frances was certain he felt the same as she did, so how could this be the end of their story? Part of her longed to drive out to the farm, but then she remembered his face as he had left her in the car. She couldn't bear it if he pushed her away again. But, she wondered, would it be better than the way things were, better than not knowing? She tried to imagine her life if somehow John did accept their love. She couldn't leave Alan. John couldn't leave his farm. Were they to live in sin forever? Frances knew she couldn't do that.

On the fifth day, the decision was taken out of her hands. Miss Nagle told her that the canon would like to see Frances in his study. There was something in the way she spoke that unsettled Frances. She seemed dismissive almost to the point of rudeness. She had left without even closing the door to Frances's bedroom.

Downstairs, Alan was standing behind his desk, his back to her.

'You wanted to see—'

Alan's face when he turned stole the words from her mouth. She had seen him look angry before, but this was different.

He seemed murderous. Even in the half-light the hatred in his eyes was clear.

'My wife.' He placed his hands on the desk, the way he sometimes did in the pulpit. 'My wife has come to see me. Oh, what a marvellous choice of a wife I made.' His mouth formed a sarcastic smile.

'Alan?' Frances whispered. 'What are you talking—'

'A parishioner!' he barked loudly, silencing her, then continued in a more reasonable tone, 'A parishioner came to see me.' He paused and raised an eyebrow, waiting to see if this provoked any response. A chill ran through Frances. She felt an awful dread that she knew where this was going. She reached out to steady herself on the side of the sofa.

'A Mr Sullivan. A Mr Sullivan of Stranach. A fisherman. You know to whom I'm referring?'

Her mouth was dry. She wanted to run from the room. Instead she nodded her head. Yes, she did.

Alan moved to the side of his desk and slowly rubbed at the wood with one hand.

'He tells me you tried to visit, but missed him. Is that correct?'

Another nod. Frances felt the tickle of burgeoning tears.

'So!' Another bark. It seemed as if Alan was enjoying this. 'So when he saw your car go by his cottage the other day, he assumed you had missed him yet again.' He paused and watched as Frances began to weep.

'Mr Sullivan, good Samaritan that he is, decided to follow your car up the hill, to inform you of your mistake.' Another pause. 'When he reached your car, do you know what he saw?' This last question was a low growl.

Frances couldn't speak. She longed for Alan to get this torture over with, but understood that he was relishing every moment of her humiliation.

'He saw . . . dear Lord, he stood in this room and told me that he saw,' Alan's voice was building in volume, 'my wife fornicating with some farmhand!'

'No!' Frances interrupted. 'That's not true!'

'Isn't it?' Alan had stepped forward. 'You were not being a low slut, a common harlot?'

Frances didn't answer. 'Weren't you?' he asked again. When Frances just sobbed without speaking, he turned and went back to his desk.

'You are convicted by your silence. My wife, my wife the alley cat.' He turned back to look at her. 'You disgust me. You have brought such shame on this house, on this parish and on myself.' Alan had begun to tremble with anger. Raising a finger, he pointed at Frances and declared, 'I renounce you.'

There was something about this phrase that brought Frances back into the room. This was more than an accusation. What did he mean by renouncing her? She lifted her head and wiped the wet away from her eyes and nose.

'I don't understand.'

He glared at her. 'I renounce you. You are no longer my wife.' He spoke slowly and loudly as if addressing a simpleton.

'What?' Frances wasn't following. Marriages didn't just end.

'Miss Nagle is packing your things. You'll leave this house tonight.'

'But, Alan . . .' She didn't know what to say. The shame of it. What would her aunt and uncle think?

'But,' she tried again, 'what will we tell people?'

'Tell people?' he snarled. 'I very much doubt we'll need to tell people anything. Mr Sullivan and Miss Nagle will do that for us. Soon the whole parish will know that I had the misfortune to marry a woman with the morals of a common prostitute.' He sank heavily into his chair, clearly pleased with his speech.

This final accusation was too much for Frances. She fought back. 'Oh? And what about Rachel Thornton? Is she a prostitute?'

Alan leapt to his feet. 'Don't you dare sully the name of a fine woman like Mrs Thornton!'

Frances approached the desk. 'You know what I saw.' Her anger flashed. Alan rushed forward, knocking his chair sideways, and grabbed her roughly. 'You saw nothing!' he spat into her face and pushed her to the door. There in the hallway stood Miss Nagle, holding Frances's case, her heavy winter coat draped over it. The old woman looked at Frances as if she was a dog that had just proven it wasn't housetrained.

'I think that's everything.' Miss Nagle pointed to the case.

Frances looked from Alan to Miss Nagle. Everything was moving at such speed. Was she to be left dragging her case down the hill into the village?

'But where am I to go?' she asked in a voice that even to her own ears sounded pathetic.

As if waiting for its cue, the doorbell rang, vibrating through the hall. Miss Nagle smoothed her hairnet as she went to the door. When she opened it, there stood Uncle Derek and Aunt Mona. Both their clothes and their demeanour suggested they were attending a funeral, thought Frances, and what made it worse was that it was hers.

Wapping, 2024

'What did you do?' Damian asked quietly.

'Well, you know yourself,' Frankie replied, shifting in her chair as if to break the link between herself and the young woman she had been remembering. 'I picked up that case and got into the back seat of the car like the child I was.' A tight smile.

'And then?'

'And then?' Frankie laughed. 'Enough talk now. Nor will be here soon.'

Outside, the weak morning light lurked in a fog that had rolled in from the river. Looking through the kitchen window, Damian could still picture the wilds of West Cork, where he and Frankie had spent the last few hours.

He enjoyed hearing her stories, set in places with names that would always mean more to him than 'Walthamstow' or 'Shadwell', no matter how long he lived in London. Young as he was, there was a nostalgia he felt in talking about home, but her stories brought back other feelings, too. The reaction of his parents when someone had tagged him in photographs taken on a night out in Chambers. He remembered looking from his parents' stony faces to the pictures of him, sweaty-faced and smiling, arms around shirtless friends, and he knew that those faces could never co-exist. Things had calmed down, of course, this was not the Ireland of Frankie Howe, but his mother always seemed nervous and on edge when Damian came home. He knew it was because she was worried he might upset his father, and he understood. Growing up, not sparking his father's anger had been the whole family's main concern, but it had begun to feel like the person his mother was frightened of was Damian. His presence was a ticking bomb in his parents' house, which no longer felt like home. That was when he'd decided to remove himself and come to London. His mother had wept when she'd said goodbye and slipped a hundred euros into his hand, but he suspected that a part of her, just a small part, was also relieved.

Not long after dawn, Damian had heard Frankie moving around in her bedroom. When he had come into the hall to see if she needed anything, she had opened her door with a flourish. 'You're up! Jesus, does no one sleep in this house?' Frankie sounded as though she'd been waiting for him.

Damian noticed that she was fully dressed, even her sock. How had she managed that, he wondered.

'I'm paid not to sleep, what's your excuse?'

'Well, I'd pay good money to be able to. I blame this thing.' She brandished her crutch and then pointed towards the kitchen. 'Toast?'

'Sure.'

Frankie had showed Damian how to rub a peeled clove of garlic against the rough surface of the hot toast and then drizzle a little olive oil over it.

'Isn't that only gorgeous?'

Damian agreed with an enthusiastic 'Mmmm,' his mouth full.

The kettle was boiled and Frankie supervised the heating of the pot and the measuring out of the loose leaves. They sat together at the kitchen table that was so small it was hard to imagine for what purpose it had ever been built. Damian had to sit sideways to avoid his knees becoming entwined in Frankie's legs.

'Was it your sister you said lived in Stranach?' Frankie asked him, and so began the tale of Frankie's marriage and her infatuation with John O'Sullivan. Damian had been in Stranach more than once, he would have said that he knew it, but he had no idea where the lane Frankie had described was located. He doubted that the cottage had survived. He wondered if his parents would remember it. He should call them – they'd like these stories. Tales of an old Ireland that was long gone.

Damian made another pot of tea in anticipation of Nor's arrival and squeezed himself back down at the table.

'And did you ever explain? I mean, to your aunt and uncle, what happened?'

Frankie rolled her eyes. 'Explain? There was no explaining. Everything was my fault. I had brought shame on the family, the memory of my parents, the parish – you name it and I had brought shame on it. I swear from the moment I got in that car till I left I only heard my uncle speak in Bible verses.'

'You left?'

'Banished would be closer to the truth.' Her face hardened. 'If it hadn't been for Nor's mother taking pity on me, I don't know what I would have done.'

'You lived with them?'

'No, God no.' Frankie sipped her tea. 'They bought me a ticket for the boat train to London and gave me Nor's address.'

'Reunited!' Damian grinned, eager for a happy end to the tale.

'It wasn't quite as simple as that. I don't think Nor was thrilled to have a gormless ghost from her Irish past turning up on her doorstep, cramping her style. Nor had her own secrets.'

Frankie leaned back. 'Maybe we should wait for her before I tell you any more.'

London, 1958

I

The city hadn't just changed Norah Dean, it appeared to have turned her into someone else entirely. Frances struggled to recognise her friend when she eventually opened the door of the large white stucco house on Alderney Street in Pimlico. Norah stood in the doorway looking cool and crisp, a white shirt tucked into some high-waisted black trousers, a short string of pearls at her neck, face lightly dusted with make-up, her hair glossy and short. Frances dreaded to think how she looked after her journey from Cork to Victoria station. Lurching to one side to balance her heavy case, she swiped at her hair in an effort to make herself less bedraggled.

'Frances, darling! It's so wonderful to see you. Come in, come in.'

The voice. What had happened to Norah's voice? It sounded so loud and unnatural. Her normal accent had been pitched up into a clipped English bark. It reminded Frances of a record being played at the wrong speed. Norah climbed the wide stairs and Frances followed, heaving her case from step to step.

'The girls are all dying to meet you.' The strange voice echoed through the hall.

Upstairs, the room Norah ushered Frances into could best be described as floral. The long curtains at the floor-to-ceiling windows matched the rose-strewn fabric of the battered sofa. Two tired-looking armchairs came from an equally bright part of the garden.

Three young women of a similar age were scattered across the room. If they were excited to greet their visitor, they hid it very well. Various cups and glasses were on the coffee table, and discarded newspapers covered the floor. Only one of the women looked up from the magazine in her lap as they entered the room.

'Oh, who's this, Nor?'

'Nor?' Frances asked but was shocked to find how unfamiliar her own voice sounded in this room.

Her friend rolled her eyes as if bored by having to explain. 'Oh, everyone in London calls me Nor. Van came up with it and it stuck. I rather like it.'

Frances ignored the use of *rather* and simply asked, 'Van?'

'Van Everden. She's a friend. You'll meet her tonight at her party.'

The word *party* immediately reminded Frances of how tired she was after her journey. She had hoped that her first night might be just herself and Norah, catching up. In fact, if she was being completely honest, she had imagined Norah reacting with suitable outrage as Frances described the many injustices of her life in Castlekeen. 'A party?' she asked with as much enthusiasm as she could muster.

One of the other women sitting on the sofa turned to look at Frances and Norah.

'I didn't know you were going.' Her drawl suggested that she didn't care either way.

'Yes, yes, she insisted. But I'm being so rude – this is my friend from Ireland, Frances, and these are my flatmates. Hilda . . .' The first woman gave a little wave. 'Honor . . .' A tight smile from the sofa. 'And Tilly . . .' The third woman finally acknowledged Frances. 'Hello, dear,' she said as if she were much older, her voice husky and low. 'Please excuse my appearance' – she indicated her pale blue pyjamas – 'but your friend appears to have used all the hot water.'

Norah gave an exaggerated gasp. 'Did I? Oh, I'm so sorry, but I wanted to have a bath before Frances arrived.'

Honor spoke from the sofa. 'And how long is Frances staying with us?' She pronounced her name as if it were an assumed identity.

Frances didn't know what to say. Mrs Dean had just told her that she could stay with Norah when she got to London. She hadn't considered what would come next, which now made her feel extremely foolish. Thankfully Norah spoke for her. 'Not long. Just till she gets a job and back on her feet. She's bunking in with me and I promise you she is quiet as a mouse. I told you about Frances. Remember, my friend who has had a beastly time?' She stressed the words to jog Honor's memory. It must have worked because suddenly Honor's whole demeanour changed. She leapt from the sofa and rushed forward to hug Frances.

'I'm so terribly sorry about what happened to you. Awful, just awful.' She held Frances at arm's length. 'Welcome to London.'

'Thank you. Thank you so much.' This small gesture of kindness was almost enough to make her cry.

'Come on,' Norah said, 'let's get you settled.'

Norah's room was small but bright with a tall window looking out on Alderney Street. Frances got the sense that it had been recently and swiftly tidied, with clothes jutting unevenly from a rail, and books pushed into piles against the wall. Norah explained that she worked with Honor in the Delfont offices, assisting the producers for West End shows. When a room had become available in the flat, Norah had left her aunt and moved in. Tilly and Hilda were the original flatmates.

'They're great fun, when you get to know them,' Norah assured her friend. 'Now, what do you want to do? There's a lovely little Portuguese café around the corner. Are you hungry?'

Frances was hungry, but even more than that she needed to rest.

'Do you mind if I just have a little sleep?'

'Oh, I forgot – you didn't fly.' Norah said this as if she herself was constantly jetting back and forth to Cork. Frances resisted pointing out that Norah herself had been on a plane only once.

'I'll pull the curtains. The bathroom is the door opposite. I'll bring you back some *pastel de nata*!' Norah had closed the door before Frances could ask her what on earth she was talking about.

She sat on the bed, too tired to even take her coat off. She had assumed that being reunited with Norah would make everything, if not better, then at least familiar, but her friend was too busy trying to be a new sort of Norah. And this place, this London, was so much more than she had envisaged. It wasn't just another location, a change of scenery, it was a different world. Every sight and sound, the smell of chimneys and traffic – which even now she seemed to be breathing in from the bedclothes – were all so unfamiliar to Frances that she felt completely unbalanced. How could she ever call this place home? It was as if she was running after a ball she would never be able to catch. She put her head on the pillow and within minutes she was in a deep, dreamless sleep.

When she woke she could hear traffic outside the window, where the daylight seemed to be fading. Had she slept all day? She became aware of Norah sitting on the edge of the bed.

'Hello.'

'Sorry. I didn't want to wake you, but the others want to dress and have food before we go to Van's party. You must be starving.'

Frances pulled herself up to sit with her back against the wall.

'I am, but . . . I don't think I said thank you before. Thanks for having me. I'll get out of your way as soon as I can. Thank you so much. Your mammy was so kind to me.'

Norah nodded. 'She explained what happened. Quite the drama!'

Frances reddened. She hated her life being made public like this. 'Do the girls know everything?'

'Only some. I just told them you had to escape an awful husband. Which is true, isn't it?'

Frances shrugged. Was it? If the awful husband kicked you out, did that still count as escaping? 'I suppose.' She wondered when she and Norah might spend some time alone together so that she could explain fully what had gone on. She longed to talk to someone about John, someone who might understand her feelings.

Norah stood up abruptly and turned on the light. Frances wondered if her friend was avoiding anything resembling a heart-to-heart. Was there something about Frances's story she didn't want to hear?

'Well, you're in London now and nobody knows you or your story, so you can be whoever you want to be.' Norah held Frances's gaze for a moment and then laughed.

Frances wanted to ask Norah who *she* had decided to be and why that person was so very different from the Norah she had known. The idea of getting lost in the big city appealed to Frances, but she didn't want to stop being herself.

Norah darted between the bathroom and the rail of clothes that leaned precariously against the wall. Soon she had swapped her white shirt for a black one with a high collar. A thin glittery scarf was wrapped around her neck, the same red as her dramatic lipstick.

'Well? Am I ready for a party?' she asked and, despite her newfound sophistication, Frances saw a shadow of the girl she had known back in Ballytoor.

'You look beautiful.' Frances didn't think she had ever seen someone look so glamorous in actual real life. She imagined that Norah would have stopped traffic in the square back home.

'I'll leave you to get ready. See you in the sitting room. Hurry, or we'll have finished the Dubonnet.' Norah's breezy confidence felt a little forced. Frances wondered if it was because of her or the party or the prospect of attending one with the other.

She opened her case and selected a grey wool skirt and a peach twinset with pretty pearl buttons. She inspected the top half of her outfit in the mirror above Norah's chest of drawers: it was a bit rumpled, but she was sure it would be presentable by the time she arrived at the party.

Laughter and up-tempo music drifted down the hall. Nervously, Frances peered around the door and then stepped into the room. While the music played on, the chatter stopped abruptly. Norah looked at her friend and the other girls looked from Frances to Norah.

'What?' she asked. 'What's wrong?'

Norah put down her drink and ushered Frances back out of the door.

'Come with me.'

Back in the bedroom, Norah was swiping through the hangers on her clothes rail.

'It's fine, darling. I'll find you something,' she called over her shoulder.

Frances was still unsure of the problem. 'I know it's a bit creased, but they'll fall out, I'm sure.' She patted her cardigan.

Norah turned and smiled. 'It's not that. You just look . . .' She looked Frances up and down. 'Well, a bit square. It's a fun party. A London party, you know?'

Frances did not know, but nodded, trusting her friend.

'It happened to me when I arrived too. Ballytoor is different.

Here, what you wear to church isn't what you wear to go out. Try this.' She handed Frances a blue shirt-waisted dress with an extravagant skirt. It was made from a thick cotton and she liked the way it felt.

'Oh, and maybe this in your hair.' Norah proffered a pale blue scarf dotted with yellow stars. Frances smiled as she took it. 'Thank you. It's all so pretty.'

'Hurry!' Norah called as she left her to get changed. 'We'll be leaving in a minute.'

When she re-entered the sitting room, the dress hugging her waist, the scarf framing her face, the girls gave her a round of applause. Frances could feel herself blushing as she gave an awkward curtsey. Honor jumped from her chair.

'You could have stepped out of *Tatler*! You look smashing.'

Frances noticed that the others were all wearing slacks and shirts. She was fairly certain that Tilly's jacket was part of a man's suit.

'Drinkie?' Hilda asked, sloshing what was left of the Dubonnet into a glass.

'Thank you.'

The girls all clinked her glass with a chorus of cheers, and Frances allowed herself to believe that everything might be all right.

Dinner was pasta in a tiny Italian restaurant where the air seemed to be mostly made up of steam and cigarette smoke. Frances was squashed on a bench with Hilda and Tilly while Norah and Honor sat opposite them on bentwood chairs. The red wine was served in small goblets and everything tasted delicious. Cream and garlic, vibrant leaves of basil, tomatoes that had so much more flavour than the ones Frances had bought in Galvins only a couple of weeks earlier. Frances wanted to talk about the food but the others ate as if someone was holding a stopwatch. They teased Tilly when she ordered garlic bread.

'No kisses for you tonight.'

It was only then that Frances considered who might be at the party. There were her four companions and their hostess Van, but of course there must be others.

'Who's going to be at the party?' she asked no one in particular, and the rest of the table turned to Norah.

'Well, Van is a literary agent, she looks after playwrights and directors mostly, but I suppose there might be some actors as well.' She sounded a little unsure about this and Honor interrupted her with a snigger.

'But it will mostly be women. I mean, Van knows everyone, so who knows.'

Hilda squeezed Frances's arm. 'Don't worry. We'll take care of you.'

Frances wondered why she would need looking after. A party full of women sounded ideal to her.

When they left the restaurant, the damp night air felt cool and refreshing on Frances's skin, and she noticed how the lights were reflected in the wet pavements. Their little group made its way past the elegant shopfronts of Jermyn Street, and then down a short hill into an imposing square lined with large mansions, all lit from within. As the others hurried on, Frances tried to catch a glimpse of the interiors. Heavy drapes, the tops of ornate chairbacks, the sparkle of a chandelier.

'Where is this?' she asked.

'St James's Square,' Hilda replied without slowing down.

'Nancy Astor used to live here,' Tilly added, slightly out of breath.

Frances wasn't entirely sure who that was. 'Oh.'

And then they had turned right out of the square into a darker street. Three or four buildings along, they reached a large stone-pillared porch and stopped.

'This is it,' Norah said. Frances looked up at the building in disbelief.

'Your friend lives here?'

'She has a flat,' Norah explained and ushered everyone inside.

'How do you know her?' Frances asked. It seemed very unlikely that any of these girls would be friends with someone who lived in this place.

'Through my aunt. She's been a great friend. She helped me get my job at Delfont.'

Had Frances imagined it or had the other girls just exchanged an amused look?

Inside the wide wood-panelled hallway, an old man in a uniform that wasn't quite military stood by the stairs with a clipboard.

'Yes?' His voice croaked like a neglected engine.

'The Everden party? Dean, Norah Dean.' Frances could scarcely believe the sound that was coming out of her friend's mouth. It was now completely British with not a hint of Ballytoor.

'Second floor. There is a lift if you prefer.' The man pointed to his left.

'Stairs are fine. Thank you.' Frances and the others scampered after Norah up the staircase, their footsteps muffled by thick carpet. On the second floor at the end of the hallway, a large panelled door was ajar. The sounds of a party drifted towards them. Loud voices and laughter. Someone was playing a piano.

Inside was a small vestibule with double doors leading into a large reception room with the highest ceilings Frances had ever seen. One of the tall windows had been propped open and the lace curtain swirled across the room on the night breeze. What seemed like hundreds of candles made warm dents in the thick, smoke-filled air, and every flat surface was piled high with books and stacks of paper. Frances hid behind the others while Norah scanned the crowd.

'I can't see Van, can you?' Norah asked Honor.

Frances gave the crowd a surreptitious glance. It did seem to be mostly women, but this was not like any female gathering she had encountered before. There were no sherry glasses here, no polite chatter. These women were holding tumblers and wine glasses, emitting long plumes of cigarette smoke, their laughter full-throated, their bodies leaning unselfconsciously against walls or draped across chairs. She spotted a few men but they were all very young and slight-seeming. Looking again, Frances wondered if the men were in fact also women.

'There she is,' Norah said and waved towards the far end of the room.

A tall, angular woman had just come through the narrow door by the furthest window. Frances guessed that she was in her mid- to late forties. Disconcertingly, she was dressed almost identically to Norah but in a heightened manner. Her pearls were a double strand, her shirt collar was higher, the long scarf a liquid gold. Catching sight of Norah, she called out, 'Nor!' and handed the plate of canapés she had been carrying to a young man, or maybe woman, who was standing next to her. She strode towards them.

'Nor! *Bonjour*, priestess!' She took Norah in a tight embrace and kissed her on the cheek. Stepping back, she looked at the others. 'And you've brought the little sisters of hilarity with you. Welcome, girls!'

Honor, Tilly and Hilda stepped forward to kiss their hostess on her proffered cheek. Frances wasn't sure if she should do the same. Was that something people did on a first meeting? Before she had a chance to decide, Van had a hand on the side of her face. 'This one is new. What's your name, darling?'

'Frances. Thank you for inviting me.'

Van grabbed at her gold scarf. 'The voice. That adorable accent.

Oh, little Frankie! And how long have you been in London, Frankie?'

Frances was sure that her face must be bright red. Why was this stranger calling her Frankie? 'Today. I arrived today.'

Without warning, Van hugged her. 'No. That is too much. How marvellous. Welcome to Sodom!'

Norah quickly interrupted by touching Van on the arm. 'This is Frances, my friend from Ireland. I asked if she could come.'

'Of course, of course. Frankie is so welcome.' She gave Frances a warm smile and touched her face once more. '*Boissons pour les filles!* Come with me – there's plonk, a fairly lethal punch and there was gin but the early birds may have polished that off already.'

The little group was led into a large kitchen. The wide sash window was also pushed open and two women were sitting on the windowsill, smoking. A table was covered in various bottles and a random selection of glassware. The others began to pour themselves drinks but Frances held back. Van turned to her, a bottle in her hand.

'And Frankie, what will she have to drink?'

Frances surveyed the table nervously. 'Maybe some wine, red wine?'

'Of course! I couldn't refuse that voice anything. She sounds the way you used to, Nor.'

'You were the one who encouraged me to change,' Norah said defensively.

'Well, you wanted to work, and Bernie Delfont sends things to the provinces, he doesn't import them. How are things at Delfont Towers?'

'Good. Busy. It's all Talk of the Town these days.' Norah had acquired a cigarette from someone and the way she was smoking reminded Frances of the way they had pretended to smoke as girls.

'Quite the success. I find that Eartha Kitt so intriguing.'

'Do you?' Norah stretched out her vowels in a way that seemed meaningful, but Frances was unclear as to what that meaning might be.

Van gave a short laugh. 'Oh, not that intriguing. Not the way I find your little pal Frankie intriguing.' Van leaned towards Frances and raised her drink. 'Cheers, Frankie.' They clinked glasses.

Norah's face became serious and she took their hostess's arm. 'Van, come with me. I need to show you something in the other room.'

Van giggled in a mildly inebriated way. 'Of course! My eyes have it.'

The two women left Frances, so she rejoined Honor and the others, who were leaning against the kitchen counter.

'Enjoying yourself?' Honor asked. She was now smoking too.

'Yes. I've never been to a party like this before,' Frances said, sipping her bitter wine and pretending to enjoy it.

'I'm going to see Barbara next door,' Tilly announced, dropping a lit cigarette into a discarded glass of white wine.

'Isn't she with Amanda now?' Hilda asked.

'I'm still allowed to talk to her!' It was the most spirited Tilly had sounded since Frances had met her. Honor turned away and went back to the table to refill her glass.

The three women had only been making small talk in the kitchen for a few moments when Tilly burst back into the room.

'They're dancing next door. Come on!'

Obeying her command, they put down their drinks and went back into the large room, which now contained many more bodies than before. A young woman in a vibrant red polka-dot blouse was playing the piano but there was also music coming from a record player. It was not the most mellifluous sound but the crowd didn't seem to care. They moved as one. It reminded Frances of the way seaweed moved when it was caught in the shallows.

The others began to dance and Frances, grateful for the couple of glasses of red wine she had drunk with dinner, joined them. Dancing with women wasn't new, she had done it at school, but it was the first occasion in a very long time that she hadn't had to think about the male gaze. The others seemed to feel the freedom as well: limbs flailed, hair flew, sweaty faces smiled with pure joy and none of the self-consciousness that comes from trying to look pretty. Frances gave herself over to the strange rhythmic noise that was passing for music. Her world became the happy faces of Hilda and Honor and the three of them laughed for no reason as they danced. Shaking her limbs, Frances felt like she was saying goodbye to all the restraints of Ballytoor and Castlekeen. She was shaking loose Alan and her aunt and her uncle, letting go of the disapproving looks of pale-faced parishioners. This was going to be her new life. She paused for a moment and looked around at the bodies moving to the thin sound of the piano layered over some dance record she couldn't identify.

By the door, she noticed two people in a passionate embrace. Frances tried not to feel shocked. This was London and people could do what they wanted. Then she realised that the figures were two women and could barely suppress her prudish surprise. She looked to see if anyone else had noticed the couple, but it was like a contagion. There were other pairs of women doing the same thing in other corners of the room. Frances turned to gauge the reaction of Honor and Hilda, but they were gone and in their place was a clear-skinned woman with dark hair slicked up and back into an Elvis quiff. She smiled at Frances and tried to take her hand to dance. Frances pulled away and pushed past people into the small hallway. What was this place that Norah had brought her to? She found she was struggling to catch her breath, more from a vague sense of panic than the exertion of dancing. Exhausted from her travels and tired of feeling foolish, she closed her eyes. All she wanted was to be transported to Norah's flat and to lie down away from this cacophony and these people, but she had no keys, no money and no idea where in the city she was.

'Hello.' A clipped British voice.

Frances opened her eyes. A short woman with large glasses was standing in front of her.

'Are you in charge of the coats?' she asked.

'No!' Frances snapped and pushed passed her, only to bump into Norah.

'I was looking for you.' Strands of Norah's hair were stuck to the sweat on her forehead. Her red scarf was gone. 'I saw you run off.'

'What is this place? What's going on?' Frances hated how thin and whiney her voice sounded.

Norah looked away at the dancers. 'It's a party,' she declared brightly, but then, turning back to Frances, added softly, 'I'm sorry. I wanted to explain. I didn't know how to.' She stood looking into her friend's face. Frances assumed she was waiting for some sort of understanding or forgiveness.

'I want to go home.' It was the only response she could think of.

Norah gave a quick glance over her shoulder. 'Of course – I'll come with you. Let me just tell the others.' She darted away and was immediately swallowed up by the thicket of dancers.

Now that Frances knew she was leaving, she felt slightly deflated. As she looked again at the couples wrapped around each other, they already seemed less shocking to her. Norah re-emerged from the crowd and, taking her friend's arm, led her out of the door and down the wide staircase. Frances felt grateful to be leaving but also sheepish that she had caused a scene and yet again appeared to need looking after.

'I'm sorry. I'm just so tired.'

'Of course. I'm sorry. I should have realised.' Norah's voice was soft and more Irish.

They clattered across the tiled reception and then they were retracing their steps in the chill night air.

'I wasn't . . . you know . . . I just wish you'd warned me, that's all.'

Norah was quiet for a moment. 'I know. I meant to. I kept thinking I would. This afternoon, before dinner, on the way to the party, but suddenly we were in Van's flat and it was too late. I'm sorry.'

They were heading towards the brighter lights of Piccadilly.

'We can catch a bus up here,' Norah explained.

As they walked side by side, Frances waited for further explanation, but none came. They were at the bus stop when she finally summoned the courage to ask some questions.

'Do you not like boys any more?'

Norah studied the pavement, but a smile crept across her face. 'I don't not like boys, it's just that now I might like girls too.'

Frances nodded.

'Is this too much? I know it's a lot but I'm not a different person. You understand?'

'Yes. Of course I do.' Frances couldn't make eye contact because that had been precisely what she had been thinking. Norah *was* a different person. 'I want to know more.' She took a deep breath. 'Is Van your . . . your . . . ?' The correct word failed her.

'No. No, she's not. Well, maybe a little, maybe I thought she was, but Van, well, she has lots of friends.'

Frances thought about this for a moment.

'And the others in the flat, are they all . . . what do I say?

Lesbians?' She found herself giggling. The word seemed so un-familiar and scientific.

'No. Well, Honor is a lesbian, and Tilly, but Hilda, well she isn't sure.'

'Wouldn't you know? I mean wouldn't Hilda know that about herself?'

'It's complicated. I knew I had feelings but I didn't know that I was different until I met Van.' She found Frances's eyes. 'Taking you to that party, it was silly. I'm really sorry. I suppose I just wanted you to see my new life.'

'That's your new life?' Frances sounded more judgemental than she felt.

'Part of it, yes. Frances, I can't talk to you if you want me to apologise or defend myself. I'm happy – happier than I've ever been in my life.'

Frances couldn't help thinking that Norah didn't seem very happy. Unsure if she was still allowed to hug her friend, she did it anyway. Sudden jagged sobs shook Norah's shoulders as Frances stroked her hair. It felt good to be the comforter for a change.

'Do you love Van? Is that it?' she whispered.

Norah pulled her tear-stained face away. 'Maybe. I certainly like her more than she likes me, and then when she started flirting with you—'

'Me?'

'You know she was.'

Frances squirmed. 'A bit. I don't know. She was pure fooling, I'm sure.'

Norah was laughing. 'Oh, not fooling. She told me my friend Frankie was going to be a heartbreaker and— Oh, here's our bus!' She stepped towards the kerb and the warmth and light of the bus that, in the still of the night, looked like home.

*   *   *

The next morning Frances pretended to be asleep as Norah moved around in the shadows, getting ready for work. She waited until she had heard the heavy door slam multiple times and a silence descend on the flat before getting up. Just the walk to the kitchen left her longing to return to bed. Unused as she was to drinking, she deeply regretted the red wine of the night before. Her mouth felt like she had swallowed an old woollen glove and her head throbbed. She did not envy the others having to spend the whole day in an office.

Tea and toast partially restored her and a long hot bath did the rest. She knew that she should look for a job but the enormity of the task was so daunting that she convinced herself she should wait and ask the other girls for help in focusing her search. The only thing she had even approaching a qualification was a few weeks on a cookery course in Cork, and she very much doubted that would be enough for her to secure a job in a London restaurant. Instead, she spent several hours in the Tate Gallery. It seemed like such a luxury to just sit on a polished wooden bench and stare at the enormous canvases. It took some time before she realised that no one was looking at her or judging her for spending so much time in each room. She was no longer the canon's wife, and her newfound anonymity made her feel quite giddy.

Eventually she made her way back to the flat, not wanting to spend money for tea in the gallery café. When she opened the front door there was yet another delivery of letters on the floor. How often did post arrive in London? She picked them up and sorted through them, placing most of the envelopes on the hall table because they were addressed to other flats in the building, but one, the most expensive-seeming, light blue and grained, was addressed to her, care of Norah. There was no stamp – who could it be from? Not waiting to head upstairs, she tore it open.

Inside was a small piece of paper neatly typed and signed with a flourish above the printed name 'Van Everden'. Sitting on the stairs, Frances read.

> *Everden and Associates,*
> *22 Suffolk Street,*
> *London SW1*

> *Dear Frankie,*
> *May I call you Frankie? I hope so, because I want to imagine a future where you and I are friends.*
>
> *I feel I owe you an apology for last night. It was never my intention to make you feel uncomfortable. I fear the party spirit may have got the better of me.*
>
> *Perhaps it is guilt, but I prefer to believe it's my superior sense of intuition, because I think I may have a role for you working at the agency. Please make yourself known to the receptionist on Monday morning at ten. Nor knows where we are.*
>
> *With apologies and the hope of making a better second impression,*
> *Van Everden*

A job? Her first full day in London and somebody was offering her a job? Life was not meant to be this easy, something surely would go wrong. What sort of job? Maybe the girls could tell her more about Everden and Associates when they got back from work. Running up the stairs, she tried to suppress her excitement but it was impossible. She was in the biggest city in the world and she was succeeding. It rankled her that the first person she wanted to tell was Alan. What did it matter what he thought? Still, the idea of him hearing of

her success in a world that made Castlekeen look as insignificant as it was was too enjoyable to deny herself. Frances threw
herself down on the floral sofa and looked up at the ornate
ceiling. She thought about John O'Sullivan. Could she write
to him and tell him about her job? Could he leave his life
behind and come and join her in London? She sighed. That
would be like inviting a . . . she tried to think of a creature,
maybe an otter or a fox, to wear clothes and perch on a sofa.
He had to stay where he was.

'You?' Honor said, as if accusing Frances of something. It
seemed that the others did not share her excitement at the prospect of her new job.

'But what can you do?' Tilly asked. 'Have you shorthand or
typing?' Frances shook her head. 'Well then,' Tilly continued,
'I very much doubt this will come to anything.' She threw her
coat across one of the armchairs. 'Sorry,' she added as an after-
thought. 'Cruel, really, of Van to offer something without
knowing all the facts.'

Norah was staring at the letter. 'She told me that she wanted
to apologise but she never mentioned anything about a job. What
could it be? I don't mean to be rude, Frankie, but you don't know
the first thing about the theatre, do you?'

Frances wasn't sure she wanted to become Frankie, but decided
to ignore it. 'Well, did you know anything before you got your
job at Delfont?' She wasn't going to give up on her fantasy without
a fight.

'Well, no, but I had secretarial skills. I'm a secretary, so is
Honor, it's what we do. I can't imagine Van is so smitten with
you that she's going to put you through secretarial college.'

'She might,' Hilda said, walking into the room, having heard
the conversation through the open doors. 'You of all people know
what she's like.'

Norah turned on Hilda, clearly irritated. 'We were friends. Good friends. We still are. Frances . . . well, Frances, you know, she's not interested in that, not like that. It's a very different situation.'

Frances didn't like being discussed as if she was no longer in the room and, despite her growing fear that the others might be right about Van's motivation, she refused to allow them to make assumptions for her. 'Well, I won't know till I go in on Monday morning.'

'True,' Tilly announced with a sense of finality. She was ready to talk about something else. 'Now, what shall we do for food? I can do a pot of my savoury mince or we could get takeaway from the Pagoda.'

'Chinese!' the girls chorused and, not for the last time, Frances found herself unsure of what was happening.

II

Suffolk Street consisted of an elegant selection of white stucco buildings tucked in behind Haymarket. Frances found it easily and it was impossible to miss the large brass plaque on number twenty-two declaring it to be the home of Everden and Associates. The reception area was on the ground floor. A man – it was definitely a man, despite his slim frame and blond hair so long that it curled under his ears – was sitting behind an imposing wooden desk. He looked up and removed his glasses. Frances was struck by his pale eyes and even, white teeth. He had the air of a friendly matinee idol. 'May I help you?'

'Yes,' Frances declared with a confidence and volume that she immediately realised was not appropriate for this hushed room. 'I have an appointment,' she continued, now in almost a whisper, 'with . . .' She hesitated. Van or Miss Everden? She opted for the latter. The man smiled warmly. 'Frankie? We've been expecting you. I couldn't mistake that lovely accent.'

Frances wasn't sure how to respond, so she didn't.

'If you'd like to take a seat, I'll let Van know you're here.' He stepped through a door behind his desk and, almost before Frances had taken a seat, Van came striding into the room. She was wearing a strange sleeveless cardigan that came down to her knees over a silky grey blouse and wide-legged pinstriped trousers. She rushed forward and shook Frances's hand.

'You find me a woman transformed, Frankie. Professional, clear-headed, efficient.' She turned to the young man settling back into his chair. 'Dear Dennis, I got a little excited on Thursday night and I fear I may have frightened young Frankie here.'

Dennis gave a little laugh. 'Oh, no need to be frightened. Careful, yes, but never frightened.' Van gave him a playful slap to the back of his head and led Frances through the door.

Surprisingly, this second room seemed slightly smaller than the reception, and, judging from the size of the desk spanning the back window, this was Van's office. Frances had assumed that Everden and Associates took up the entire building, but it seemed that the only associates were on the brass plaque outside. Van retreated behind the battlements of books and manuscripts on her desk and indicated the small leather chair to the side. Frances sat. Just then there was the sound of a toilet flushing and a young woman emerged from a second door that Frances hadn't noticed.

'Ruby, this is Frankie. Frankie, Ruby.' A brief handshake and a flash of white teeth. Ruby looked remarkably normal. She wouldn't have looked out of place at a bring-and-buy sale in Castlekeen. She wore a pastel twinset over a brown tweed skirt, and her hair looked like it had an artificial wave. She wasn't what anyone would describe as glamorous, but she was pretty in an unthreatening way.

'Ruby, would you please take these to the post office?' Van held up a thick pile of large envelopes. 'You can get petty cash from Dennis.' Ruby seemed mildly put out by this request, as if she had something else she would prefer to be doing. She didn't sigh or roll her eyes, but that was the impression she gave as she left the room. Van held her forefinger to her lips until she heard the outer door close.

'She is driving me insane. It's irrational, I know, but I want to hurt her, physically hurt her. Do you know what I mean?' Happily, she didn't seem to require Frances to answer because she continued, 'My question to you is, would you like to replace her?' This time Van did look at Frances expectantly.

'Well, yes, but I don't know if I can do her job.'

Van waved her hand in the air. 'Trust me, if Ruby can manage, a small dog in a hat could do the job. For the most part you will be on the phone. It's arranging meetings, making sure my diary is correct, sometimes booking travel. *Parlez-vous français?*'

Suddenly transported back to school, Frances automatically blurted out '*Oui, un peu.*'

'Well, *un peu* is all you'll need. Dennis does the invoices, and do you type?'

'Well, I have typed; but not really, no.'

'Not to worry. You can learn on the job. We're not exactly rushed off our feet here, so you can take your time.'

Van's enthusiasm was making Frances very uncomfortable. She needed a job, but this was clearly a position she was wholly unsuited for.

'This is so kind of you, but I'm sure you could find someone better qualified . . .'

'Oh, Frankie, aren't you . . .' Van reached out a hand to touch her, but then quickly withdrew it. 'That's why I want you to work here. So straightforward. You remind me of Nor. I wish I'd given her a job, but of course that became complicated.' Van raised her eyebrows and smiled. 'We can give you a trial period if you prefer? Two months, say?'

Frances was relieved. 'That sounds wonderful.' She thought about Ruby. Presumably Van had been keen on her at some point. Would she turn on Frances in the same way?

'Let's start you tomorrow, Frankie. Ruby can show you the few ropes she has grasped, but Dennis is the one who knows everything.'

Before she knew it, Frances was back on the street. She felt different, as if the people striding purposefully along the pavement could tell that she was one of them now. As she walked towards Trafalgar Square, she passed Ruby, who appeared not to recognise her. Did she even know that she was leaving?

Wapping, 2024

Damian knew he shouldn't be drinking at work but Nor had insisted. 'It's Calvados. Just a little sip. Even if you don't like brandy, you'll love this.'

Damian sheepishly agreed.

'I hope there isn't an emergency during the night,' Frankie said with a wink.

'Stop it! I won't have it then. I'm grand.'

Nor turned back to the table. 'You are having some! Now, Frankie, have you such a thing as brandy glasses?'

'Brandy glasses? I have not. I have too much in this place as it is without brandy glasses. Use the good china.'

Nor placed three pretty green and gold teacups on the table. 'Very rustic!' She poured out generous measures of the amber liquid. The smell was enough for Damian – it assaulted his nose and brought tears to his eyes.

'Wow, that's strong.'

'Oh my God, Nor, did you make it yourself? That smells like petrol.' Frankie put down her cup.

Nor gasped with indignation. 'It's from a little farm just outside Bayeux. Teddy swore by it.' She poured the rest of the two cups into her own and gave the contents an exaggerated sip. '*Délicieux!*'

'You sound like Van Everden.'

Nor put down her cup. 'Strange old Van. I was very fond of her. I know you had your problems with her, but she was always kind to me.'

'Problems? Yes, let's call them problems.' Frankie wiped some crumbs from the table.

'Did you not get to keep the job?' Damian asked. He liked this turn in the story, full of lesbians and Frankie working in show business. It was the sort of London he had hoped to discover when he had first arrived. 'Was it the typing?'

'No, no. To begin with I was a great success. I managed to learn some basic typing and I was organised. I worked there for over a year. I suppose I was more mature in some ways than most of the London girls my age, so I wasn't distracted.'

'Damian, you have no idea. Frankie was like a new woman,' Nor said, perching on the windowsill. 'And I'd never seen Van so happy. She brought her Frankie everywhere.'

'And no funny business?'

'No. Well, that's not quite true. She would have a drink and then start making suggestions, but she knew I wasn't the one for her.'

Nor let out a whoop that made Damian jump in his chair. 'The one for her? Van was madly in love with her, completely besotted. Everyone just assumed they were together.'

'Did they?' Frankie asked.

'Yes, of course they did. You were what we'd call now a lesbian power couple. Van dressed you and made sure you were at every opening night with her. I was wildly jealous!'

'And where did you live?' Damian was struggling to imagine Frankie living the life Nor was describing.

'Oh, I stayed on at Alderney Street. The other girl from Delfont moved out.'

'Honor,' Nor reminded her. 'She headed back to Wiltshire

when she got herself pregnant. Turns out she wasn't quite as committed to the sapphic arts as she had led us to believe.'

Damian suddenly remembered something.

'But you got married, didn't you?' he asked Nor.

'Well, someone has been very chatty.' She threw a glance at Frankie. 'That's a story for another day. I must go – the driver will think I've been kidnapped.' She began gathering her coat and bag.

'Sorry, I didn't realise . . .' Damian said quickly, embarrassed that he might have overstepped the mark.

'Don't be silly. I'll tell you all about it next time. Unless of course madam beats me to it.' Nor was speaking over her shoulder at the kitchen door.

'Did you ever see Honor again?' Frankie wondered. Her demeanour had changed. She seemed quieter.

'You know, I don't think I did. She got married, I know that, but I seem to remember illness. Cancer, maybe?'

'Sad. Wait long enough and it's all sad.' Frankie heaved herself up from the table and leaned on her crutch. 'I'm so glad we're still friends, Nor. It means so much.' She leaned forward and gave the other woman a hug. Damian felt awkward. The kitchen was too small for all three of them to share this moment. Nor didn't look very comfortable with the hug either, and Damian wondered why. It did seem like a farewell of sorts.

Nor pushed Frankie away and kissed the top of her head. 'Look at you, getting all sentimental. You're supposed to be the tough one.' She turned to Damian. 'Time to get madam off to bed, I think.'

Later in the bedroom, with Frankie sitting on the bed and Damian finally being allowed, after much persuasion, to put lotion on her uncovered foot, he returned to the subject of Van Everden.

'What did Nor mean by "your problems with Van"?'

Frankie looked to the ceiling and then down at the young man busy at her feet.

'It was a misunderstanding, I'll give her that, but her reaction? I'm not sure I can ever forgive that.'

'What happened?'

'Now? You want that story now? Aren't you bored of hearing tales about dead people you don't know?'

Damian smiled. 'Would you stop. I know you, and I like hearing about your wild youth. Anyway, I'm not tired yet. Are you?' He swung her feet up and under the covers and she lay back on the pillow.

'Not especially. But we'll need tea.'

'Sorted,' he said as he jumped up.

London, 1960

I

The spring season had been a great success for the clients of Everden and Associates. Two experimental French writers had long runs with absurdist comedies that Frankie couldn't understand, even though they had been translated into English. A show by one of Van's biggest clients that had been a hit at the Royal Court a couple of years earlier was being turned into a film, and a long-forgotten South African writer had been commissioned to write a series of radio plays about the Coalbrook mining disaster. The phones rang constantly with people wanting meetings with the great Miss Everden, or enquiring after touring rights, or simply trying to get tickets to some sold-out show.

'It's never normally like this,' Dennis told Frankie late one Friday afternoon. He gave her his best smile. 'I mean, we muddle through, but hits – more than one hit – that never happens.'

Frankie could hear Van on the phone in the office next door, so kept her voice low. 'But her flat, these rooms, us – how does she pay for it all?'

'Only daughter of the Everdens of Kent.' He leaned towards Frankie and whispered, 'Top secret, of course. But I see cheques arriving. Big cheques. Not a word!'

Frankie was confused. Van exuded confidence and success. 'But, why do they help?'

Dennis listened for a moment to ensure Van was still on the phone.

'Guilt. Little Miss Everden wanted to be an actress but that news was not received well in Kent, so they got her a job with an agency and then set her up in her own business. Something they can tell people about at the golf club.'

Frankie wasn't sure what to think. Running a literary agency had to be better than being married to Canon Frost, but it was still Van's parents dictating what she did. Frankie had never expected to feel sorry for Van, but she did.

A few nights later, Van and Frankie were sitting in Quaglino's after seeing a starry but dull play on Shaftesbury Avenue. Frankie had become used to eating in nice restaurants but this seemed a little grander. A small band was playing by the stairs, and the candlelight glittered in the jewellery of the female diners. When Dennis had overheard Frankie making the reservation, he couldn't wait to tell her that Princess Margaret sometimes ate there.

'Is it a special occasion?' she asked Van, contemplating their lavish surroundings.

'No . . . well, maybe, we'll see. I'll taste the wine.' She barked this last command at the wine waiter hesitating by their table.

'Of course, madam.'

A tiny pour followed by a quick sniff.

'Lovely, thank you.'

Frankie found herself thinking how much easier life was with a man. It didn't matter how successful Van became, there would always be a wine waiter or a maître d' to remind her that she wasn't enough. Not for the first time, Frankie resolved to do something about going on a date, or indeed just meeting a man. Her world had become so female-centric that presumably, if she was to meet an interested man, he would just assume Van was more than her boss.

'You'll like it. It's sweet.' Van smiled at Frankie.

They clinked their glasses.

'Oh God.' Van looked down at the table. 'John Calder is over there. No, don't look!' she hissed at Frankie as she moved in her chair to see who Van was talking about.

'Do you need to go over and say hello?'

'Christ, no. He loathes me with a passion.'

Frankie wanted to ask why, but had learned that Van didn't respond well to questions she felt were too personal.

'About a hundred years ago I used to work for him. He's never forgiven me for starting up for myself. And I took Claude with me.' Claude was one of the French absurdists enjoying great success.

Van leaned back in her chair and looked across at Frankie meaningfully. 'I must learn to trust my intuition more often.'

Frankie didn't understand. 'Oh, yes.'

'You, you dozy doat! You've been a good-luck charm. Thank you!' She raised her glass once more for a brief toast. 'You enjoy working for me, don't you?'

'Yes,' Frankie said enthusiastically and without hesitation. She could scarcely remember the woman she had been barely a year earlier, the washed-out waif dragging her suitcase through the streets of Pimlico. Van Everden had taught her so much, not just about the world, but also about herself. Hapless Frances had become Frankie, who was good at her job and from time to time might even have been described as confident. It seemed that Frankie enjoyed details, could easily retain information, and was well liked. It didn't quite give her the pure satisfaction of cooking or baking but it was pretty close.

'Good, I'm glad.'

After their starter plates had been cleared away, Van refolded her napkin and then announced, 'I had quite a tempting invitation today.'

Again, Frankie just waited for Van to expand.

'My friend David, David Higham?' This was Van's way of indicating it was a name Frankie, or whoever was listening, should be familiar with. Frankie had no idea who David was but just nodded.

'Well, one of his clients, Tim, Tim White?'

Another nod in the dark.

'His book is being turned into a Broadway musical, I mean a big one. It's Lerner and Loewe.'

Even Frankie had heard those names before.

'Rehearsals start in New York later in the year, and David feels Tim may need some hand-holding' – Van mimed downing several drinks – 'but David doesn't feel up to the journey. He's offered me a two-week jolly, air fare, hotel. What do you think?'

Frankie wasn't sure what to think. Was this an invitation? Was Van asking her to go to America, on a plane? She knew she mustn't seem too excited in case she had misunderstood and the whole conversation descended into humiliation. She took a sip of her wine to steady herself.

'Aren't you too busy?'

'Too busy for New York? Never! Dennis can hold the fort here and besides, everyone will think I'm there being a hotshot agent rather than a glorified babysitter.' She leaned forward. 'I would love to show you New York. Honestly, Broadway makes us look like a bunch of am-dram hacks.'

'Me? Seriously?'

Van laughed. 'Oh Frankie, yes, you. We'll see some shows, I've got a couple of friends there; I might even do a little work.'

If she hadn't been worried about what it might mean, Frankie would have hugged her boss.

'Thank you! Thank you so much. I can't believe it. When?'

'Rehearsals begin right after the Labor Day weekend, whenever that is – early September I think.' She reached forward and clasped Frankie's hand. 'Something to look forward to.'

Frankie did her best to hold her smile steady and mask her discomfort. Were other diners looking at the two women holding hands? Was a waiter going to say something? She lowered her gaze to avoid eye contact but Van seemed to misunderstand the gesture because she squeezed her hand tighter.

II

The next two months were shrouded in a veil of furtive planning. All thoughts were on New York but the trip was rarely discussed. In the office, Dennis had been less than pleased when he had heard about the plan, and, back at Alderney Street, Frankie knew that the girls would not want to hear about Van whisking her off to Manhattan. Van seemed to enjoy the secrecy. 'Wait till Broadway' became her whispered catchphrase, as if their lives were going to change completely once they got to New York. It was a side of her boss she had not seen before and Van seemed reduced by it, girlish and silly. Frankie's excitement came more and more to feel like trepidation.

Her constant guide through the early weeks and months at Everden and Associates had been Norah. Each morning Frankie would stand for inspection while Norah decided if what she was wearing would pass the Van test.

'I've got some brogues you can borrow.'

'She hates yellow and roses, so this is a disaster.'

'Plain, navy, boxy – top of the class, Miss Howe!'

It was part of their routine, a way of re-establishing their friendship after so long apart. Frankie would report back in the evening on what had gone well, or the mistakes she had made, whether Van was pleased or not. Norah seemed happy for her friend, despite that initial prickle of envy. She laughed along, teasing her about how much Van seemed to have taken her under her wing. It was only as Frankie became more comfortable that tensions seemed to build again. An excited report from an opening night would be met with silence or an uninterested 'Good night.' A new outfit that was clearly a gift from Van might be ignored. Frankie understood that her friend, who had once been so close with Van, was probably jealous, so she tried to compensate by asking Norah about her work or where she was spending her weekends, but the replies seemed deliberately disengaged. Bookings were up or they were down at Talk of the Town; an American star had made a fuss about moving hotels; she was just going for drinks at The Gates. 'Busy?' Frankie would ask. 'Packed.' Then the conversation was over.

When news of the American trip broke, Norah came into Frankie's room one night and sat on the edge of the bed.

'What?' Frankie immediately feared the worst. Was she going to be asked to move out?

Norah bit her lip. 'I didn't know if I should say anything, but please be careful.'

'Careful?'

'Van. She can . . . well, just don't get too close. She can change.'

Frankie waited for more details. 'In what way?'

'Snap. She can turn. I mean, it happened a bit like that with me, but we weren't that close. I mean you must have seen it, the way she can run hot and then cold.'

Frankie tried to remember. 'Not really. I mean, I've seen her lose her temper.'

In the half-light of the bedside lamp, Norah bore a striking resemblance to the long-necked silhouette of Frankie's boss. It was as if the spirit of Van past had come to warn against the Van of the future. 'Well, for example, the way she treated Ruby.'

'Ruby?' If Frankie was being completely honest, she hadn't given Ruby a second thought since she had cleared her desk for the last time. 'What about her? Van is allowed to fire people, isn't she?'

'Oh God, Frankie.' Norah looked over her shoulder as though there might be someone else in the room. 'Ruby was Van's girlfriend.'

'What? Twinset Ruby and Van? No!'

'Yes. And she was sent packing the moment you walked through the door.'

Frankie pulled herself up in the bed. 'But I'm not . . . you must believe me, it's not like that between me and Van.'

Norah raised her arms in surrender. 'I know, I know. But that's what I'm trying to tell you. It's not about what you are or aren't doing with Van, it's how she feels about you, and the closer you get, the more chance of her pushing you away. Pushing hard.' Norah widened her eyes for emphasis.

'Ruby was her girlfriend?' Frankie was still struggling to process this piece of information.

Norah stood. 'I just felt I should warn you.' She sounded weary.

'Thank you,' Frankie said, but only because it felt like the appropriate response.

The door clicked shut as Norah left the room.

These words of warning echoed in Frankie's mind as she sat beside Van in the taxi on their way to the airport. A large handbag was on the floor of the cab and Van was rifling through it with a running commentary. Every item on their itinerary, the length of their flight, where was the letter from the Drake Hotel confirming their reservations? Frankie attempted to answer all of Van's questions as calmly as she could. She had their passports and the cardboard wallet with the tickets from Pan Am. Van seemed determined to unearth the mistake she was convinced Frankie had made.

The airport didn't improve matters. It was a building site, and the obstacle course of metal barriers and temporary signs seemed to send Van into a further tailspin. Even though Frankie was the one who had never flown before, it became instantly clear that she needed to take charge, guiding Van through the maze of stairs and corridors. Frankie struggled to reconcile the self-assured boss she was accustomed to with the head-twisting, wide-eyed woman she was barely managing to herd through the passport checks.

The inside of the plane was Frankie's reward. It made her gasp. The cabin looked so ultra-modern and new. The hostesses in their blue uniforms, the little blankets, the trays of drinks; even Van was briefly hushed by it. Frankie gave their coats to the hostess, made sure that Van had her book and glasses, and then put their bags in the overhead lockers. Announcements were made in deep American voices and then the plane was thundering down the runway at an alarming speed, the rattling of glasses in the galley, a stomach lurch and then it was happening, really and truly happening – the plane was flying. Out of the window, west London became so small it made Frankie want to laugh. She turned to say something about it all to Van but was shocked to find her boss clutching the arms of her seat with her head pushed back, eyes closed, her skin bathed in sweat.

'Van, are you all right?'

The question seemed to give her permission to breathe, and Van took a great gulp of air.

'Yes. Not a lover of that bit. Silly, I know. Now, where is the hostess? We need drinks.'

The two women clinked their funny little doll's house champagne flutes. 'New York!' Frankie began to relax as the Van she knew seemed to return. She flicked through the pages of the *Clipper Travel* magazine and sipped her drink. To her left, she was aware that Van was on her second drink and then, with what seemed like unseemly haste, her third. Frankie cringed as Van's voice became louder, her demands more frequent and petty. She needed help with her seat, her light, the blanket. How many more hours was the flight? What time was it in New York? Eventually her head slumped forward in an alcohol-induced slumber. Frankie and one of the hostesses exchanged a furtive look of relief.

The prospect of two weeks alone with Van had begun to seem like a very long time. Frankie wondered how fourteen full days and nights might be filled. Was this what it was going to be like for the whole trip? She felt more like a nursemaid than any kind of professional colleague. Whatever gratitude or excitement she might have felt had already evaporated. She studied Van's face, the skin hanging loose, the red lipstick smeared, the traces of downy hair above her lip. Frankie thought about all the advantages Van enjoyed in life thanks to her wealthy, indulgent parents and yet, here she was – an object of pity. She looked more like a creature that had limped to the verge after being hit by a car than a woman who could mark up manuscripts or negotiate deals. Perhaps she just didn't travel well. Frankie hoped that New York would restore Van Everden, and then she too slipped into sleep.

A river of yellow taxis sat waiting in the sultry evening air outside the airport. A strong wind carrying strange dank smells blew past the doors as the two women left the terminal with their porter.

A flustered Van offered the man some notes after he had placed their luggage in a taxi.

'Thank you, ma'am. Thank you,' he said, beaming. 'Enjoy your stay.'

As Van slid into the back seat beside Frankie, she grumbled, 'I must have given him too much. Did you see how thrilled he was? Did you?'

'How much did you give him?'

Van settled herself and stared straight ahead. 'I'm not sure.'

The traffic was unlike anything Frankie had seen. The cars were as big as boats and the road was four or five roads stitched together. Every billboard, row of storefronts or drab motel seemed wildly exotic. She wanted to share her excitement, but Van seemed distant and unmoved by the journey. Then, there it was: the skyline of Manhattan drawn in glittering lights up and down the night sky. Frankie held her breath. She had seen photographs of New York, watched it in movies, but the reality of it was overwhelming. Nothing could have prepared her for the sheer scale of it all.

'Impressive, isn't it?' Van acknowledged.

'Gorgeous! It's just gorgeous – oh, that's the Chrysler Building, isn't it?'

Van moved her head slightly before confirming that it was indeed.

The road dipped, concealing the view of the skyscrapers, and then the taxi was in a tunnel, which fed them into the stone canyons of Manhattan itself. Frankie abandoned any attempt to appear blasé. She leaned across Van without apology to stare open-mouthed from the cab window. The restaurants, the department-store windows, the awnings outside the apartment blocks, the lights reaching impossibly high in the sky – this city made London seem like Ballytoor.

'You're going to love it here, Frankie,' Van said, smiling widely, and for the first time since they had got in the cab in Suffolk Street Frankie felt her friend and mentor was her old self.

The chill of the air-conditioning in their hotel room was both strange and comforting. Dim lamps threw shadows over the two large beds that sat side by side. In the corner of the room was a small round table that held a bowl of fruit and a bottle of red wine with two glasses. When Van stepped out of the bathroom in a pair of pale blue pyjamas, Frankie had a terrible feeling of déjà vu and was momentarily transported back to her wedding night with Alan in Kerry.

'Nightcap?' Van said, indicating the wine.

The question seemed loaded but clearly Van wanted a drink, and Frankie didn't wish to make things awkward.

'Yes please. I'll just get ready for bed.'

When Frankie emerged from the bathroom, hair and teeth brushed, she felt suitably unsexed in a floor-length brushed-cotton nightdress. It had never actually belonged to her Aunt Mona, but it could have. Van arched an eyebrow.

'Very convent chic.'

'What? It's comfortable.'

'I'm sure there must be some *bon mot* about bad habits, but I'm too tired to think of it. Here.' Van held out a glass of red wine for Frankie.

'Cheers.'

Their windows on the seventeenth floor of the Drake Hotel looked north onto 57th Street and beyond. Below them to the right they could see Park Avenue. The traffic rushing by looked like a stream of white and red lights, and the yellow of the cabs was already becoming familiar.

'I can't believe I'm here. Thank you so much, Van.' When Frankie turned from the window she found Van gazing at her.

'It's wonderful to see it all through your eyes.' Van looked down for a moment. 'I'm not sure if I owe you an apology or not.'

'An apology?' Frankie couldn't help feeling anxious. What had Van done?

'For today. I'm not the best traveller and I took some pills I got from a girlfriend. You know, to calm me down, but I'm not entirely sure they agreed with me.'

Frankie thought back to the crazed woman in the back of the taxi and the barked commands on the plane.

'Don't be silly. You were grand.'

Van gave a sheepish smile, as if acknowledging Frankie's kind lie.

'Grand. Oh, Frankie, I'm so very glad you're here.' As she spoke, she touched the side of Frankie's face and kissed her cheek. Before Frankie could react in any way, Van was apologising again.

'No. I told myself there would be none of that. You've been very clear, I know that, but you must understand I can't stop myself from wishing this was more.'

Frankie had no idea how to respond. She had agreed to this trip aware of Van's feelings for her, so she had no right to act shocked, but if she were too understanding she feared it might escalate matters. For a moment she thought she saw tears in Van's eyes, but then her boss was on her feet, busying herself with pillows and switching off lamps.

'We should probably get to bed. God knows what time it is back home. Tomorrow, we have a lunch with Tim White and then you'll need to pack a small bag because we're off to a party.'

'A party?' Frankie said, putting down her glass.

'Yes, just north of the city. A friend – well . . . a friend now, you follow?'

Frankie nodded. She felt she did know what Van was intimating.

'She's a lighting designer on Broadway and she's invited us to a house party for the weekend.'

'The weekend?' Frankie wasn't sure she liked the sound of this.

'Don't worry, it's not far away – we can come back into the city if we're not enjoying it. Now, are you ready for lights out?'

III

The next day the women made their way through the dense hot air towards Fifth Avenue and their lunch rendezvous. The sight of Tim White sitting by the window in the restaurant made Frankie feel like a native New Yorker in comparison. His thatch of hair was white and he was sporting a thick beard yellowed around the mouth by cigarette smoke. Despite the oppressive heat outside, his jacket was brown tweed, and he was already holding a large glass of red wine.

Van fussed around the table making introductions.

'I know this is so terribly touristy but my friend Jean recommended it, and I have to say the view is quite remarkable.'

The white-haired man glanced out of the window as if only just noticing he was on the forty-first floor. 'Yes. Very impressive. Why is it called Top of the Sixes?' He peered at his female companions as he took a swig of wine, a red blush now added to his already stained beard.

'Well, this building is six six six Fifth Avenue.'

'The mark of the beast,' he said ominously before picking up his menu. Van and Frankie exchanged a look of alarm. 'Shall we order?' Mr White asked from behind the large menu.

After their waitress had left the table, a silence descended. It seemed to Frankie that the presence of two women at his table was making Mr White uncomfortable and, try as she might, Van was incapable of putting him at his ease. The only things that seemed to interest him were his cigarettes and refilling his wine glass. Happily, their food appeared with remarkable speed.

'Shrimp salad bowls?' the waitress enquired without enthusiasm.

'For the ladies. I'm the grill.' It appeared that food was also capable of attracting his attention. He stuffed his napkin into his shirt collar in a way that reminded Frankie of seeing farmers eating in Langton's Hotel back home.

'Where are you staying?' Van asked brightly.

'With Julie and Tony.'

'Julie?'

'Julie Andrews, the leading actress in the production,' he explained, surprised to learn Van didn't know who that was.

'Of course I know who Julie Andrews is; I just wasn't aware you were so . . . so close,' said Van.

Mr White was now attacking his mixed grill with gusto.

'Lovely couple. They came to stay with me on Alderney.'

'Oh, I live on Alderney Street.' It was the first time Frankie had spoken and almost immediately she regretted doing so. The others swivelled towards her expectantly, but she found she had nothing more to add. After a lengthy pause, the writer simply said, 'I see.'

Frankie stared intently at her shrimp salad bowl.

'And are you happy with the adaptation?' Van persevered.

'I haven't read it yet but I really don't mind what they do. *Pygmalion* fared all right as *My Fair Lady*, so I trust they will do right by me.'

'Tim wrote the most wonderful book about the court of King Arthur,' Van explained to Frankie.

'Yes, I know,' she said with an air of surprise. Of course she knew all about the book and the musical adaptation – that was why they were here, after all.

Wine did not oil the wheels of conversation but it did manage to fuel a monologue from Van about their trip, her agency, the productions she had been involved with, both past and present, and finally her memories of a family holiday she had spent on Jersey when she was a child.

His grill dispatched, Tim wiped his mouth and beard vigorously with his napkin. It was unclear if he had heard anything Van had said.

'Well, this has been very pleasant, but I told Tony I'd be back at the apartment before Julie returns.'

They all stood.

'Will I be seeing you on Monday?' he asked.

'Monday?'

'They call it the read-through. Just around the corner from here, I believe. Fifty-Fourth Street if I'm not mistaken.'

Van managed to smile and assure Mr White that they would be there, even though Frankie was sure this was the first they had heard of any read-through.

Tim White, his shoulders slightly hunched, made his lumbering way through the tables, like an overgrown schoolboy on the last day of term.

'Thank God that's over. More wine?' Van said as she fell back into her chair. 'What was David Higham thinking? What hand-holding does that man need? He's best friends with Julie Andrews! And what was all that about the read-through? Nobody mentioned it to me.' A waitress appeared. 'Yes, please. Actually, I might have one of your cocktails . . . a French 75, please? Frankie?' Van was smiling now so Frankie chose to keep the mood light and asked for the same. Van clapped her hands.

'Well, I think that makes me a free woman. Tim White can look after himself, and New York is all ours. My friend Jean said she would pick us up at the hotel around five.'

* * *

Despite the thick warm air, the streets were still crowded as the two women slowly made their way back towards the Drake.

'I'm not certain how many will be at this little party,' Van began, 'but it will be a group of like-minded ladies. What they used to call a sewing-circle party?' Van glanced at Frankie to gauge if this seemed acceptable.

'Fine. That's fine with me,' Frankie assured her boss, though she really didn't mean it. She knew that all the guests would assume she and Van were a couple and, while she felt far more comfortable now than when she had first arrived in London, she knew she wouldn't be able to relax or enjoy herself. She could already imagine the awkward smiles, the in-jokes she wouldn't understand, the dread of unwelcome compliments. Trying to remain positive, she told herself that these women would be interesting, and it was a chance for her to see a little more of the city. She felt confident she could handle this weekend. After all, here she was striding down 56th Street and no one was staring at her as if she were an interloper.

All trepidation vanished as their hostess Jean ferried them across the George Washington Bridge with all of Manhattan posed proudly along the banks of the Hudson. Frankie kept her head craned around for as long as she could to take in the spectacle, the way the sun glittered on the water and the towers that rose above it. In the front of the car, Jean, a compact woman with short dark hair and owl-like eyes, was informing Van about the party.

'Have you met Kit Cornell before?'

'Should I have?'

'Kit? Katharine Cornell? Huge Broadway star – well, she was. She's claiming she has retired.'

'Yes, of course, of course. No, we haven't met, but isn't she friends with Gertrude?'

'Yes, yes. Gert Macy. She's a very old pal of Kit's. Doubtless she'll be there. She has a house in Sneden's too.'

By this time the car was across the bridge and Frankie was paying attention.

'Is Sneden's another town?' she asked.

'No, it's not even a village. I don't know what you'd call it. Just a collection of houses in the woods above the Hudson. Kit has been out here for years. I think everyone likes to imagine it's bohemian, but it's the wealthier class of artist you'll find in this neck of the woods. Sorry, that sounds bitchy. It is really magical. You're going to enjoy it.'

'I'm looking forward to it,' Van said, letting the wind from the open window catch her hair. 'Who is she married to? I'm drawing a blank. He's a director, isn't he?'

'Kit? Guthrie McClintic.'

'That's him. Will he be there?'

'I doubt it. I'm sure he'll be staying in the city. It'll just be Kit – and Nancy, of course.'

The large sedan made its way north from the bridge with Frankie catching glimpses of the river through the trees. Then after about half an hour, Jean turned right and the roads became steadily smaller until they were driving down a dirt track through some woods. At one point it seemed as if they were driving away from the river, but then they came to two large stone pillars each topped by an ornate lantern and a driveway that ended at a long low house perched high above the Hudson. The setting sun had turned the opposite bank a startling shade of amber. They parked beside a few other cars and made their way to the white-columned arbour that led to the wide front door.

'Kit!' Jean called out and hurried towards the elegant woman who had appeared in the doorway. Frankie would have guessed she was in her fifties and she had clearly been a great beauty.

Her dark hair was swept back, her eyebrows elegantly arched over eyes that glittered and a mouth from a Renaissance painting. Even if Frankie hadn't been forewarned, she felt confident she would have known this woman was a star. Katharine Cornell strode forward, arms outstretched, three dachshunds weaving between her legs.

'I'm Kit.'

'Van. Van Everden.'

'Delighted you could come. And this lovely creature?'

Frankie felt herself redden. 'Frankie Howe. Pleased to meet you.'

'Oh!' Kit emitted a theatrical squawk that prompted the dogs to start yapping at her feet. 'That voice. Just delicious. Where are you from, sweet thing?'

'Ireland. Cork?'

'*Coark!*' she repeated in a strangled imitation of Frankie's voice. Putting her arm around her shoulders, she steered Frankie into the house. 'Come in and meet everyone.' Frankie allowed herself to be led away, but she could sense Van's proprietorial glare.

Inside, a wide hall led down into a vast living room littered with antiques, and then through French windows onto a large terrace where various women were scattered across sun loungers and garden chairs. Their laughter sounded small and tinny against the enormous darkening sky behind them.

'Fresh blood!' Kit announced loudly as they stepped through the French windows. 'This is Frankie, that's Van, and you all know Jean Rosenthal?'

The women waved and called out their individual greetings. Kit walked over to a younger woman with short grey hair and mannish features. She placed a hand on her shoulder. 'This is Nancy. That's my old friend Gert' – she pointed towards a crumpled-looking older lady – 'and that's Peggy and Dee.' The youngest and prettiest women in the group smiled broadly. 'And we're still waiting for Pam and Stella. Now, drinks.' Kit walked over to a glass-topped table covered with bottles and jugs. 'Judy made up jugs of Tom Collins before she left. Yes?' She held up an empty glass and waved it enticingly.

Soon the three new arrivals were sipping their gin, and Frankie began to relax as the alcohol made its way into her system and she was no longer the focus of attention. The others were gossiping about Broadway and telling stories about people she didn't know. Occasionally she heard names like Orson and Bernstein and was briefly able to follow the conversation before getting lost again.

Just before it became dark, the final guests arrived. Pam was about the same age as Kit and dressed in a flamboyant silk dress that could have doubled as a tent. Stella was all long tanned legs in flannel shorts and a halter-necked top that showed off her toned arms and strong shoulders. From what Frankie could glean from snatches of talk, Pam owned some theatres and Stella was a tennis player or perhaps a coach. They settled in as another jug of cocktails was poured.

Kit went into the house and returned with a large box of matches, then began lighting a line of tiki torches that edged the patio.

'That's better. And I do think they help with the mosquitoes. Would anyone like DEET?'

Stella immediately raised her hand. 'Oh, yes please! They love me.'

Gert threw back the remains of her drink. 'I can see why!'

'Steady, Gert,' Nancy said, taking the older woman's glass. 'Maybe a break?'

'How dare you? I don't have to be drunk to pay a compliment!'

Nancy laughed. 'I feel poor Stella should be more concerned about you than the mosquitoes.'

'Don't worry about me,' Stella called across the patio as she rubbed the DEET lotion into her long limbs. Her glossy skin reflected the light from the burning torches and for a moment it seemed that the whole group was lost in her beauty.

'Want some?' She was offering the DEET to Frankie.

'Oh, you must!' Kit commanded. 'Your virgin Irish skin must be protected.'

Frankie smiled sheepishly and held out her hand to take the lotion.

'Save your hands,' Stella said. 'Mine are already messed up. Let me.' And without waiting for Frankie to speak, she was rubbing Frankie's arms and then she was on her knees massaging the lotion into her legs.

'The luck of the Irish!' Gert cackled.

No one else spoke and, while Frankie could feel all eyes on her, she was especially aware of Van's. She didn't dare look up.

'I should bring our bags in. Jean?' Van was on her feet, her English accent sounding stiff and brittle in the mellow evening air.

'Sure, sure.' Jean got out of her chair.

Frankie knew that this was her cue. 'Thanks. Thank you very much. I should go and help.' She stepped away from Stella's hands and followed Jean and Van into the glow of the living room. She could hear Gert's rasping laugh echoing behind her. 'Well, someone doesn't like to share!'

As she walked towards the car, Frankie realised how drunk she was. She hoped that some food might be served soon. Van was waiting by the back door of the car.

'Your bag,' she said curtly.

'Thank you.' Before Frankie could walk away, Van grabbed her arm. 'I didn't like that.'

'I'm sorry. I couldn't—'

'I know,' Van said, interrupting her. 'I know it wasn't your fault, but . . . I don't know. I suppose I'm just saying that I find it difficult seeing you like that. I . . . oh, ignore me, I'm being a fool. Let's enjoy ourselves. They're a fun bunch, aren't they?'

Frankie felt her tense shoulders relax. 'Yes, yes they are.'

As she hurried back to the house, the front door was suddenly lit up by the headlights of a large car being driven by a young dark-haired man.

'That's Joe, my driver. He sometimes stays above the garage,' Kit explained as they entered the hallway. 'Now, ladies, come this way.' She led them into a dark red room lined with books. 'Will you girls be sharing a room?'

'No,' Van said, a little too loudly.

'I see.' Kit raised an eyebrow. 'In that case, Van you can stay through here in Guthrie's room.' She opened a tall door into another red room dominated by a painting of a much younger Kit in Egyptian garb.

'Sorry about that,' said their hostess with a dismissive wave of her hand. 'My Cleopatra. It was a gift and Guthrie claims he likes it.' She turned and spoke to Frankie: 'And I'll set you up on the couch in his study.' She indicated the wide, low sofa in the room they had just come through.

'That's great. Thank you so much,' Frankie said, hoping her words weren't slurred. She gave a little bob of her head as if addressing royalty.

'Now I must set out supper!' Kit said and strode from the room.

The ten women dined at a long candlelit table on the patio. Bowls of salad and platters of cold meat were passed around. Wine flowed freely. Their laughter and chatter was punctuated by the mournful call of trains echoing across from the far bank of the river. One by one the candles burned out and people started to head off to find their various beds for the night. Peggy and Dee stood as one and bade everyone a good night before sauntering into the house. Pam pushed herself away from the table. 'They're still like honeymooners. Sweet.' She reached out her hand to Stella, who was now wrapped in a light shawl. 'Dance with me?' She sounded a little drunk.

'Leave me. Dance by yourself.' Stella held her arms in the air to evade Pam's grasp.

'I will, I will.' The older lady managed to stand with some effort and then began to slowly twirl around the table. Her wide silky dress fanned out, and despite her unsteadiness there was a strange beauty to the way Pam moved, her shadow playing against the wall.

Kit and Nancy were the next couple to wish everyone a good night's sleep. 'Leave everything. Judy will be back in the morning to tidy up,' Kit called as she wandered back into the house, glass in hand.

Gert had tried to engage Frankie in conversation, but Frankie found she had little she wanted to say about where she came from or what she did. When Gert asked about her friendship with Van, Van interjected sharply, 'We work together. Frankie works at the agency.' Frankie was aware of various looks being exchanged but was unsure what any of them meant.

'Well, I'll see you all for breakfast. I must head home,' Gert announced, slipping on her jacket.

'You're not staying here?' Van asked.

'No, but I'm just down the hill. The car knows its way.' Her rough chuckle echoed across the terrace as she left.

Exhausted from her efforts, Pam was now slumped in her chair and appeared to be asleep. Stella picked up Pam's abandoned cigarette and inhaled.

'And then there were three,' she said into a long plume of smoke.

Frankie was aware of a change in the atmosphere. She glanced at Van, who immediately stood.

'Well, it's too late for me. My bed is calling.'

Frankie hesitated for a moment but then stood as well.

'Me too. Good night,' she said to Stella. She wondered if she should have offered to help her get Pam to bed, but she could hear Van's shoes making their way across the terrace.

'Sleep well, ladies,' Stella said as if it was a joke. Frankie glanced back but it was hard to see the expression on Stella's face in the stuttering light of the lone candle still burning at that end of the table. She waved and Frankie waved back before following Van into the house.

Nothing was said as they got ready for bed but clearly the evening had left Van irritated. She closed doors just a little too sharply, tugged at the drapes impatiently and gave the most perfunctory 'Good night' when Frankie wished her a good night's sleep. When Van finally retreated into Guthrie's room and closed the door, Frankie almost expected to hear a key turning in the lock.

Perhaps it was the relief at having survived the evening, or maybe it was just the cocktails and wine, but Frankie fell into a most welcome deep sleep. She had no idea how many hours had passed when she felt a hand on her shoulder. Morning sunshine was edging the heavy drapes and as she opened her eyes she saw that Stella was lounging at the foot of the sofa.

'I heard you were in here,' she said, her voice low and seductive. She leaned forward and ran her fingers through Frankie's hair. Startled, Frankie pushed herself back and into a sitting position. She struggled to find words. 'Sorry, I . . . I've just . . . Good morning.' She patted her hair down as if trying to make herself more presentable.

Stella smiled. 'Sleepyhead.' She pulled back the quilt and tried to lie down. Frankie pushed her back. 'Please. I'm not like that. Van is next door.'

'I know you're not together. Come on. Just a morning cuddle.' She pushed herself closer to Frankie and kissed her neck.

'No,' Frankie said, trying to keep her voice down. She squirmed free but in doing so caused Stella's silk kimono to slip from her shoulders, exposing one startlingly white breast. Frankie looked away to spare Stella any embarrassment, but clearly that was not what Stella was feeling as she now wriggled entirely free of her kimono and pressed her nakedness against Frankie, who let out an involuntary yelp. 'Please!'

Suddenly a door burst open, and it was as if a bomb of fury had exploded. A dishevelled Van was standing framed by the red of the room behind, her face almost matching the colour of the walls.

'You little slut!' she bellowed. At first Frankie thought the anger was directed at Stella, but then she hissed, 'Ungrateful little cunt. Just go. Go!' Her voice was a full scream now and she was tugging wildly at the long drapes, allowing the sun to reveal fully the seemingly debauched tableau on the sofa. Stella grabbed her kimono and, clutching it to herself, fled out into the hallway. Kit's voice could be heard asking, 'What is it? What on earth is going on?' And then she was in the doorway, peering at Frankie, who was now pressed into the arm of the sofa holding her knees, her eyes shut in an effort to achieve invisibility. Van was breathing heavily, her arms at an awkward angle to her body. She looked like she might kill.

'Our Irish friend is leaving us,' she snapped.

Kit looked at Frankie cowering on the sofa and then back to Van.

'I see, but where is she to go?' Kit asked with the forced brightness of a hostess trying to rescue her party.

'I really don't care.' Van picked up Frankie's small bag and threw it on the sofa. 'But she's leaving.'

'Yes. Yes, I see. Perhaps we might have breakfast first and then—' Kit's suggestion was cut off by Van barking, 'She was here as my guest and she is going.'

Frankie had never seen Van in a rage like this. She had hoped that she might be able to sit with Van, try to explain, but that was clearly not going to be possible.

'Pack and get out!' Van pointed at the bag for emphasis, then marched out into the hallway followed by Kit, who gently closed the doors behind her.

Left alone in the silent room, Frankie became aware of her heart beating furiously. She stood and looked around the room as if it might contain some solution. What could she do? Wait until Van had calmed down and seen sense? There was no way Van was going to allow her to stay long enough for that to happen. She pulled her nightdress over her head and reached for the light summer dress she had been wearing the day before. Where on earth was she supposed to go? Frankie wondered if one of the others might take pity on her and offer her a place to stay. This was all Stella's fault, after all – maybe she would feel obliged to help? The whole situation was so wildly unfair and yet it also felt strangely inevitable. Standing in this book-lined red room, Frankie felt a sense of resignation as if, somehow, this was how her time with Van was always going to end. She had flown too close to the sun and now it was time for her great fall.

She zipped up her bag and quietly stepped out into the hallway. Beyond the gloom of the living room she could see some of the other guests having breakfast on the patio. There was no sign of Stella or Pam. Van looked unhinged, pacing the terrace in her pyjamas, her hair as wild as Frankie had ever seen it.

Jean noticed her and a few of the older women made their

way to the hallway. Frankie hoped there might be the possibility of some sort of reprieve, but then she saw the expression on Van's face.

'Gert says if you walk up to the main road there's a bus back to Manhattan.'

'Other side of the road. You need to head south,' Gert said quietly and stepped back from the group. Frankie wasn't sure what the rest of the women thought had happened. A lovers' tiff? Did they really believe that she was some sort of harlot?

'Here.' Van was holding out a small wad of notes. 'This should be enough for a few days.'

The realisation that Van's threat was becoming a reality brought tears to Frankie's eyes. 'But Van, should I go to the Drake or—'

Van grabbed her roughly by the arm roughly and almost dragged her to the front door. 'I never want to see your lying face again,' she spat. Her lips were curled back and Frankie could feel the spray of spittle landing on her face. 'But Van, I'm not a liar. You know I didn't lie – ask Stella!'

'Save your breath. Pamela is almost as furious as I am. You make me feel sick to my stomach.' Van pulled the door open. 'Now walk. Walk away and find some other fool.'

Frankie looked at the driveway stretching out before her towards the large pillars at the end. She turned back one last time.

'Please, Van. You can't make me—'

'Goodbye.' And with a push, Frankie was on the doorstep, the slam of the door echoing behind her.

For a moment she stood in disbelief, and then, with seemingly no other options, she began to walk. It was already warm and Frankie walked slowly, staying under the shade of the trees that canopied the track. In the still of the morning air, the only sounds were the crunch of her footsteps on the gravel and the excited chirps and squawks of birds darting through the tree branches. Frankie moved one foot in front of the other, swapping her bag from hand to hand every few steps. At the end of the rough track there was a triangle of grass where the road split into two. She looked left and right. There was no sign of any bus stop. To her left was a small church built of white clapboard; she could see various families making their way towards it. A lonely bell began to toll, calling the faithful.

Frankie saw the churchgoers staring at her, no doubt wondering what she might be doing at this hour of the morning trudging along these rural roads with her small bag. A young couple stopped. 'Are you all right, miss? Do you need help?' the man asked, his female companion gripping his arm tightly as if Frankie could whisk him away without warning.

'The bus. I'm looking for the bus stop.'

'Bus stop is up there on the main road.' He pointed to Frankie's right. 'It's just a few steps up that way.' He looked at the woman. 'But I'm not certain the bus—' The woman tugged him forward. 'Good morning,' she said politely as they walked on.

On the main road she found two bus stops, both of them with small wooden shelters. Remembering Gert's advice, she crossed the road and sat in the shade to wait. The church bell had stopped and even the birds seemed to have lost their enthusiasm. There was just the buzz of summer insects and the occasional roar as a car drove by. Frankie could feel the sweat trickling down her back and she wiped the perspiration from her brow. She wished she had something to drink.

Time passed. Fifteen minutes, then half an hour and still no sign of a bus. Frankie felt numb. She willed the bus to come, but what then? Could she go back to the hotel? She counted her money and found that Van had given her fifty dollars. That made her feel a little better. She imagined she could survive for a while on that – after all, there must be cheaper hotels that she could find. She wondered what was being said about her, back at Katharine Cornell's house. Was Stella blaming her for what had happened? She imagined them laughing at the downfall of the fake lesbian. She sighed and leaned against the wooden bench. She was so far from home and yet something about this whole experience felt familiar. All at once she remembered and let out a honk of laughter: this was her sitting in the back of her aunt and uncle's car being driven away from the rectory in Castlekeen. She was being banished *again*. At least on that occasion she had been guilty of something, but this time – well, maybe she *was* at fault. Not where Stella was concerned, but guilty of not taking Van's feelings seriously enough. Norah had tried to warn her, and now it felt as though the whole universe was saying, 'I told you so.'

Frankie heard an engine and saw a large car edge out from the small road opposite. It turned and pulled up alongside her, and the dark-haired man at the wheel lowered the window and called out, 'The city?'

Frankie tried not to think what she must look like, her unbrushed hair sticking to her face, sweat patches darkening her dress.

'I'm waiting for the bus.'

The driver took a drag from his cigarette. 'Sunday. There are no buses. Hop in.'

Frankie stood, but then thought better of the idea. Getting into a car with a stranger was very likely to make her predicament even worse. 'I'm not sure. That's very kind of you, but . . .' Her voice trailed away, unable to come up with an excuse for not getting into the car that didn't involve calling the driver some sort of deviant killer.

'I'm Joe.' He gave her a smile and Frankie noticed for the first time how handsome he was. 'I'm Miss Cornell's driver. I heard about your troubles. Get in.' He leaned across and swung the passenger door open. Frankie was appalled to think this stranger knew of the morning's events, but she picked up her small bag and slid into the front seat.

They drove in silence for a few minutes before Joe spoke.

'So what happened? Trouble with your gal pal?'

'No!' Frankie said at once, but then tried to explain: 'Well, yes, but she's not my . . . she's my boss. I'm not . . . the others. I'm not like the others. I'm . . .' She hesitated and then said the only word she could think of: 'Normal.'

Joe gave a low whistle and tapped some ash from his cigarette out of the window. 'I see. I know it's none of my business, but that was never going to end well, was it?' He looked at Frankie and grinned. She found herself laughing. 'No. No, it wasn't. I was a fool and now I've no idea what I'm going to do.'

'You know anyone in the city?'

'No.' Her voice was little more than a whisper. 'I suppose I'll go back to the Drake Hotel. It's on 56th Street.'

'I know it,' Joe said, throwing the stub of his cigarette from the car.

Driving back over the George Washington Bridge, the island of Manhattan looked very different to Frankie. Less than twenty-four hours earlier it had glittered like a glamorous wonderland of opportunity. Now it loomed over the river, grey and impenetrable. Frankie felt her lips begin to quiver and then tears filled her eyes. She hoped that Joe wouldn't notice, but her erratic breathing must have betrayed her because he silently offered his pack of cigarettes.

'No, thank you.' She rubbed her hand across her face.

'So what do they call you?'

Frankie was dismayed by her rudeness. 'I'm so sorry – I should have said. Frankie. Frankie Howe.'

'Pleasure to meet you, Frankie Howe. Where you from?'

'I'm from Ireland, but I live in London now.' As she said this, she wondered if it was still true. Was she going to have to return to Ireland, trailing even more shame and failure?

'Italian.' Joe gestured to himself with his thumb. 'Well, my grandparents came over, then my mother married a German, so I'm Joe Haffen.'

'Hello, Joe Haffen. Thanks for the lift.' Frankie managed a little grin. Despite the circumstances, it felt good to be in male company.

The car was now travelling along East River Drive. Frankie watched the various exit signs and the numbers of the streets getting lower. When Joe drove past the turning for 53rd Street, she hesitated, unsure of herself, then asked Joe if he had perhaps gone too far.

'No.'

'But the Drake is back there.' She pointed feebly over her shoulder.

Joe gave a long sigh. 'Please don't get upset, but you aren't staying at the Drake.'

'What?'

'Miss Cornell asked me to come fetch you. She knew there was no bus on a Sunday and your English friend . . . well, apparently she rang the Drake and checked you out.'

'No. She can't have.' But even as she said it, Frankie knew that it was true.

'Again, none of my business, but that English lady of yours is a first-class bitch, excuse my French.'

'What am I . . .' But as she spoke, Frankie could feel the tightness behind her nose and knew that her tears were about to return. 'This is awful. Just awful. What am I going to do?' she asked through sobs.

'There's some Kleenex in the glove compartment.' Joe leaned across and pressed a button, allowing Frankie to find the paper tissues.

He waited while she blew her nose and then glanced at her with an encouraging smile.

'I tell you what. Me and my sis have a place down in the Village. You can bunk up with her for a day or two. Betty won't mind. She works late. Then you can get your stuff from the hotel. Maybe patch things up with your boss lady?'

'That's not going to happen,' Frankie said, dabbing at her eyes. 'It's so kind of you to give me a lift. I really can't ask for more from you.'

Joe shook his head. 'I think maybe you have the wrong idea about our apartment. It's pretty bare bones and we have what you might call an open house. People crash all the time. You'd be no trouble and I swear my sister is the total opposite of those women out in Sneden's.'

'Crash?' Frankie hated to sound like an unsophisticated bumpkin but was also keen to make sure she hadn't misunderstood.

'Sleep over, you know, for a night or two.'

Frankie considered this offer. He'd obviously come to pick her up from the bus stop with this plan in mind. Maybe Kit Cornell was even paying him extra to take care of her for a few days. 'Well, if you're sure it isn't any trouble.'

The Village felt more familiar to Frankie than the granite and glass of Midtown. The buildings weren't scraping the sky and some of the streets even had curves in them. It wasn't that it looked like London but the scale of it seemed more human. Even the people on the streets were different. On Fifth Avenue everyone walked with purpose, as if keen to complete an important mission, whereas here she could see that they stood on street corners chatting, or sat on the front steps of their buildings. Frankie felt herself relax a little as the car cruised along the narrow streets.

'Here we are. Let me just run up and warn Betty. Maybe tidy up a bit.' Joe flashed her a smile and jumped out of the car. She watched him go into a brown doorway. The building above was four storeys high and the pale brick front was zigzagged with a metal fire escape. Two young children were engrossed in their chalk drawing on the footpath. 'Sidewalk,' Frankie said aloud to see what the word felt like in her mouth. She liked it. Across the street, a man in a leather apron was sweeping in front of a narrow store selling newspapers and magazines. A dog with no obvious owner was observing the brushing with an air of judgement. Next door, two women were sitting at a small table fanning themselves, their legs splayed out in front of them, favouring comfort over propriety. A group of young people wandered by, a few of them carrying books. Frankie assumed they were students. It didn't feel like an Irish, or even a London, Sunday.

'Come on up, Miss Frankie Howe!' Joe opened her door and grabbed the small bag from the back seat. He moved with the grace of a dancer, swinging around to close the car door behind Frankie and then placing an arm on her back to shepherd her towards the deep shade of the doorway. Inside, they climbed stairs that leaned out from the wall at an angle, small amber wall lights guiding them up through the shadows. Three flights up, Frankie was breathing heavily.

'You'll get used to it,' Joe told her as he pushed open a door marked '4A'. Inside, a young woman with black hair tied in a bun put down a book and jumped up from the kitchen table. With the small upturned twist of her mouth and the same high cheekbones, she was obviously Joe's sister.

'Welcome! I'm Betty.' Her handshake was strong and hearty. Frankie liked her immediately.

'Frankie. Thank you so much for taking me in.'

Betty pulled a chair away from the table. 'Sit down. Happy to have you. Joe told me about your drama. Now, I've just put on a pot of coffee. You want some? What about you, Joe?'

Frankie happily accepted, but Joe shook his head.

'No thanks. I better get back out to Sneden's. Miss Cornell is back in Beekman Place tonight. I won't be late – maybe we can all have dinner?'

'Sure. I'll make something.'

'*Ciao*, Frankie,' Joe said as he went out of the door. Frankie thanked him; she knew she was blushing. To distract herself, she looked around the cramped room. It had everything one might have expected from a kitchen, but wedged between the stove and the window was what looked like an oddly truncated bathtub. Frankie must have been staring at it because Betty confirmed it was a bath. 'Weird, I know, but it's kind of a thing here in the city. I don't know why. Plumbing, maybe?' She shrugged and returned to her place at the table.

The women sat with their coffee, talking easily. Betty wanted to know Frankie's whole story, so Frankie explained about the work she had been doing in London and how she had come to New York with Van, and what had happened that morning. In return, Betty told how she planned to go to teacher training college at Fordham, but was currently trying to save money by helping out at a small French restaurant a couple of blocks away.

'And Joe drives full time?' Frankie asked.

'For now. He started with Katharine Cornell earlier this year when she was on Broadway and she's kept him on. He likes her well enough. Of course, what he really wants to be is an artist, but . . .' Betty looked up, so Frankie followed suit. She gasped. How had she not noticed the ceiling before now? The whole thing was like an enormous child's drawing, only so much more than that. Fantastical plants chased each other around the light fixture, the leaves and stalks coming to life like twisted green creatures. The blossoms burst open into glittering mosaics made up of pottery fragments and glass.

'He did all this? It's gorgeous!' She strained in her chair to get a better look. 'So beautiful.'

'Oh, he's talented, I'll give you that,' Betty said with a shrug, 'but the ceiling in your own kitchen is never going to pay the rent. Look at his room.' She stood and opened one of the three doors in the phonebooth-sized hallway.

This room was even more extravagant, with plant creatures cavorting across the walls as well as the ceiling. It felt alive, as if the smiling tendrils were still growing.

'I've never seen anything like it.' Frankie was trying to take it all in. She would never have guessed that this had all come from the mind of the kind man who had driven her here.

'I know, I know. It is amazing but I'm his sister, so I'm bound to worry about him. This is the bathroom, by the way.' Another door opened to reveal a tiny room with a toilet and basin. The walls were covered in more mosaics above ordinary bathroom tiles that had been painted over with wild scenes of alien greenery. The whole ceiling was a yellow sun made of metal fragments nailed into position.

'He found the hood of a cab on the street and that's the result,' Betty explained, stepping back into the kitchen.

'I like it.'

'Well, I think he likes you too.'

Frankie turned swiftly. 'What? What do you mean?'

Betty laughed. 'Up here, making sure we had enough bathroom tissue. He even wiped down the counter in the kitchen. Joe has never cleaned up. Trust me, he likes you.'

Frankie was surprised by how pleased this made her, even if she thought it wasn't true.

'I'm sure he's just being nice.'

Betty rolled her eyes. 'If that's what you want to believe. You can leave your bag in my room.' She opened the third door. 'It's just a camping cot we use for guests. I'll put it up later. I can give you a towel and you'll be good with just a sheet. Too hot for blankets.'

IV

All the windows and doors in the small apartment were open to allow a feeble breeze to move through the rooms. Drifting conversations and an occasional car horn or siren made the trio aware of the world beyond their candlelit dinner, sitting knees crushed together at the small table.

'You can cook.' Frankie was impressed by the simple meal of pork chops with a mustard sauce, and a tomato and onion salad.

'Thanks. If I can it's only thanks to Madame Barre at the restaurant. Our mother wasn't exactly an Italian mama,' said Betty.

Joe laughed as he wiped his plate with bread. 'She went full Wasp the second she married Dad. It was all American cheese and lunch meat growing up.'

'Where was that?'

'Upstate near Albany. Our grandparents are in Jersey, though. Now they're *real* Italians. Visiting them was such a trip. Everything we ate was new and our grandmother would spend the whole time screaming at Mom in Italian.'

'Remember when they came to visit us and Grandma opened her case and there was nothing in there except meat and cheese?'

Joe and Betty laughed at the memory and Frankie felt so lucky to have found these two kind people in this vast, unfamiliar city.

Joe was standing by the sink, opening a second bottle of wine.

'Someone is trying to impress somebody,' Betty said archly.

'What? It's just wine.'

'Chianti?'

'You complaining?'

'Oh, I'm not complaining!' Betty said, holding out her glass.

Joe turned his attention to Frankie. 'So, you going to get your case from the Drake tomorrow?'

'And my passport. I'll go in the afternoon, I suppose – give Van time to pack it up. Can I walk?'

'You could but the subway is right around the corner and the ten train will take you straight up there.'

'Great!' Frankie said enthusiastically, fully aware that she was going to walk rather than face the subterranean mysteries of the subway.

'What's the plan then?' asked Betty.

'My return flight is almost two weeks away, so I'll try and change that. If I can't, then I'm not sure what I'll do. Find a cheap hotel?' Frankie said uncertainly, knowing that her fifty dollars was unlikely to last that long.

'You could always pick up a shift or two at the restaurant – I mean, it would just be pot-washing or vegetable prep, but it's a nice enough place and Madame Barre would pay you cash, no questions asked.'

'Thank you, but hopefully I'll be on my way.'

Joe leaned his elbow on the table. He seemed a little drunk.

'Don't be in such a rush. Stay awhile. I'd like to show you the sights.'

Frankie saw Betty raise her eyebrows. 'I think it might be time for bed, don't you, Frankie?' she said with a wink.

Joe slapped the table. 'Bed? It's early. How's about we all head down the block to the Bon Soir? I know the kid on the door, he'll get us in and we can stand at the bar.'

Frankie looked to Betty for guidance.

'Maybe tomorrow night, Joe. I'm working lunch in the morning and, by the sound of things, Miss Frankie here has had quite the day. Let's get your cot sorted.'

With nothing more than a 'Good night and thanks for today,' Frankie stood and followed Betty into her darkened room.

Tired as she was, Frankie found that she lay awake on her narrow cot. It was very hot compared to the cool air of the Drake and the noise of traffic and people yelling and laughing that carried on the still night air gave no hint at the lateness of the hour. She could hear Joe moving around the apartment, stacking dishes, arranging the kitchen chairs, turning off lights. Then there was the creak of his mattress as he went to bed. Frankie wasn't sure why, but just the knowledge of Joe lying in the dark on the other side of the thin wall made her feel much better than she had a right to.

V

Frankie had assumed she had the apartment all to herself as she sat at the kitchen table the next day, tears pouring down her face. But suddenly the door swung open and there was Betty, full of concern and bending over Frankie, wanting to know what was wrong. Her gentle hug and the kindness in her voice was enough to set Frankie off once more. She tried to speak through gulping sobs, and haltingly told Betty what had happened in exchange for a growing pile of paper tissues.

When she had arrived at the Drake it seemed that all Van had left with the concierge was Frankie's case. Inside it she found most of her belongings along with her passport, but no airline ticket. The man at the desk was very kind but Miss Everden was not answering the phone in her room. He took a message and promised to pass it on.

Frankie had remembered about the *Camelot* read-through that was happening on 54th Street. Carrying her case and sweating profusely, she made her way down to the theatre. Sure enough, the read-through was still going on. She asked a man in the lobby if he could please fetch Miss Everden for her. The chill of the air-conditioning was soothing. She told herself that it must be a mix-up and Van had simply forgotten to put the ticket in her case. The man had returned looking slightly flustered. Miss Everden did not wish to be disturbed. With no other option, Frankie declared that she would wait for Miss Everden. The man had simply nodded and left her perched on her case, then moments later he was back. Miss Everden had asked for her to please leave the building. Frankie stood and protested. She tried to explain her predicament but before she could finish the man had informed her that he would be forced to call for security if she refused to leave. Unable to control herself, she had begun to cry and hadn't really stopped since. She was certain the people in the auditorium must have heard her. The man, despite being embarrassed and apologetic, still led her firmly towards the doors.

'How did you get home?' Betty had run a cloth under the cold tap and was patting it over Frankie's brow.

'I walked.'

'All that way and with your case?' Betty asked incredulously. The stiff brown case, looking like a tombstone with a handle, sat by the door where Frankie had dropped it.

'What am I going to do? How much is a ticket home going to be?' Frankie twisted in her chair as if she was already planning her escape.

'Is there no one to wire you money? A friend? Your folks?'

Frankie balled her fists and pressed them firmly into her eye sockets.

'No! No one.' And the brutal truth of this set her tears in motion once more.

Betty stood and draped her arms over her shoulders. 'It will all work out. You'll see. We'll get you home, don't you worry.' She bent down and pulled Frankie's hands away from her face. 'Look at it this way. You've got somewhere to stay—'

'I can't stay here!' Frankie protested.

'You can and you will.' Betty's voice was calm and firm. 'We won't let you starve, and tomorrow we can contact the airline and maybe they can reissue the ticket.' She smoothed Frankie's hair.

'Really? They can do that?'

Betty hesitated. 'Maybe. It's worth asking at least.'

'Here.' Betty put a glass on the table. 'Have the last of Joe's wine and take a little nap. I've got to get back to work but Joe shouldn't be too late.'

Frankie looked at the glass and then picked it up and sipped obediently.

'Thank you.'

'Are you going to be all right?' Betty asked, one hand on the door.

'Yes. I'm so sorry to be such a nuisance.' Frankie attempted a smile.

'Don't be silly. Wine and sleep make everything seem better. See you later.' And then Betty was gone, leaving Frankie alone with her problems.

None of it seemed real. The drive out to Sneden's Landing with Van and Jean could have happened months before rather than a couple of days. Frankie thought back to how the city had felt then, glamorous and welcoming, as Van herself had been that first night in London. Now, New York felt like her adversary, and Frankie knew she was woefully ill-equipped for the fight ahead. She imagined how pitiful she would seem wandering into a Manhattan travel agency, asking about her plane ticket. Why would anyone believe her? Maybe she could get a message to Norah. But no, Norah had warned her about the dangers of this trip – how could she ask for her help? Frankie thought about Ruby from the office. At least when Van was done with her she was able to get the bus home. This was so much worse.

Sleep helped. When Frankie had folded herself fully dressed across the low cot, she imagined that she would lie there wide awake, but the exhaustion from her seemingly endless sweat-soaked walk had quickly caught up with her.

Frankie wasn't sure what time it was when she woke. It was still light outside, but she could tell the sun was nearly gone from the sky. Emerging from Betty's room, she called out to see if anyone was home, but her voice was met with silence. She brushed her teeth and splashed water on her face, which made her feel a little better. She realised how hungry she was, but looking around the kitchen she couldn't see anything to eat. She contemplated the bathtub and longed to wash off the grime of her day but didn't dare, in case Joe came home and found her.

Frankie did the best she could with a flannel standing at the sink in the little bathroom and then changed into the lightest of her dresses, a lemon slip dress that Norah had lent her for the trip. Without thinking, she continued to get ready for some unspecified evening. She brushed her hair and tied it back. A little lipstick was applied. Had she done it all in anticipation of Joe's return? That was perhaps what it looked like when he came through the door a little later, to find her sitting at the table in the gathering dusk.

'Don't want the lights on?'

'I don't mind. This seemed cooler.'

Joe pulled out a chair and sat down.

'I called in at the Pomme. Betty told me what happened. What kind of person does that?'

There was no answer to that, so instead Frankie asked, 'What's the Pomme?'

'Oh, La Petite Pomme – it's the name of the restaurant where Betty works. It's nice. I mean, I've only ever had leftovers, bit out of my league, but it's good food. Popular.'

'Have you had dinner?' Frankie asked, hoping that he hadn't.

'No. You?'

'Not yet. I could try and cook us something.' They both looked at the stove in the near darkness.

'Or we could go out for a slice?' Joe suggested.

'Slice?' Frankie was annoyed at herself for being so clueless about every little thing.

'Pizza. You got pizza in Ireland?'

'Not in my bit of Ireland, that's for sure, but I had some in London. I liked it.'

'You haven't had pizza till you've had it in New York City.' Joe stood and held out his hand to her. 'Shall we?'

Frankie accepted it and followed him down the stairs as though it had always been the plan that Joe was going to take her out for dinner.

Outside it was that strange transition between the end of the day and the cusp of night. People walked by carrying bags of groceries, while groups, buoyed up by what their evening might hold, jostled each other with loud chatter and yelps. Joe led Frankie across Sixth Avenue to a shop window, where he ordered slices of pizza from a man he seemed to know. They continued down the block to a brightly lit bodega, where Joe held up a six-pack of beer and asked, 'This all right? I can get us a quart of something if you prefer?'

Frankie wasn't sure what choices she was being offered, so she just smiled and agreed to the beer.

As they walked, Joe pointed down a small tree-lined street.

'Betty works down there.'

Frankie looked obediently but couldn't spot anything that looked like a restaurant.

'Why is it called La Petite Pomme?'

Joe shrugged. 'Something to do with the owner's husband. He was a jazz musician. They met just after the war in France and she followed him back here. They got married but then he was touring down South and the band's bus got hit by an army truck. The whole band was killed. Five of them. So sad and stupid. You survive an entire war only to get home and be killed by your own army. Madame Barre got stuck here, a war widow without a war. Still, she got some big government pay-out because of the crash, and opened her little bistro.'

Joe stopped. 'We should cross here.'

They hurried back across Sixth Avenue and headed down a small, dimly lit street.

'And did Madame Barre ever meet anyone else?' Frankie wondered.

'No. I mean, I don't know that for sure, but she's by herself now. I guess she married her restaurant. OK, here we are.'

They were standing by a large open space dotted with trees and park benches. Ahead, Frankie could see a large arch. The sound of drums was coming from somewhere nearby.

'Washington Square. I thought it would be nice to sit outside for a while.'

'Lovely,' Frankie said as they walked towards a vacant bench. She wondered how many other girls Joe had brought here.

They sat and Joe began tearing at his pizza slice with his teeth. Frankie tried to do the same, even though she could feel cheese and grease smearing her face. She chewed her food with no sign of enjoyment.

Joe laughed. 'You managing?' He picked a string of cheese from her cheek.

'Sorry! I've never eaten it like this before,' she explained.

'How did you eat it before?'

'Well, you know, with a knife and fork.'

Joe was incredulous. 'In that case, Miss Frankie, I think we can say that you have never eaten pizza before.' He threw the string of cheese over his shoulder with a laugh. He handed her a beer. 'Would you like a crystal glass for this?'

'Stop. I'm not like that.' To prove her point she took a long draught from the bottle, but managed to spill a large quantity down the front of her dress.

'Yeah, right.' Joe was laughing and, after a moment's hesitation, so was she. Frankie swiped at her dress and looked around the park. A couple on another bench were kissing. She could see that the drummer was a Black man sitting on the ground by a nearby fountain. A loud siren was wailing in the distance.

'Oh Joe, if you only knew how different this all is from what I've known. I mean, I like it, I really do, but it's all so new.'

Joe took a slurp of his beer.

'Tell me about yourself. What's life like in London? You got a sweetheart waiting for you?'

Frankie tried not to betray her embarrassment when she said, 'No.'

'Hey – I don't either. Nothing wrong with that.' Joe leaned back against the bench. 'I did, for five years. A girl from back home. We came to the city together but it didn't work out. You know how it is.'

Frankie had no idea how it was but nodded in a way that she hoped conveyed a certain worldliness.

'She got sick of waiting. She thought this' – he indicated the park and the buildings that surrounded it – 'was just some sort of wild adventure, but then we'd go back home to Albany and do the whole husband and wife thing. Kids. I think for a while that's what I wanted too, but I'm not ready to give up yet.'

'Your art?'

'You've seen it?'

'Difficult not to!'

They both laughed. 'True enough,' Joe said.

'I really like it,' she added quickly.

Was Joe the one blushing now?

'Thanks.'

They sat and chewed and drank in silence for a little while. A small dog on a long leash came and sniffed around them as they ate, till the owner tugged it away with an apology. Frankie swallowed. She knew her face must be shiny from the greasy food, and there were probably sweat stains on her dress. Clearly this was not the time to try to impress a boy, but she felt an urge to reveal herself to Joe. She had only had a couple of sips of beer and the glass of wine hours before, yet she felt giddy and daring.

'The husband-and-wife thing. I've done that.'

Joe's eyes widened with surprise.

'I was not expecting to hear that. You're a dark horse. Who'd you marry? What happened?'

Frankie put down her beer. She was unused to talking about herself – no one had ever seemed interested enough to ask her questions. Even her conversations with Van seemed to be entirely made up of information about Van or the world that Van thought Frankie might need. She tried to gather her thoughts.

'He was an older clergyman. A widower, but he never loved me.'

'Did you love him?' Joe was leaning closer, his voice low.

'No. I mean I thought I might learn to, but he was in love with someone else.'

Joe raised an eyebrow and took a drink of his beer.

'So what happened? Did he leave you?'

Frankie surprised herself with a burst of giggles.

'No. He threw me out because he thought I was in love with someone else.'

'And were you?'

Had Frankie been in love with John O'Sullivan? No. She had desired him, yes, but she was fairly certain it hadn't been love.

'There was someone else but it wasn't serious.'

Joe considered this for a moment.

'And this was all back in Ireland?'

'Yes, that's when I went to London. Met Van.'

'You don't have much luck, do you?'

Frankie looked at the face of the man sitting beside her. The street lamp was casting a shadow so that one dark eye glinted while the other seemed lost. The hair that was lit by the lamp was glossy and thick, and the bristles around his mouth almost sparkled. His left arm was behind her where he was resting his hand on the back of the bench. This was the sort of situation that would normally have sent Frankie into a spiral of fear and uncertainty. What was he thinking? How did she look? Did she want something to happen? But tonight in Washington Square Park she knew the answer to all of those questions. She pressed herself against Joe's arm.

'I feel lucky now.'

The drumming stopped and Joe Haffen kissed Frankie Howe.

VI

They managed to keep their secret for less than a day.

That first night when they had got back from Washington Square, they had been careful. Betty had still been at work, but in case she came home early, when Joe led Frankie into his room, he had pulled her down to the floor rather than his creaking bed. As they unbuttoned each other's clothes and ran hands and lips across flesh, not a word had been spoken. It was as if everything had been pre-agreed during some conversation neither of them could recall. Frankie found a physical confidence she had never experienced before, nor had the opportunity to. When Joe had slipped his fingers into her, she had leaned into him. When he had placed himself over her, she had spread her legs and raised her hips to him. The sweat from his brow had dripped down onto her face and she had licked at it hungrily. There was nothing about him that she didn't want.

Afterwards they had lain together, their nakedness causing Frankie no embarrassment or shame. She scarcely recognised herself. With her hand she had traced the stripes of light and shadow that crossed Joe's chest and hips. He had kissed her breasts, her mouth, her shoulder, and then pulled her to her feet. She should be asleep on the cot next door before Betty got home. A final kiss and then she was alone, her mind bombarded by thoughts of all that had gone on that night. She could feel the ache where he had played with her nipples, the unfamiliar sensation between her legs. She wanted him back inside her. When Betty had crept in later, Frankie pretended to be asleep, and then before too long she was.

The next morning, Frankie and Joe tried to act as if nothing had happened but failed miserably because, of course, something had. How could Betty not notice that everything Joe said was just a little too loud, and how Frankie, seated at the table, was both awkward and expectant? Betty looked from one to the other as she stood by the stove with the coffee pot.

'Good night?' she asked casually.

'Nice. Yeah. Me and Miss Frankie had a couple of beers in the park. Not a late one.'

A few hours later, all of Betty's questions were answered when she came back to the apartment from the restaurant to see if Frankie wanted to pick up a shift that evening, and found her brother sitting on a kitchen chair with his hands up the skirt of their visitor. He jumped to his feet while Frankie turned quickly, covering her body with her hands as if she were naked.

'Joe!' Betty said sternly.

'What? It just happened.' He looked to Frankie, who could only stare at the floor.

'Honest to God, Joe, I can't. I just can't.' Betty stepped forward and ushered Frankie out of the kitchen and into her bedroom. She shut the door firmly behind them.

Using one hand, Betty gently raised Frankie's chin till they were eye to eye.

'Are you OK?'

'Yes.'

'You're sure? You've been through a lot in the last few days. I don't want him taking advantage of you.'

Betty's words made Frankie question what had gone on. Was this just a man making use of the nearest woman? She didn't think so. Before Betty had interrupted them, he had been saying such lovely things to her, making her feel special for the first time since she could remember, making plans for the next afternoon when he would be free. She had loved the feel of his hands roaming across her body, his lips on hers. Whatever his intentions might be, Frankie was more than happy to play along.

'Don't worry about me. He's been very kind. I'm sorry if we upset you.'

Betty smiled and brushed Frankie's hair away from her face in a way that stirred a distant memory of her mother.

'I'm not upset. If you're happy then so am I. It can just be a bit of a shock when I remember that my brother is also a man.'

Frankie felt as though Betty had left something unsaid. She remembered Joe telling her about the girlfriend who had gone back home. She wondered if Joe had behaved badly towards her.

There was a gentle tap.

'You ladies all right in there?'

Betty threw open the door. 'Yes. I was just having a little chat with Frankie.'

'It's fine, Joe,' Frankie said, then he slid an arm around her waist and it felt like they were officially a couple. It was as simple as that.

'Well, if you aren't too busy being a lovebird,' said Betty, 'I came back to see if you wanted to pick up a shift at La Pomme tonight? Just dishes and a bit of salad-washing. If you work till close, Madame Barre will give you four dollars. Sound good?'

Frankie looked to Joe to gauge his reaction, and immediately hated herself for doing it. If the whole mess with Van was going to mean something, surely it was that she should not rely on others but stand on her own two feet.

'Yes! That sounds great. What time do they want me?'

'Come around five and that way you'll get fed before you start work.'

Frankie nodded enthusiastically and Joe squeezed her tight.

'You know where it is, right?'

'The street after the pizza place on Sixth Avenue?'

'That's the one.'

'Well remembered!' Joe chimed in.

For Frankie this was almost an out-of-body experience. She saw herself in the small New York apartment being offered work, while being held by a man who desired her. She wished that everyone – Van, Norah, Alan, her aunt and uncle – could witness her in this moment.

VII

Washing a few crumb-covered plates after a meeting in Castlekeen parish hall had not prepared Frankie for her shift at the deep metal sink in the back of La Petite Pomme. The restaurant was on the corner of a three-way crossroads to the west of Sixth Avenue, in amongst the handsome maze of brownstone houses. It was flat-roofed, single-storeyed and appeared to be made of wood. It had the air of a building that had never been intended to stand for as long as it had. The door, surrounded by what was surely borrowed carved cornicing, stood between two large windows that revealed the neat dining room within, while the kitchen was accessed through a litter-strewn alley at the rear. Betty had explained the history of the restaurant to Frankie: originally it had been owned by an old Russian couple, émigrés, who had lived in one of the brownstones a couple of streets away. Madame Barre had been renting from them, but when the old man died the widow wanted to sell up. She agreed what everyone thought was a bargain price with Madame Barre, who bought the place using the insurance money from her husband's accident. The Russian lady was long gone from the neighbourhood now, leaving Madame Barre to be the new old lady.

Large saucepans were now piling up and there weren't even customers in the restaurant yet. Frankie was pouring with sweat and already the amount she was being paid for her labour seemed measly. Betty sidled up to her and said, not unkindly, 'Frankie, you're going to have to step it up a bit. Madame Barre gets back at seven and she hates to see a pot pile at the start of service.'

Frankie just grunted and wiped some sweat from her brow. She couldn't see how much faster it was possible to clean the sauce-encrusted pots. She didn't care how ungrateful it might seem; she had already decided she would politely decline if Betty ever offered her another shift.

The four women who were working at the two metal counters and the double-width stove moved quickly and steadily but rarely spoke. Apart from the occasional sizzle of something in a pan, the only sounds were from the clink of bowls and the clank of metal spoons as the women prepared trays of vegetables and bowls of garnishes for the dinner service. Through the small round window of the door into the dining room, Frankie could see the waiters darting around with trays of wine glasses and piles of napkins. It looked more fun out there.

'Fuck.' Betty's voice was shocking not just because of the word she had used but also its volume. Frankie turned from her sink, expecting to see blood or at least a burn.

'What is it?'

Betty was whisking furiously at a bowl on the stove. 'This béarnaise sauce just won't work. It looks like scrambled eggs and this is the second batch I've tried. Madame Barre is going to go crazy when she sees all the eggs I've wasted.'

Frankie recalled an afternoon at Mrs Hurley's Ecole Gastronomique on Oliver Plunkett Street dealing with this very problem.

'I . . .' She hesitated to be so bold but the thought of doing something other than scrubbing pots spurred her on. 'I could help if you want.'

Betty looked at her doubtfully. 'You know how to make béarn-aise sauce?' she said in a voice that suggested she was now wondering what else she didn't know about this Irish woman.

'Yes. I studied cooking for a while. I think you're overheating it; I was taught to heat the butter separately and then add it to the yolks. Do you want me to try?'

Betty looked around and then stepped back from the stove. 'Please. Make yourself at home.'

Frankie washed out the bowls Betty had been using and placed a small pan of clarified butter on the stove. She mixed the other ingredients in a bowl, enjoying the feel of the whisk in her hand as it worked the egg yolks. Then, once she had decided the butter was hot enough, she dribbled it into her egg mixture, whisking with a fury she hadn't managed to muster when scrubbing the pots. After a minute or two, she was satisfied. She added salt and pepper and asked Betty where to find the tarragon.

'I usually add a few chives too. Will I?'

Betty couldn't quite seem to believe what she had just witnessed. 'Mmmm, sure, yeah, why not?'

Frankie whisked in the herbs, then transferred the contents back into the pot and put a lid on it.

'There you go.'

Betty gave a small round of applause. 'Thank you so much. That was a life-saver. Oh, and now I know you can cook, the kitchen back at the apartment is all yours.'

Frankie laughed. She felt the rush of pleasure that came from a job well done, a feeling that instantly evaporated when she turned to see how the pile of dirty pots by the sink had grown.

Waiters started to bring in the first few orders and an older lady with a husky voice began to call them out, prompting the others to open fridges or place pans on the stove. Not long after-wards Madame Barre herself came into the kitchen. Frankie was surprised. She had been expecting some sort of voluptuous *gour-mande*, a glass of wine in one hand and a pungent cigarette in the other. In fact, Madame Barre was positively bird-like. Her fine grey hair was scraped back and held with a black wooden clasp, and her tiny wrists protruded from her white chef's jacket. She looked more like a ballet teacher than a cook.

'*Bonsoir!*' she called, in a voice that seemed too deep for her body.

'*Bonsoir*, Madame Barre,' the others parroted back.

She moved behind the serving counter before noticing Frankie.

'And this is?' she asked, looking around.

'My friend, Frankie,' Betty replied. 'Bruno couldn't make it tonight.'

Madame Barre sighed, obviously displeased by this news. She looked directly at Frankie. 'Fast, fast, fast,' she instructed, clapping her hands on each word.

'Yes, *madame*,' Frankie said with as much confidence as she could summon, and then turned back to the sink.

Her back ached and her eyes were stinging from the sweat dripping into them, but she had found a sort of rhythm that drowned out thought. Her mind was almost blank, lost in a stubborn group of lentils that wouldn't shift or the cheese clinging to the prongs of a fork. Frankie had no idea what time it was. The waiters were flapping in and out through the dining-room door and, each time they opened it, the dense chatter of the diners hit her like the blast of heat from an oven. The chaotic monotony was suddenly interrupted by Madame Barre hitting a pot with a metal spoon.

'Who is making this?' she called and then repeated the question till she had everyone's attention. Betty didn't hesitate. She thrust out her finger to point at Frankie. 'She did.' It sounded more like an accusation than the awarding of any credit.

Still holding the pot, Madame Barre stepped around the counter to the sink. She was so close, Frankie could see the way her pale pink lipstick was bleeding into the wrinkles around her mouth.

'You make this?'

Frankie assumed that it must be the chives. She should never have added them.

'Sorry, yes.' She kept her head bowed.

'Is good. Is very, very good.'

Frankie looked up to find the old woman smiling at her. She glanced over at Betty and she was smiling too.

'Thank you.'

'Your name again?'

'Frankie.'

Madame Barre nodded with her lips slightly pursed.

'*Bien fait*, Frankie. *Bien fait.*'

Wapping, 2024

'How did you get on with Shona?'

'Fine.'

Damian raised an eyebrow. Shona had covered his shift the night before because he had been on a rare second date.

'Really? Because she told me you never said a word to her the whole night.'

Frankie shrugged and pulled her light woollen shawl across her shoulders.

'I wasn't in the mood.'

'Tell the truth now, Frankie – you missed me, didn't you?'

Frankie's mouth gave an involuntary twitch.

'You missed me like mad, didn't you?'

Frankie let out a honk of laughter.

'I'm used to you is all. A person can get used to anything, even a pain in the neck.'

Damian picked up her tray. 'Well, that's me told.'

As he walked towards the kitchen, Frankie called after him, 'How was your night?'

Damian wasn't sure how much he should tell her but then he considered how much Frankie had told him about her love life.

'I went on a date.'

'And?'

He was in the kitchen now.

'Kettle?'

'Please.'

'It was fine. Second date. I don't think there will be a third.'

'Where did you meet?'

'Wait, I'll come back in.'

The single lamp by Frankie's chair lit up the steam from their cups of tea.

'I'm on the apps. That's where I found him,' Damian explained.

Frankie thought about this for a moment. 'So, it's all about how they look? Nothing else?'

'You get a feeling about them from their messages, too – and anyway, don't pretend it was ever any different. I'm sure you liked the look of Joe before you ever spoke to him.'

'Well, yes, you're right, but there was a romance to it too. Fate had brought him into my life. I didn't just go to a big filing cabinet marked "Boys".'

'I don't know. I think the apps just give fate a helping hand. Anyway, last night's date was not the one. He likes to party too much to ever date someone who works nights like me.'

'His loss,' Frankie said and patted Damian's hand. 'You are an unclaimed treasure, that's what you are.'

'Ah, stop it. Now back to you. Last time I left you stuck in New York. How did you manage to escape?'

Frankie took a long sip of tea. 'You'll find as you get older that often problems turn out to be their own solutions. Van Everden did me the favour of my life. Once I'd found Joe I only wanted to be with him, and then a job at the restaurant with Madame Barre fell into my lap and . . .' She paused as she recalled those early days in New York. 'And I had never been happier.'

'What? So you just stayed?'

'I mean, I contacted the airline but I was so relieved when they told me that they couldn't help. I wrote to Nor but there was no reply. It felt like London had been a false start, and Joe and Betty and the Pomme were the real beginning of my life.'

'But how could you stay? Did you not need a visa or something?'

Frankie leaned her head back and exhaled.

'The madness of youth. We got married. I know, I know – less than two weeks, that's how long we'd been together when we went down to City Hall and tied the knot. I remember the girls in their big white dresses sitting in the chairs staring at me in my gingham skirt. I felt so guilty. They were taking it all very seriously and myself and Joe had scarcely brushed our hair. We told ourselves it was just so I could stay in the States but oh, we were giddy with the excitement of it all. There was a photographer outside taking snaps of all the newlyweds and we posed up a storm. They must be in one of those boxes in your room. If you'd asked me that day if I loved Joe, I'd have said yes, but we were probably just in love with the drama. Joe bought champagne and we drank it out of paper cups in Washington Square with Betty. We thought we were so special. No one had ever been as wild as us. Such a happy time.' Frankie peered into her teacup and repeated, 'A happy time.'

Damian looked at the old woman in her chair with one leg in a cast. It made him happy to think of her young and in love, but sad that it clearly hadn't lasted.

'And did you all just live in the apartment together, the two of you and Betty?'

Frankie raised her head from her cup and looked at Damian as if she was surprised to find him still sitting beside her.

'Yes, for a few months. Then Betty started at Fordham to do her teacher training and moved into a cheaper place with girls from her class. Joe used her old room as his art studio and we settled into, I don't know what you'd call it, a sort of domestic routine. Life seemed to all happen very late at night when I got home from the restaurant and Joe had finished driving. Or some nights, my favourite nights, he'd come by the Pomme after closing and we would all sit around talking about God knows what, drinking the unfinished bottles of wine. Madame Barre would tell us stories about the war, about coming to America. I think that's why she was so kind to me. It wasn't just that I could cook, but that I was new to the city, like she had been, and in love. I was her project. She taught me so much about French food and I loved it, loved it.' Her eyes glittered with the happy memories. 'Did you never work in restaurants?' she asked Damian.

'Not really. A bit of bar work back home, and I worked in an American-themed place when I got to London first, but I couldn't stick it, too stressful for me.'

Frankie swept a loose strand of hair behind her left ear. 'I know what you mean. I can't believe I was the sort of person who thrived on all that pressure. I mean, the Pomme wasn't big, but it was busy and I was running that kitchen.'

'Wait,' Damian interrupted her, 'when did that happen?'

Frankie chuckled. 'After the béarnaise sauce incident, Madame Barre took me under her wing and showed me every rope she could think of. I never washed dishes again, and slowly I made my way up the kitchen ladder till I was standing in when Madame Barre had a night off. I suppose it went on like that for, I don't know, two or three years? Time is so strange when you get to my age. Those years in New York seemed endless and yet they shot by at the same time. Do you know what I mean?'

Damian thought that he did. He felt the same way about his time in London. Eight years was not an insignificant time to have lived somewhere, but most of the time he felt as if he had just arrived in the city. When he thought about his future life in London, it wasn't the one he was currently living. He imagined he might still be helping people, but the Damian of the future didn't live in a shared house in Shadwell, and he wasn't single. There was a vague expectation that his parents might eventually be proud of him. Despite the passing years, he still felt confident in this vision of his future and he wondered if, when he finally got there, all the years spent waiting would concertina in the way that Frankie was describing.

'Hello!' It was Nor's voice coming from the hallway.

'In here!' Frankie called.

When Nor appeared in the doorway, Damian let out an involuntary 'Wow!'

She was wearing a tuxedo made from black moire silk. Under it she wore a complicated white satin blouse, and her enormous diamond earrings matched the glittering brooch on her lapel. The expensive musk of her perfume filled the room.

'Oh good. I hoped you two would be awake still.'

'Where have you been, all dolled up?' Frankie asked, pulling herself up in her chair.

'The worst opera I have ever seen – and I have sat through some godawful operas. A revival of *The Knot Garden*. I wanted to self-harm. I'm ashamed to say I claimed illness and bowed out at the second interval. Have you still got that Calvados?'

'Help yourself. Who were you there with?' Frankie called after her friend as she ducked into the kitchen.

'The Wickhams. Mad as a box of frogs, the two of them. I mean, if she wasn't worth a fortune she'd be in a mental home by now,' Nor replied, carrying a bottle and three china cups back into the living room. 'Everyone?' She held the bottle aloft.

'Go on then.'

'You're going to get me fired,' Damian said with a smirk.

'Well, I'm not going to tell. And Frankie is well on the mend now,' Nor said brightly, but Damian and Frankie exchanged a look. Their time together might soon be at an end.

'Cheers!' The trio clinked cups.

'What brings you here?' Frankie asked her friend.

Nor shrugged. 'I wasn't ready to go home. Some nights the house just seems too big. You know.'

Frankie choked on her brandy. 'No. No, I do not know. Look around, Nor. Do you want any of this furniture back?'

Nor dismissed the question with a wave of her hand. 'I didn't want it any more and you needed some.'

'How long have you lived here, Frankie?' Damian asked and was surprised that the question hadn't come up before.

'Oh, she hasn't told you the story of her return?' Nor sat on a stiff wooden chair.

'No. She was just telling me about her time in New York.'

Nor clapped her hands. 'Oh, you should have seen our Frankie then. A proper businesswoman, owning her own restaurant in Manhattan. So impressive!'

'Stop!' Frankie interjected. 'I haven't got there yet. You haven't even come back into the story yet.'

Damian put down his empty cup and looked from Nor to Frankie. 'Yes, I wondered when that was going to happen.'

New York, 1965

I

The male form had been a mystery to Frankie for most of her life. Apart from her fully clothed encounters with Alan and John, the closest she had come to glimpsing a man's body was the occasional swimmer on the beach being clumsy with his towel, or at school, walking past the boys' changing rooms when the door opened unexpectedly. Having access to Joe and his musky skin and forbidden patches of thick dark hair, even now after four years, was still wildly erotic to Frankie. One of her greatest pleasures was to sit in the steam-filled kitchen and watch while he washed himself in the tub. Sometimes she would take the hard bar of soap from him and press it into his flesh, fanning her hands on the expanse of his back. She would stand and wait with a towel as he rose up from the bath like a mythical creature, water dripping from every part of him, and then she would wrap the towel around his body and rub him dry.

Since Betty had moved in with her college mates, the apartment had become Joe and Frankie's private paradise. Sex was no longer confined to his bedroom. Clothes had been shed on every inch of the floor and Frankie felt as if there wasn't a single surface she hadn't been pressed against. Similarly, Joe's art, like the tendrils he painted, had crept from the bedroom to take over the entire apartment. Even the doors all displayed vistas of Joe's rampant alien gardens. He worked for hours, never judging any corner of any room to be entirely finished. Joe could always find space for another animated leaf or unnatural blossom. Frankie found it difficult to express how she felt about Joe's art. Living in the apartment was like being inside him. When she looked at the walls it felt as if she were permanently surrounded by his love.

The other relationship that had grown nearly as important to her was with Madame Barre in the restaurant. While Joe worked on his art, Frankie would potter around their tiny apartment kitchen perfecting sauces, trying out new recipes, experimenting with combinations of flavours, and when she considered something was good enough she would bring it to Madame Barre, who almost invariably put the new dish on the specials board. Frankie's chicken breasts wrapped in ham and stuffed with Camembert had even made it as far as the permanent menu. The unexpected arrival of Frankie had been like a gift for the old lady. In the afternoon while the other women were prepping for the evening service, Madame Barre could be found huddled with Frankie, teaching her some obscure technique or variations on a classic. Frankie knew it was fanciful but she allowed herself to believe that this was what it must have been like as a little girl with her mother in the kitchen in Ballytoor.

After the last customer had left, the two women might share a glass of wine while Frankie heard stories about the jazz musician who had lured Madame Barre from Paris to New York. Charlie Wise and his orchestra, in reality just four other musicians, had seemed on the cusp of great things when it had all ended with the bus crash on a stretch of highway still under construction outside Huntsville, Alabama. Two vinyl albums in frames hung behind the short bar in the dining room of La Petite Pomme, named after the bigger apple that jazz musicians spoke of when referring to New York. When Charlie had died, part of Madame Barre's grief had been about losing the chance of ever becoming a mother, and now, so late in her life, along came this young woman so eager to learn and carry on her traditions. Frankie was the daughter Madame Barre had never dared to dream of.

It was hard sometimes for Frankie to really remember who she had been before she'd met Joe and Madame Barre. Obviously she knew that she'd been naïve and unfulfilled, but how had that felt? She was like a sponge now for all the new experiences the city and its people had to offer, and somehow, as she soaked them up, they silenced her memories of who she had been before. The re-invention wasn't just confined to her carnal life with Joe or her culinary one with Madame Barre. She discovered thrift stores and slowly developed a New York look. Her old clothes, a mixture of mousy and slightly more preppy from her time at Everden and Associates, gave way to bold prints and full skirts. There was nearly always a bright scarf in her hair, and her winter coat had clearly belonged to a man before she had claimed it. She no longer looked out of place walking past the bohemians of Washington Square on her way to work at La Petite Pomme.

Neither Joe nor Frankie ever brought up the subject of the future. It was as if just speaking about it would accelerate it into being, and Frankie suspected that this current state of bliss couldn't go on indefinitely. Yes, they had got married, but still nothing felt permanent. Frankie knew too well that happiness was not to be trusted. She loved Joe and she truly believed that he loved her back, but that wasn't going to be enough. New York could never be her home, not really. She had arrived here by chance, so a part of her assumed that that same fate would eventually intervene to take her away again. Easier to just enjoy the pleasures that each day provided. She was making a decent wage for her long hours at the restaurant and Joe too was earning more money. Katharine Cornell had left her Sneden's Landing house after the death of her husband and decamped to Martha's Vineyard. Free from her full-time demands, Joe was now just a driver for hire with a high-end car service. He had more control of his hours, and, while the wages were less, he more than made up for it with tips.

One night, early in the dinner service, Frankie had been behind the little bar borrowing some vermouth for a sauce. Outside, the occasional passer-by hurried through the heavy rain that bounced high off the pavement and drummed in waves against the restaurant windows. It was the sort of night where the mood in the dining room was relaxed. The staff knew that there wouldn't be any walk-ins in this weather and it was likely that some of the reservations would be no-shows. The maître d', a tall slender Black man called Wendell, was sorting through the menus, discarding any that were too stained with smudges of sauce or wine-glass rings. Being accepted by Wendell had been another rite of passage for Frankie. She wasn't sure if he was actually related to Madame Barre's dead husband, but she knew that he had lived with her when he had first come to the city from Augusta, Georgia. His accent still had a slight Southern lilt. He looked across the room and, catching Frankie's eye, smiled conspiratorially. He took his job just seriously enough.

Through the wet window, a large black sedan could be seen pulling up outside. Although the restaurant attracted an affluent crowd, it was still unusual to see a chauffeur-driven car at the door. Frankie assumed it was Joe dropping by to say hello or to cajole her into making him a sandwich. But when the driver stepped out, it wasn't Joe. The driver made a great fuss of opening a gigantic umbrella before allowing his passenger to step from the car. Intrigued, Frankie waited behind the bar for a moment longer to see who it was and if they were coming into the dining room. Sure enough, the driver and umbrella moved steadily towards the door and then at the last moment the passenger stepped free and ducked into the restaurant. Wendell moved forward but, before he could greet the customer, Frankie called out, 'Norah?'

The woman in the doorway let out a shriek of delight.

'Frankie! It's true – I've found you!'

The two women rushed at each other and embraced. Then they each took a step back to examine the other. Norah Dean looked like the version of her adult self that she might have fantasised about in her childhood bedroom, a fur draped across her shoulders and jewelled earrings that seemed to find every piece of light in the room. Frankie wondered fleetingly what impression she was making on Nor. She knew that she must be exuding a confidence that Nor would never have dreamed possible. She was glad she had chosen that night to wear her bright red bandana and matching lipstick. Despite Nor's glamour, Frankie didn't feel overwhelmed. It seemed that they had both done something with their lives.

'I can't really stay. I've got a dinner on the Upper East Side. But—'

'Well, I'm working,' Frankie interjected. 'But maybe . . . Wendell, when's the next table due?'

He glanced down at his reservations book.

'Mm, a two-top in twenty minutes and then steady for the rest of the night.'

'Thanks. Do you have time for a quick drink?' Frankie asked her old friend hopefully.

Nor looked at her watch. 'Why not? I can be a little late.'

Frankie pulled out one of the bentwood barstools and gestured for Nor to sit. 'What can I get you? Gin?'

'Vodka! I switched. Vodka rocks, a dash of lime if you have it, please.'

'Did you get that?' Frankie asked Sidney, the bespectacled young man behind the bar. He nodded. 'And I'll have a small claret. Thank you.'

Frankie sat up beside Nor.

'So how did you find me? I wrote to you but that was before I got the job here.'

'Oh God. I never got it – we all moved out of Alderney Street. You must have thought I was a complete monster, not writing back.'

They both laughed.

'It's fine, Nor. Everything has turned out for the best and I'm so happy you found me.'

Their drinks were put on the bar.

'Thanks, Sid. Don't forget to write them in the book. Cheers!'

'Cheers. I'm so happy I found you too.'

They both took a sip.

'Van was poisonous about you, vile. I mean, I knew what she was like so I assumed it wasn't true but, well, you know, I was so jealous of your trip with her that I almost wanted to believe her story, but then I met a woman called Gert Macy. Do you remember her?'

Frankie shook her head.

'A producer. She's done some work with my husband—'

'Husband?' Frankie almost shrieked with surprise. The couple at the nearest table turned around.

'Shh!' Nor said with a laugh. 'We'll get to him. The point is Gert was at Katharine Cornell's house on the night in question.'

'Oh. Grey hair, solid-looking?'

'That's probably her. Well, Van's name came up and she told the story of the Irish Jezebel sent packing and her version of events made a lot more sense. It was Gert who mentioned this place.'

'I still can't believe Van was so vindictive. Anything could have happened to me.'

Nor shook the ice in her glass. 'I feel awful that I didn't help.'

'If you had I wouldn't be here. Anyway, who is this husband of yours? Have you . . .' She hesitated. 'I mean, are you not the same as before?'

Nor slapped her thigh. 'Oh, Frankie darling, I haven't changed, not a bit. But then the man I married is – well, if you stuck feathers in his hair he couldn't be more obvious. A total screamer. Ted Forrester. He's an American but he spends a lot of time hiding from his family, pretending to be a theatrical producer in the West End. I met him through Bernard Delfont and we got on like a house on fire. He's very funny, wonderful company, but his family made an ultimatum. If he carried on his shameless bachelor lifestyle he would be disinherited. His family are the Forresters of Forresters department stores, and they own most of the Canadian railway – certainly not the sort of will anyone wants to be written out of. So please step forward the blushing bride, Miss Norah Dean!'

Frankie tried to think of an objection to what seemed like such a mercenary plan, but it really did seem to benefit all the parties involved.

'And that car, that's his?'

'Indeed it is. But you'll meet him. We come over from London all the time, his family insist on it. And what's this about Katharine Cornell's driver? Gert had all the gossip.'

Frankie looked down into her wine glass and placed a finger on the rim. She felt like a schoolgirl again.

'His name is Joe and we're very happy. The years have just flown by.'

'Well, you look wonderful. And here? You're the chef?'

'Tonight I am. Madame Barre – she's the owner – last year she semi-retired, so now we share the job. You and . . . oh, I'm so sorry, I've forgotten already. Your husband?'

'Ted, Teddy Forrester.'

'Of course. You and Ted must come here to eat.'

'Absolutely. Next time.' Nor slipped off her barstool. 'But now I must fly. I think I'm what they call unfashionably late!'

They kissed each other on the cheek and Frankie watched as her old friend disappeared into the night like a glamorous apparition.

From then on, Nor popped into La Petite Pomme every few months and on every visit the jewels in her ears and around her throat seemed to have grown larger, the sheen on her fur coats even glossier. She introduced Joe and Frankie to her husband, Ted Forrester, who was just as Nor had described. The only thing about him that even hinted at heterosexuality was his ability to refer to Nor as his *wifey*. He wore his thinning blond hair long and feathered around his plump, permanently flushed face. Frankie guessed he must have been in his forties, and Nor had been right, he was very good company. Enthusiastic, interested, generous and clearly besotted by Nor in every way apart from the one his wealthy parents had hoped for. Despite Frankie and Joe knowing the truth, they soon began to think of Nor and Teddy as an actual couple.

Perhaps as a favour to Nor, or maybe because he genuinely did admire Frankie's cooking, Teddy occasionally brought wealthy friends and prospective colleagues to the restaurant for dinner. La Petite Pomme got a couple of favourable mentions in the *New York Times*, and Frankie suspected it was somehow connected to Teddy. Not that she minded. The restaurant was fully booked nearly every night of the week and any remaining sense of boss and employee between Madame Barre and Frankie evaporated. Almost completely retired since the start of the new year, especially since the kitchen had become so busy, the old lady would sit at the bar sipping her small glass of Pernod and beaming at the waiters as they hip-swerved their way through the packed dining room, trays of food and drinks held aloft. This was the restaurant that she had always dreamed of owning and Frankie, her sweet Irish Frankie, had made it all come true.

Frankie wished that Joe could share more in her happiness at work. She was sure he was proud of her but, now that money was less of a problem for them, it gave Joe more time to worry about other things, mostly himself. The arrival of spring only seemed to make things worse.

'You think I'm talented, don't you?' It was almost two in the morning and Joe seemed to be in one of his self-pitying moods.

'Of course I do!' Frankie answered quickly. She sat beside him on the bed. 'You're the most creative person I know. You've made whole worlds.' She smiled as she indicated the murals all around them.

'I just wish I could share it, get my vision beyond our apartment. I bumped into Marian Zazeela the other day. Remember her? We met her at that thing on Chambers Street with La Monte?'

Frankie nodded. It had been one of the longest nights of her life, sitting on the floor listening for hours to sounds that she failed to recognise as music.

'Well, she works with light, and she uses photographs to show galleries, so I was trying it out. Can I show you?' His face looked childish with its mix of eagerness and nerves.

'Of course.'

From under the bed, Joe pulled out a large hard-backed folder, with photographs carefully mounted inside. Frankie's heart broke a little to think of Joe doing all this work without telling her.

'These are beautiful, Joe, beautiful.' And she was being sincere. Sunlight danced off the mosaics and strange shadows made the murals look even more enticing and alive. 'You've got to show these to people.'

'You really think so? They don't look too amateur?'

'No, not at all. Where will you go?'

Joe produced a sheet of paper with a long list on it. Frankie felt a squeeze of her heart.

'I thought I'd mail some copies out and then there's a bunch of small galleries uptown I can visit – you know, maybe talk to the owners.'

'Yes! That sounds like a great plan.'

Frankie hugged him, pleased to see him so enthused. Maybe her success in the restaurant might rub off on him.

The days went by and a pattern quickly emerged.

'Anything?' Frankie would ask when she came home from work.

'Nothing.' Joe at this point just sounded sad or disappointed. Later, as the quantity of bourbon he drank accumulated, it would turn to anger. On this particular night Frankie knew that he had done more than wait in for the mail. He had taken some of his folders uptown to a building on Madison Avenue that housed several prestigious galleries.

'What about the Fuller Building?' she asked, keeping her voice bright.

'Waste of time. Most of them wouldn't even take a look. "You need an appointment." Can I make an appointment? "You need to be invited to make an appointment." Such horseshit. One kid behind the desk at Charles Egan took a look and said he liked them.'

'Well, that's something.'

'Refused to come and see the works here on the walls. Suggested I try working on canvas.'

The scorn in Joe's voice warned Frankie to bite her tongue, but she agreed with the kid at Charles Egan. Surely if you wanted to sell your art, you should make it easier to buy? When she had naïvely suggested this as an idea, many months before, she had quickly learned that it was not the sort of thing one said to an artist. It was almost a physical pain for Frankie, being relegated to the status of everyone else, from family to strangers in the street, and not considered capable of helping the man she loved. Their intimacy was so intense and overwhelming apart from in this one area. What hurt was not so much being disagreed with, but being disregarded.

Nor, too, had tried to help. She brought a wealthy friend who was remodelling a dated fin-de-siècle Park Avenue apartment all the way down to the Village to see Joe's work in situ. The woman had been enthusiastic and commissioned him on the spot to decorate both of her guest bathrooms. They had all arrived at La Pomme giddy with the news. Nor ordered champagne and Frankie had had to hide in the kitchen when she found she was crying. The happiness on Joe's face broke her heart. Why couldn't she make him look like that any more? She was sure that she used to.

The euphoria was short-lived. A few nights later, Frankie had asked to see the design sketches that she knew Joe had been so excited by. He'd talked of little else. He was polishing his work shoes over the sink, and he just shrugged in an offhand way. 'Not happening.'

'What? Why?'

'She called here this afternoon. Still loves what I do, but her decorator has different ideas, yadda, yadda, not happening.'

'I'm so sorry.' Frankie stepped across the kitchen to wrap her arms around Joe. He squirmed free. 'It doesn't matter. It's not a big deal.' He walked away, carrying his shoes into the bedroom.

Frankie wanted to follow him and tell him that it did matter, and that it was a huge deal, and he had every right to feel upset, but something warned her to stay where she was, silent in the kitchen.

II

'What about a baby?' Nor asked as she clinked the ice in her drink. 'That happy sound,' she continued, without waiting for Frankie to respond. 'Are you having one?'

'A baby?'

'A drink.' Nor laughed. 'My God, I hope you'd tell me if you were pregnant.'

'I might tell you, but no drink for me thanks. May I remind you, I'm working.'

'Not for an hour or so.'

'Even so, I need a clear head and I should set an example to the new girl.' Frankie glanced over at a serious-looking young woman, her tight curly hair scraped back from her face.

'What happened to Sidney? I liked him.'

'As far as I know he's in Canada. They tried to call him up for Vietnam. One of the busboys is down in South Carolina training already. Every day I hear stories. Thank God Wendell is too old.' Frankie shook her head in disbelief that such a thing could be happening.

'So sad,' Nor agreed. 'They tried to get a cousin of Teddy's but lo and behold he was diagnosed with asthma.'

'Lucky,' Frankie said drily.

Nor took a small sip of her drink. 'You're avoiding my question. I think being a father could solve all of Joe's problems.'

Frankie glanced across the dining room. Wendell was talking

to the new girl, and the other waiter was at their station polishing cutlery. She could speak freely.

'I don't think that's going to happen.'

'Have you talked about it?'

'Well, no, but if it was going to happen I'm pretty sure it would have happened by now.' Frankie peered at her friend. 'If you know what I mean.'

'He doesn't use anything?'

Frankie slapped Nor's arm. 'God, I hate talking about these things but no, no he doesn't. Never has.'

'Never?' Nor was incredulous.

'I know. Madness, but no baby, so I don't think papa Joe is the— Shut up! Here he is.'

Joe walked through the door, freshly shaved, hair slicked back and wearing a dark suit over a crisp white shirt.

'Ladies.'

'Joe, you look so handsome!' Frankie liked it when Joe made an effort.

'Well, I wanted to look my best for my date.' He put an arm around a smiling Nor.

'I'm jealous.' Frankie fanned herself playfully. 'You're going to make Teddy jealous too.'

'He's going to make Teddy something, but I'm not sure it'll be jealous.' The three of them laughed.

'Nor, you're awful. Now I should get into the kitchen. Have fun, you two.'

Joe leaned forward and kissed his wife. 'We will.' He turned to Nor. 'I guess we aren't taking the subway.'

'Correct. But Teddy has the car, so let's just grab a taxi on Sixth. Don't work too hard, Frankie.'

'I won't.' She watched them leave. She smiled and waved, but, even before she had turned to go into the kitchen, she had an uneasy feeling. It had been very kind of Teddy and Nor to get Joe an invitation for the opening of a fancy new contemporary art museum uptown, but Frankie already knew that her husband would return home in a resentful sulk.

Joe's list of what was wrong with the new Whitney Museum was exhaustive. Everything from the lighting and the artists they'd selected all the way to the canapés and the line for the cloakroom – everything was ill-conceived. Frankie tried to listen to it all, making the appropriate responses, but, worn out after a busy shift, had ended up falling asleep. This had not improved Joe's mood and he'd spent another hour drinking bourbon and muttering his many and varied grievances to the apartment walls covered in his far superior work.

What occurred next could not be described as good. It wasn't. It was sad, and yet things have a strange way of never being just one thing. Madame Barre was found dead in her apartment. Despite her old age, it still came as a heartbreaking shock to Frankie. Wendell, who had known Madame the longest, was distraught. After they got the call in the restaurant he had sat at an empty table, his face contorted with tears. Frankie had sat beside him and held his hand. 'My momma only let me come to this city because of that woman. She took care of me.'

'I know. I know she did. Me too.' And somehow the realisation of what a mother Madame Barre had been to her made Frankie cry even harder.

Wendell busied himself calling the people in the reservations book to explain, while Frankie made a sign for the door to tell people why they were closed for the night. The staff who arrived expecting to start their shift gathered around two tables. Frankie opened a few bottles of red wine. The women from the kitchen, along with Bruno the dish-washer, looked sheepish as they joined the waiters, but soon they too were swapping their stories of Madame Barre, the way she had always taken a shot of brandy for every one she put in a sauce or in her tarte aux pommes, the money she had lent people, the time she had ordered rabbit and it had been delivered alive. They laughed and tried to explain her to the newer staff who hadn't really known her. Frankie didn't attempt to hide her tears when she spoke about her mentor and all that she had taught her. Toast followed toast.

As the small impromptu wake drew to a close, Rebecca, the newest member of the team, asked, 'How long are we going to be closed for?'

Frankie and Wendell looked at each other. It wasn't just a question of what was respectful but also an uncertainty about the future of La Petite Pomme. If they reopened, who were they working for?

Wendell cleared his throat. 'Let's say definitely closed tomorrow.' He looked to Frankie for agreement.

'Yes,' she said, just to be clear.

'And then assume we'll be open again for the Saturday dinner service.'

'Unless we call you to say otherwise,' Frankie added. In her mind's eye she saw herself arriving at the restaurant to find the doors padlocked and eviction notices stuck to the windows.

Joe was working that night, so the apartment was empty when she got home. He had offered to drop his shift, but she insisted she would be fine. In reality, she wished he had been there to hold her, cradle her in her grief, but the truth was that they might need every cent if La Pomme was closed down.

The next morning, Frankie left Joe in bed and, with no particular plan in mind, crossed Sixth Avenue and made her way to the restaurant. The chairs were upturned on the tables. The dirty wine glasses from the day before were on the bar, waiting to be washed. She shrugged off her coat and began loading them into the small glass-washer. It felt good to be doing something useful. The phone rang. She remembered she needed to try to call the customers they had failed to reach the day before.

'La Petite Pomme, how may I help you?' she parroted down the line.

'Is this Mrs Haffen? Frances Haffen?' It was the voice of an older man. Frankie wondered what more bad news she was about to receive.

'Yes. To whom am I speaking?' Her voice seemed very small and tight in the empty room. Even to her own ear she sounded like a canon's wife answering the phone in Castlekeen.

'I'm Mr Myers of Wexler and Cohen. I tried you at home but your husband told me I could find you on this number. Is this a convenient time?'

Frankie said, 'Yes,' but wondered if she meant it.

'We represent the estate of the late Mrs Wise.'

'Mrs Wise? Sorry, I don't know any—'

'Ah, you would have known her as Madame Barre, I believe.'

Frankie pulled a chair off a table and sat down. 'Yes. I knew her. Is this about the funeral arrangements?'

'Well, no, though Mrs Wise has left very specific instructions so I'm sure you'll be informed in a day or two.' The man seemed slightly thrown off script. He cleared his throat and began again. 'Now, Mrs Haffen, I'm calling with what I imagine will be some rather welcome news. I'm pleased to inform you that Mrs Wise has bequeathed you her business.'

A tiny yelp escaped Frankie.

'That is to say, the building and contents, as well as any funds in the business bank account – which, I can tell you, currently amount to just over three thousand dollars.'

'Thank you. Thank you very much, Mr . . .' but she couldn't remember his name. Then she was crying. Then she was crying and running down the street, back to tell Joe the good news.

Frankie's mind went into overdrive. She had so many plans and ideas. She would change the name of the restaurant to Pomme, since that was what everyone called the place anyway. The food could be different now. Fewer of the old-fashioned French classics – she wanted to experiment, make it unexpected, the pork chops she stuffed with peaches and butter, the chicken livers in the hollowed-out brioche. But her biggest and best idea was for Joe: he would redecorate the whole dining room; it would be his masterpiece, and, best of all, she could pay him.

'I don't know,' was his disappointing response. Frankie had wanted wild, unfiltered gratitude and excitement, not these pursed lips.

'What don't you know?'

'Well, does it look a bit pathetic? My wife just feeling sorry for me . . .'

Frankie grabbed his shoulders. 'What are you talking about? *We* own a restaurant, so of course *we* will decorate it in the way *we* want. Joe, you know I love what you do, and there won't be another dining room like it in the whole city. It's exciting! So be excited! No one is feeling sorry for anyone.'

A smile crept across his face. 'I guess it could be cool. I've had this idea for making a river using just little toy cars; I suppose it could flow down the wall to the side of the bar, and then we need apples – what has pictures of apples?'

Frankie thought for a moment. 'The cider. You could use the labels off the French cider we sell.'

'Yes!' He kissed Frankie and was already reaching for his drawing pad and pencils.

The funeral was an awkward affair. Madame Barre's La Petite Pomme family, staff and customers sat on one side of the crematorium, while on the other there was a sparse scattering of members from the late Charlie Wise's family. Frankie didn't know if she was just being paranoid, but she felt as if the family members were all staring at her, the woman who had stolen their inheritance. The only bright point was when a group of elderly jazz musicians shuffled forward and, for a few minutes, became young again as they blew their horns.

At the end of October, they closed the newly named Pomme for a week and Joe got to work. The dining room was filled with pots of paint, piles of old crockery, a bucket of corks, toy cars, doll heads. Frankie and Wendell stood by the door watching Joe as he ran from his sketchbook to the wall to make light pencil marks and then back again.

'Are you sure about this?' Wendell whispered.

'What? You don't think it's a good idea?'

Wendell shrugged. 'It's pretty wild.'

'But beautiful!' Frankie insisted. 'You've seen our apartment. You love our apartment.'

'Yes, I do. But that took years, didn't it?' He looked back at Joe scribbling below the window. 'He's got a week.'

For the next six nights, Joe barely slept. Most evenings he didn't even make it back to the apartment, just sleeping on some coats under the tables. Frankie made sure he ate, and she helped however she could. She spent hours carefully steaming the labels off hundreds of cider bottles; she painted old mannequin hands that Joe had found outside a store in the garment district. They had been in the corner of their bedroom for as long as she had known him, but now they were going to be green and screwed into the wall to hold coats. A highway of small toy cars was nailed to the wall behind the little reception area, colanders were hacked apart to form strange lantern blossoms on the lights, graters were used as sconces, and everything existed in the midst of a huge fecund jungle. Hour after hour Joe worked on every leaf and stem, creating a cornucopia of alien delights. Leaves might be edged with lips, a petal could morph into a tongue, a crack in the plaster might bleed. The restaurant might have reeked of paint and glue but nevertheless it was ready to be unveiled to the world.

The staff were back and astonished. As they mopped and polished, they kept noticing new details.

'It's really something.'

'People are going to be shocked.'

'I like it.' Wendell was only too happy to eat his words. Frankie had been right. Pomme was no longer a little French bistro in the Village, it was a beautiful freak that demanded attention. And that is what it got.

Wapping, 2024

'It's in there somewhere.'

'Yeah. I'm sure it is but I'm going to need more than "some-where".' Damian was on his knees in the small room that was now known as his bedroom. Tasked by Frankie to find a scrap-book that she knew was in one of the many boxes, he was currently in the process of tackling his fifth box. So far he had found mostly bed linen and books, with the occasional theatre programme or exhibition catalogue.

'Oh! Look! I must be getting close.' He held up a piece of paper.

'Oh my God, let me see that.'

Damian handed Frankie what looked to be a handwritten menu. For a moment Frankie just held it and stared.

'This would have been the second year, I think, when Joe started doing the menus too. Sixty-six, or sixty-seven. So pretty.' She laughed. 'I mean, almost impossible to read, the waiters had to tell nearly every table what was on it. Jesus, I was keen on blue-cheese sauce. I was even serving strawberries with a blue-cheese crème anglaise. What was I thinking?'

Damian continued to lift out long-forgotten items.

'Aprons, tea towels, old newspapers . . . ah, is this it?' He was holding a slim brown volume that had a French cider label stuck to the cover.

'That's it. You brilliant boy. Come on, we'll go back and have a look.'

Frankie pushed herself away from the wall she'd been leaning against and, just using a walking stick, hobbled her way back to the living room.

When she'd settled into her usual chair, Damian sat on the floor beside her to get a better look at the book in her lap.

'It was Wendell who kept this. I was too busy cooking, and Joe, well he was proud of our success, I know he was, but he would never have kept a scrapbook like this. Look at the state of me!'

She was pointing at a photograph cut from a newspaper. She and Joe were standing arm in arm outside the restaurant; her hair was tied up in a bandana, and she was wearing an apron over some pedal pushers.

'That was the new sign Joe made. Can you see? It was broken green glass from wine bottles with lights behind it. Gorgeous.'

'I'll tell you what else is gorgeous: Joe. I mean, you said he was handsome but he was quite the catch. What a beautiful couple you made.'

Frankie put a finger on the face in the photograph. 'Yes. A beautiful young man.' She turned the page. 'All these reviews – I'd forgotten how many. The *Voice*, the *Times*, the *Post*, the *New Yorker*, everybody came, and for a little while – this will sound silly, but, just for a minute or two, Pomme felt like the centre of the world. And maybe what made it all the sweeter was how unexpected it all was. I mean, I wasn't raised to expect success, never mind happiness.' She glanced at Damian to see if he under-stood, and was surprised to find his eyes glistening with tears. 'What's wrong with you?'

Damian wiped his face with the sleeve of his sweatshirt.

'It's just sweet to hear you talk like this. It's nice.'

Frankie shut the scrapbook. 'What you're trying not to say is that it's sad. And it is.'

'Frankie!' he objected.

'Look, you know the way in life, and dear God, a young man like you must feel this, you always believe that the best is yet to come.'

He nodded.

'Well, here I am in my eighties, stuck in this flat with Nor's unwanted furniture and a man who seems only too keen to wipe my bum.'

'I only offered, I didn't insist.'

'Fair enough. My point is that there is nothing tragic in me knowing that the best days of my life are behind me, and' – she squeezed the scrapbook to her chest – 'these were the happiest years of my life. I know that now, and I'm grand with that. I was lucky to have them.'

Damian didn't know what to say. He couldn't disagree with her but it still seemed like a bleak way of looking at a life that wasn't yet finished. Frankie reached out and patted his head. 'I wish you all the happiness I had. We were a team, a proper team. After Pomme opened, Joe kept driving but he came to help out whenever he could. Madame Barre left the place to me, but for a few years there it really felt like *ours*. His art was mentioned in every review, the customers wanted to know who had decorated the place; it was lovely, *lovely* to see him glow. You never want to see someone you love feel defeated, so this was everything for me. And his family, his weird parents. For years they pretended I didn't exist, as if Joe had never got married, but suddenly they were coming to the city, bringing relations I'd never heard of to the restaurant for dinner. I didn't mind; it made Joe happy. He knew it was ridiculous, but he liked it.'

'Was the sister Betty still around?' Damian wondered.

Frankie smiled. 'No, not really, and I'm fairly certain she didn't love it – Joe and me getting all the attention. Things changed for her. By then she'd met a man called Adam, nice, a bit dull, and moved back up to Albany to teach. She had always been the golden child, even managed to have two kids, but I swear the parents were more impressed by the restaurant. And then everything else that happened.'

Damian made himself more comfortable on the floor.

'What happened to Joe?'

'What happened to Joe?' Frankie repeated the question slowly and deliberately. She pondered for a moment. 'Too much. Too much happened to Joe.'

New York, 1967

I

'Chef! Chef! Chef!'

Frankie hesitated in the kitchen. She hated making appearances in the dining room during service, but this was a special occasion and it sounded as if the diners weren't going to take no for an answer.

It was more than a year since Frankie and Joe had reopened Pomme and tonight was the latest instalment in the ongoing celebrations for Teddy Forrester's fiftieth birthday. Festivities had begun in London with a reception held in the American embassy, then a weekend house party in Sag Harbour, followed by a black-tie gala given by his parents in the St Regis Hotel. Tonight, Teddy and Nor had booked out all of Pomme for their more artistic, *downtown* friends.

Taking a deep breath, Frankie stepped out into the dining room to loud cheers. Wendell swirled a linen napkin above his head. Teddy struggled to his feet, swaying as he held his wine glass aloft. His lips were as red as Nor's. Frankie wondered if he was wearing her lipstick.

'This is Frankie Haffen, chef extraordinaire and owner of this marvellous place.'

People started to applaud but Frankie shook her head and

called over the noise, 'And happy birthday to Teddy!' She looked over her shoulder and waved out two waiters who had been waiting in the kitchen with a large square cake covered in candles. As they came forward, a chorus of 'Happy Birthday' began, and, after some cheers, Frankie slipped away, back into her domain.

She was holding her order book and going through the fridges to see what was needed for the next day, when she heard a polite cough behind her. She turned to find a serious-looking man in an expensive grey suit standing in the kitchen. He had a high, tanned forehead and heavy eyebrows that dominated his face.

'Excuse me,' he began. His voice was soft and accented. French or maybe Italian? Frankie attempted to smile. How had Wendell allowed this to happen?

'I'm sorry, but whatever you need I'm sure one of the waiters can help you.' She pointed back towards the dining room, hoping the man would follow her directions out of her kitchen.

'Actually, I wanted to speak to you.'

'I see.' What was this going to be? A complaint? Praise? The man's demeanour was hard to gauge.

'I just wanted to know who has made all of your murals.'

A sigh of relief.

'Oh, that's Joe. My husband, Joe Haffen. He did everything out there. The lights, the mosaics. It's all him.'

'Impressive. I like them a great deal.' He fished in his jacket pocket. 'I don't want to tread on any toes, but I have a small gallery uptown and I'd be very interested in talking to your husband about his work. If he'd like to, that is.' The man finally smiled. It was unsettling to see his face crack, but she took the card.

'Thank you. I'm sure he'll call you.'

The man made to leave but then turned back. 'Wonderful food, by the way. Really very good. Very.'

'Thank you.'

'Good night.'

The man was hardly out of the room before Nor had rushed in. It was clear that she had also been enjoying the wine.

'What did Leo want?'

'That man?'

'Leo Castelli. That was Leo Castelli. He has a gallery.'

'I know, he just told me. He wants to talk to Joe.'

Nor shrieked and bounded forward to hug her friend.

'Oh, we so hoped that might happen! Oh Frankie, this is the best, the best.'

Frankie was slightly irritated by this outburst. It was never easy to deal with the enthusiasm of a drunk person, though obviously working at the restaurant she had learned to tolerate it.

'Well, I'm sure Joe will be very grateful. Now I've got to finish up.' She held up her order book.

Nor grabbed her arm. 'No, Frankie, you don't understand. The Castelli gallery has the best: Rauschenberg, Jasper Johns . . .' She paused to think of more names that might impress. 'Warhol – dear God, how could I forget Warhol?'

Frankie had heard of Andy Warhol. She took the business card out of her apron pocket and looked at it properly. The card was thick, the print embossed. The address of the gallery was on 77th Street. Suddenly she felt a spark of excitement deep within herself. This might be it. This card might be Joe's passport to the future of his dreams.

Teddy was the next person to barge into the kitchen. Was Wendell asleep? The light from the small round window in the door behind him made Teddy's dishevelled hair a wispy halo. His wide face beamed with all the good things, drink, excitement, pride and joy.

'Leo told me he wants to meet with Joe.'

Nor squealed and went to hug her unlikely husband. 'I know, isn't it wonderful?'

Frankie held up the business card as if it was the winning ticket in a raffle. Her hand was shaking.

Back at the apartment, Joe was sleeping already. Frankie wasn't sure what to do but she was too excited to go to bed so she decided to wake him. For once, Joe didn't try to undermine or downplay his own good fortune. He paced around the apartment holding the business card.

'Leo Castelli. *The* Leo Castelli wants to talk to *me*!' He kissed Frankie, then looked at the card again, before covering Frankie's face with more kisses.

After they had drunk most of the bottle of champagne Frankie had brought home from Pomme, Joe slowly undressed her and, unlike their lovemaking of late, the sex didn't feel rushed or perfunctory. They weren't tired or worried about how early they had to get up, they were just happy. It was a form of bliss, something that neither of them had even known they could hope for. Of course they had felt happiness together before, but now, with all the pieces of their lives clicking into place, it was as if they were completing a puzzle. As they lay together afterwards, their breathing still laboured, Joe buried his face in Frankie's hair and repeated over and over again, 'I love you so much.' She wasn't sure, but she thought he might have been crying.

The next day, Frankie felt her excitement fade. This was too much good fortune, and she didn't trust it. She could feel a small knot of tension in her stomach as she readied herself for the disappointment she was certain would follow. What made things worse was that Joe appeared to be making no effort to put a check on his expectations. He regaled Frankie with stories from the art world of how Leo Castelli would turn artists into stars overnight, the way the Lichtenstein show had sold out before it opened, how Leo opened the door to Europe, where everyone was going crazy for the new American art. Frankie had to muster all her self-control not to try to bring Joe down to earth. What if it was just a meeting and nothing more? Maybe he just wanted Joe to decorate a child's bedroom. She hated thinking in such a negative way but she knew she would be the one who had to pick Joe up if there was a mighty fall.

On the day of the much-anticipated meeting, Frankie had to go to work, so Joe was heading uptown alone. She wished him good luck, kissed his freshly shaved face and sent him on his way. She could hear his footsteps descending the stairs, and for the first time since she was a girl she found herself praying. Please God, make this happen for Joe. Don't let him come home defeated.

Her prayers were answered.

The Castelli Gallery would host an exhibition of new works by Joseph Haffen the following March.

'It was supposed to be Donald Judd, but he says he won't be ready in time. It's me, just me. They're giving me the whole space. Leo showed me pictures of a Warhol exhibition and he covered whole rooms in wallpaper, so I'm going to do the same, only with my murals.' Joe's excitement was bursting out of his body. He moved his arms as if he was already painting the walls.

Frankie couldn't quite believe what she was hearing. She loved Joe, she believed in him, of course she did, but now some stranger was giving her husband a level of validation and joy she could never hope to achieve Her role had always been to encourage Joe, to buoy him up and help him have faith in his talent. Who was she now? Was she supposed to be the person who tried to tether him to reality? She wasn't sure she wanted this new job.

'And what will people buy? Is the gallery selling special commissions or something?'

There was a flicker of irritation on Joe's face but then his smile returned. 'I forgot to tell you: no, there will be pieces for sale.

The show is called *Fragments* and it'll be as if the art has been found or recovered from an abandoned building, you know, like a piece of wood or a torn piece of canvas that has a glimpse of the whole mural. It's so clever. It was Leo's idea.'

'I see,' Frankie said, thinking to herself that it sounded very much like an idea she had suggested a few years earlier, which Joe had dismissed without consideration.

The restaurant continued to be busy, and Frankie still worked nearly every shift, while Joe, despite his upcoming exhibition, still found time to help. Every Tuesday morning, like clockwork, he would be outside Pomme waiting for the wine delivery. He constantly checked the dining room and bathroom to make sure his décor hadn't been damaged and, if it had, he'd patch it up. Before service he'd sit at the bar sketching out ideas for the Castelli installation, and if he wasn't there then he could be found wandering the streets of the Village, looking to salvage materials he might use for the smaller pieces. Leo Castelli was paying Joe a monthly stipend, so he was no longer driving. Frankie found herself beginning to relax. She wasn't losing her husband; if anything, she was seeing more of him. Their sex life was almost as intense as it had been at the start of their relationship, and Joe seemed to be romantic in a way he'd never been before. Frankie would often get up to find that he had already been out to the bakery for treats, and when she got home from work he'd offer to massage her feet. It was never stated, but Frankie felt that all of it was Joe's way of acknowledging everything she had done to make sure he had never thrown in the towel and was ready for this opportunity. He knew how much of this moment belonged to Frankie.

The hell of a busy restaurant at Christmas passed in a blur, as it merely marked the passing of time. At the beginning of February, the staff at Pomme gathered round the bar and applauded as Joe put up the first poster for his exhibition, which, as was the practice at the gallery, had been designed by the artist. The colours on the paper seemed almost electric in their brightness. Frankie ran her hand across the gloss of the poster. It was really going to happen.

On Joe's opening night, Pomme was shut. Obviously Frankie was going to be there, and Joe had also invited Wendell, Nor and Teddy, along with his family from Albany. He had deliberately kept his guest list short. He wanted to conserve as much room as possible for collectors and reviewers.

'Do I look like an artist?' Joe asked Frankie as he stood in the kitchen doorway. He was wearing a new tan corduroy suit over a dark purple shirt that Frankie had bought him for Christmas. Frankie wanted to stay in this moment forever. This was the magic hour when he still needed her, and before the world decided if the new works by Joseph Haffen were worthy of its attention. In this moment, with Joe standing in front of her, like a teenager going to his first dance, everything was still possible.

'Yes,' she assured him. 'You look like the greatest artist in all the land.'

Joe's guest list might have been small, but the crowd at the gallery was not. Frankie knew that this was Joe's night, so, once she spotted the reassuring sight of Wendell smoking in a corner, she made a point of leaving Joe and weaving her way through the throng.

'You look beautiful,' Wendell said once she'd reached him.

'Oh, thank you.' In her nervous excitement she had forgotten that she too had made a special effort with her appearance. What did the wife of an artist wear? She'd decided on a bronze shift dress in shot silk, her hair tied back with a thrift-store scarf and small gold earrings. She knew she looked good, but at the same time it was all very plain. She hadn't wanted to stand out or distract from Joe and the art in any way.

'What do you think?' Wendell asked, gesturing towards the room with his cigarette.

'It's like being at home,' she said with a giggle.

'Or at work.'

'I know. It's so strange to see it here. It looks different, though – so bright.'

Wendell waved at someone. 'I think that's Betty.'

'No, she couldn't get away. The kids. But Joe's parents are here somewhere.'

The general din of conversation helped Frankie to relax. So far, so good. Joe had an exhibition and people had come to see it. She looked around at the crowd. It was a strange mix of people. Some, perhaps the majority, looked like Nor and Teddy, well-heeled New Yorkers who felt that embracing this new art scene made them more interesting, and, more importantly, saved them from becoming their parents. The others were mostly younger and dressed in strange bohemian ensembles. They might have come directly from Washington Square. Clearly, they were not going to buy any of this art, but they knew that this Upper East Side outpost was shaping their future as well. The only good thing about being a starving artist was when you were fed.

'Do you want to see the other room?' Wendell asked.

'Of course.' Frankie would never have admitted to Joe how surprised she was by the size of the gallery. After all the talk about Leo Castelli, she had expected something much grander, but this was really just the size of a well-proportioned apartment. The next room was much darker and was a side of Joe's work Frankie hadn't seen before. There was less of the lush foliage and more of a dark petrified forest. It made her uneasy.

'I love this stuff,' Wendell gushed. 'I mean, I wouldn't want to live in it or eat here, but it is really beautiful.'

Frankie looked around the room, the brooding shadows stitched together with decaying tendrils and horror-movie cobwebs.

'I don't like to think of this being inside Joe. I like—'

'Frankie, darling!' Nor had appeared out of the crowd, looking wildly glamorous in a black velvet opera coat. 'Where's Joe?' But before anyone could answer, she had spotted him. 'There he is with Teddy. Come.' She tugged at Wendell's arm and they both followed her across the room.

The four of them huddled around Joe, who seemed a little dazed by everything.

'I feel weird. I don't know any of these people.' He looked around distractedly. 'Leo has organised drinks at The Mark afterwards. You'll all come?'

Before the quartet could respond, Leo Castelli himself appeared.

'Mrs Haffen, lovely to see you again.'

Frankie smiled. She was under no illusion that he wanted to speak to her.

'Apologies, Joe – Ivan was taking care of Leon Kraushar, so obviously I was in hiding.' He gave a thin giggle as if the group would understand why this was amusing, but, confronted by their blank faces, he quickly added, 'Now, my lovely people, I hope to see you all at The Mark, but first I must take Joe away. The Sculls have just arrived, and I want you to meet Ileanna. She has plans to bring you to Paris.'

'OK.' Joe flashed an apologetic smile at the group before he was swallowed up by the well-tailored shoulders of all the people who wanted to congratulate him. Frankie felt the others looking at her expectantly. There was an awkwardness.

'I'm so happy for him,' she said quickly, and it was true. She really was happy for Joe. What went unsaid was how sad she felt for herself.

II

Frankie came home from the restaurant one afternoon, in between shifts, to find Joe with a screwdriver removing all the doors.

'What's going on?'

'Leo has found a buyer for them. Eight hundred and fifty dollars.' He paused for effect. 'Each!' He hugged Frankie tightly and planted a kiss on her mouth. She looked around uncertainly.

'But Joe, what will we use for doors?'

'We don't need doors!'

'The toilet.' She pointed at the tiny room as if he might need to be reminded of its existence.

'I'll shut my eyes. Five doors, baby! We're selling five doors. I'll wear a gold blindfold!'

The exhibition had begun tentatively. Nothing had sold on the opening night, and Frankie could sense that Joe feared the worst. But then the reviews had started to appear. *ARTnews*, *Art Magazine* and a rave in the *Times*. The following weekend Ethel and Robert Scull had bought four of the smaller pieces, and by the time the exhibition closed it was completely sold out. Calvin Tomkins was planning to write a large profile for the *New Yorker* and Joseph Haffen's second solo show had already been announced. It was to be held that September at the Sonnabend Gallery in Paris. Joe had started work in his newly rented studio space on Prince Street and moved all his materials down there. Frankie never imagined she would miss the smell of paint and white spirit, but she did. It felt as if Joe no longer lived in the apartment, even when he was sitting across the table from her.

Every day it seemed as if Joe was being invited to an exhibition opening or a fancy dinner held by a gallery or wealthy collector. At first he had faithfully asked Frankie if she wanted to accompany him, but there were only so many times she could take the night off, so somehow it got decided that Joe should go to these events by himself. If Frankie was being honest, she was quite happy with this arrangement. The art crowd bored her, while simultaneously making her uncomfortable. What was she supposed to say to some artist showing her bits of felt dropped on the floor? She would never have admitted it to Joe, but at most of the exhibitions they went to all she really wanted to do was tidy up. She was much happier at Pomme.

Nor and Teddy were spending more time in Europe, where Teddy had got involved with the major theatre tour of a Russian circus. This meant that Frankie's only contact with her friend were colourful letters full of stories about alcoholic clowns, a living fur coat made of trained cats and a worrying tale about a lion going missing in Paris. Frankie didn't feel she could really share her own stories when she wrote back, and certainly not her worries about Joe. Her letters were little more than lists of all the exciting things that had happened to Joe, with a brief mention of her own life at the restaurant.

In the absence of a flesh-and-blood Nor, increasingly Frankie found herself turning to Wendell as a confidante. Since Frankie had taken over the restaurant, he had been her main helper and supporter, and slowly that relationship crept into their personal lives. He would slip in and out of the kitchen before service with nuggets of news or gossip, often involving his own eventful love life. It had been Wendell who had come rushing in to deliver the news that Andy Warhol had been shot. Joe, sitting at the bar, had blurted out, 'Is he dead?' so quickly that he didn't have the time to mask the hope in his voice, nor indeed his disappointment when he heard that Warhol was still alive. Frankie and Wendell had laughed about it later that night. It hadn't felt like disloyalty to Joe, just that affectionate amusement everyone feels when someone you love reveals something unflattering about themselves.

Frankie

Frankie found that she looked forward to the end of the night when it was just herself and Wendell. Frankie doing her ordering, while he might be re-stocking the bar or finalising table plans for the following day. A glass or two of red wine was their reward after a busy shift. When they turned out the lights and locked up, Wendell usually headed off to some club or romantic assignation, while Frankie walked back to the apartment, hoping to find Joe already home from whatever party or event he'd been attending, and not too drunk, or high.

Joe spent almost two weeks in Paris, opening his show. It was the longest amount of time that he and Frankie had ever spent apart in their eight years together. He sent a postcard nearly every day, but they would arrive at the apartment in clumps of two or three. Each message was almost identical: he missed Frankie and had been to a dinner with some people whose names she felt she should know, but never did. He was away for their wedding anniversary. He telephoned, but there was such a bad delay on the line that all they could do was talk across each other for a few minutes.

'Happy anni—'

'*Je t'aime*—'

'How's it go—'

'I really miss—'

'I better—'

'You better—'

'Go!'

When he returned to New York, he did so with a caseful of gifts for Frankie: books, jewellery, perfume, lingerie. He entertained her with his jokey French and stank the apartment out with French cigarettes. Frankie didn't mind. She had her Joe back and he loved her, and they were both so lucky. For a few months after Paris, that seemed to be true. Perhaps they were becoming accustomed to all the attention that Joe was receiving, though

207

the energy around him also seemed less frenetic and stressful. He was still busy. He had been selected for a group show at the Whitney, there were plans for a spring show in LA and he'd been given the honour of designing the interior for the American Pavilion at the next Venice Biennale in 1970. There was more money in the bank than they knew what to do with and his sudden notoriety had the knock-on effect that Pomme, with its remarkable interior, was busier than ever. The crowd had become artier, with wilder hair and louder voices, but they drank and paid their cheques, so Frankie was happy. They seemed like one of those couples who had it all, and they were, until they didn't.

In France Joe had bought himself a navy beret as a joke, but Frankie noticed that he was wearing it more frequently and in a way that meant that, whatever the joke had been, it was no longer obvious. When he brought people into the restaurant for dinner, which was far more often now, he always paid, or rather told the waiter to put it on an account that no one was aware of. Frankie found herself producing cash from her purse, so the waiter at least got a tip. When she had tried to bring it up with him, he had been dismissive.

'Stop worrying. It's just money. We have money.'

'And who are all these people we're feeding?'

'Friends.'

Frankie stared at him in silence for long enough to make him look up from the magazine he was flicking through.

'What?'

'Friends I've never seen before?'

'New friends. You don't get it, Frankie . . .'

'What is there to get?' Her anger rising, she continued, 'Well, yes, no, I'll tell you what I don't get. I don't get why you don't lift a finger in this apartment, why you use the word *oeuvre* without laughing, why you wear that stupid beret. I don't get why you can't be a success and still stay the same Joe as you were before.'

'Because people change, Frankie. We're all changing all the time. Who were you when I picked you up on the side of the road? Now look at you, running your own business. Me changing isn't the problem, it's that you can't. You liked it when I was a loser; you can't cope now that I've got the money, now that I'm in demand.' He was standing, pulling on his coat.

'Where are you going?'

'Somewhere I won't annoy my wife.'

'Oh right, I can't cope? Well, I'm not the one—'

The slam of the front door as Joe left cut her short.

She had a bath to try to relax. They didn't fight often, and she hated it when they did. She took long, deliberate breaths, exhaling slowly, the steam from the water soothing her skin. He'd be home soon, full of apologies, they'd probably have sex and it would be another few weeks, maybe months, before he started bringing his *friends* back to the restaurant. With a wet finger she traced the elegant line of the tendril that bordered the wall beside the bath. She remembered when Joe had painted this part of the apartment. It was just after Betty had moved out. She could remember him bent over wearing just his undershorts, his skin taut across his back. She had licked his spine and bitten his earlobe. He had shrieked and turned around, his hard-on pressing against his shorts. She smiled at the memory. It hadn't been that long ago. They could be those people again, couldn't they?

III

It was thanks to Nor that Frankie found Donna. She had been the chalet girl for Teddy and Nor at Chamonix that winter, but the rest of the story was rather vague. Teddy and Nor often had new, usually attractive, younger people around them and Frankie had learned not to ask too many questions. Donna, with her long dark hair, trim waist and clipped English accent, never said that Nor had brought her to New York, but no other explanation was ever forthcoming either. Nor presented her plan to Frankie as if it had all been devised for her benefit.

'Just try her out.'

'She seems so young. She's just a girl. Literally a chalet *girl*. Is someone going to tell her that she can stop wearing ski pants now?'

'Trust me – you know I'm fussy, but she was cooking for eight of us and it was all delicious.'

Frankie knew this was a fight she was going to lose.

'She can have a trial shift. I'm not promising anything.'

'Frankie, you need someone. You work too much. Joe needs a wife, and if you're not playing the role . . .'

'What have you heard?' That sudden panic. A cold hand gripped her heart.

Nor just laughed loudly. 'Nothing! But it's better if you're by his side. This place can survive without you.'

It was an odd sort of disappointment, tinged with guilt, to discover that Pomme could indeed operate without Frankie at the helm. She might have still made extra amounts of certain sauces or fancy pastries that she felt were beyond Donna's talents, but Frankie had to admit that her new chef could not only cook but, perhaps even more importantly, was able to steer the kitchen calmly through the storm of a busy dinner service. Yes, Donna was disconcertingly young, but the rest of the staff, including the cheekiest of the waiters, quickly grew to respect and trust her. Frankie wondered if this was how Madame Barre had felt when the young Irish girl had first appeared in her kitchen.

Joe seemed delighted with Frankie's newfound availability. It was as if this had been his unspoken wish all along. For every party or event they went to, they would spend a night at home alone. It seemed that Nor had been right, Joe hadn't been chasing anything new. In a world where he was no longer driving people around for hours, and coming home exhausted, there was more room for his wife. With Donna covering three or four shifts a week, Frankie was happy to play her expanded role.

Once Frankie got past the way some of Joe's new circle dressed – she herself had never considered making clothes from vinyl – and the odd things they sometimes talked about – was a newly dug ditch near Seattle really a work of art? – she quickly discovered that it was all very ordinary. Yes, there was the wilder Warhol set with its drag queens and hustlers, but most of the artists Joe and Frankie mixed with were just straightforward couples. Frankie didn't recognise any of the names but she quickly learned how important Joe thought the artist was by the way he introduced them to Frankie.

'Donald Judd and Julie Finch'; 'Robert Smithson and Nancy Holt'; while others got a cursory 'Dan and Sonja' or 'Robert and Priscilla'. Being a part of this arty set was all far more pedestrian than Frankie had expected. The men stood around smoking while the women would produce big bowls of overcooked pasta or gritty salads.

She took a quiet pride in the way the men listened to Joe when he spoke, laughed at his jokes. She had worried that he might be out of his depth, or admitted into this new circle in a way that felt patronising, but no. It seemed as though his arrival on the scene had hardly caused a ripple. Some, like Robert Rauschenberg, had been a little sceptical about the work, worrying that it might have borrowed too closely from his own, but Leo Castelli reported that, once Rauschenberg saw the exhibition, he realised how little crossover there was. The important collectors weren't dropping anyone, they were simply adding Castelli's newest star to their collections. The appetite for new art seemed endless. Frankie was astonished at the sums of money being talked about, and the artists' homes she was being invited to might have been bohemian, but they were big and filled with nice things. Having always loved their little apartment, now she found that, when she opened its door after returning from one of their nights out, her heart sank.

'I love our apartment . . .' Frankie began as they walked home one night.

'I love you!' Joe grabbed her unsteadily. He was drunker than Frankie had realised.

'That's lovely, but it would be nice to have people over.'

'We have people over. Over and over. Wait a sec. Got to pee.'

He ducked into a small alley and turned his back to Frankie.

'We have Wendell, Betty and the kids, but we couldn't entertain. We couldn't have a party.'

'Party, party,' Joe echoed as he shook himself and did up his pants.

'Somewhere you could work, and we could live, and have people over.'

'Let's head to Pomme for a nightcap.'

'Really?'

'Just one,' he pleaded. She looked at her watch. There'd probably still be someone at the restaurant and she always liked to know how the night had gone.

'All right, just one.'

'Love you!'

The next morning, they were both hungover and slumped at the kitchen table. The coffee was black because there was no milk and neither of them could be bothered to head downstairs to the store.

'Did you mean what you said last night?' Joe asked.

Frankie immediately worried that she might have said something to offend someone. 'What? What did I say?'

'About here, about wanting to move.'

Frankie thought for a moment and looked around her.

'I suppose I did. I mean, I love it and it's you, so I'd understand if you didn't want to let it go, but more space – well, that would be good too.'

Frankie looked up at the ceiling that Joe had painted ten years earlier, standing on the kitchen table while Betty warned him of how angry the landlord would be. She loved living inside his paintings, surrounded by his imagination, but their lives felt too big for these small rooms now. They deserved more space.

Joe surprised her and said, 'Yeah, yeah, you're probably right. Let me ask around.'

Three weeks later, the subject of moving had hardly been mentioned again, till one day, mid-morning, just as Frankie was getting ready to head to work, Joe burst through the door.

'I thought you were at the studio.'

'I was.' He was smiling and out of breath. 'I've got something to show you. You got time?'

She glanced at her watch. 'How long do you need?'

'Twenty minutes, thirty tops.'

Frankie could sense his excitement.

'Sure, I can do that – let me grab my coat.'

She almost had to run to keep up with him as Joe strode along the street.

'OK, I need you to keep an open mind.'

'I promise. Where are we going?'

'Spring, between Broadway and Lafayette. It's just around the corner from the studio.'

'What is it?'

'It's – no, wait till you see it. An open mind, remember, that's all I ask.'

Frankie mimed locking her lips and throwing away the key.

A few minutes later they were standing on a cobbled stretch of Spring Street outside a tall cast-iron building with enormous filthy windows. Bits of garbage were being chased down the street by a cold easterly wind. On the ground floor of the building there was a forgotten-looking wholesale store that appeared to only sell hats and caps. Joe was looking up.

'This is it.'

Frankie looked at the five floors that appeared to be abandoned.

'This is what?'

Joe gave a laugh that sounded almost guilty. 'Come on.' He pushed open the large door to the side. It was metal and the black paint was peeling. Frankie followed him up the steep, rough wooden stairs. On the first landing they passed a door from behind which came the frantic rattle of industry.

'A sewing factory, I think.' Joe had to raise his voice to be heard. On the next floor he took out a bunch of keys and unlocked the rusty padlock that hung from the bolt on the large double doors. These ones had white paint peeling off them.

Inside was a vast open space. Huge floor-to-ceiling windows faced onto Spring Street, while at the back a row of smaller windows looked out at whatever industrial jumble lay beyond. The ceiling was high and some parts were covered in tin tiles, other areas had unpainted beams, and there was a small incongruous patch of Styrofoam tiles. The space was interrupted by a series of thin metal pillars. The insistent rattle of the factory downstairs could still be heard. Frankie took a few steps forward; she knew that Joe was waiting for her to speak, but she had no idea what she was meant to say. She heard Joe's footsteps behind her on the wooden floorboards.

'Well? You said you wanted more space.'

'You want us to live here?' Frankie hoped he couldn't tell from her question what a ridiculous idea she thought this was.

Frankie

'No. Well, not like this.' He strode forward. 'I thought we could put up a partition here for the bedroom' – he pointed in the vague direction of the brick wall on his left – 'and then there's plumbing back here' – he opened a small door Frankie hadn't noticed – 'and a toilet, so we can easily put in a bathroom and a kitchen along the back wall here.' He almost ran along the width of the room, tracing where worktops and a stove might go. 'So much room for me to work, and think of the parties we can have. People over all the time.' He was back at the front of the space with Frankie. He put his hands on her waist. 'What do you think? Do you love it?'

Frankie surveyed the room once more, trying and failing to imagine the various elements that Joe had conjured up.

'I mean, it might be wonderful, but it's so much work to put into a rental.' There was a slight shift in Joe's face. Not quite a twitch, more of a ripple.

'What is it? What have you done, Joe?'

He took his hands off her waist and squeezed his eyes shut.

'I bought it.'

'What?' She couldn't believe what she was hearing. 'You . . . without even mentioning . . . and why even ask me what I . . . when you . . . oh Joe, what have you done? How much was it?'

He hesitated. 'Fifteen thousand dollars.'

Her mouth hinged open and shut. 'Can we afford that?'

Joe laughed. 'Have you not been paying attention, Mrs Haffen? We have money now.'

She punched his arm.

'Had money. You've gone and spent it all on this big room in the middle of nowhere. Where will we get our groceries? How are we supposed to heat this place? We'll freeze to death.'

Joe forced a kiss on her lips as she squirmed.

'The factory downstairs has heat. Heat rises. And we're not

moving in right away. We'll get work done. Donald Judd and Julie live down the street; Dorothea Rockburne, you like her – well, she and her kid are over on Grand; Ivan has his new gallery around the corner. It's going to be great. An adventure. Trust me.'

Thus began the Spring Street years in what became known simply as the Haffens' loft. True to his word, Joe partitioned off a sleeping area and a bathroom with a shower. The walls were thin to the point of fragility and didn't go as high as the fourteen-foot ceilings, but they afforded some privacy. Open shelves lined the back wall, along which also stood a large gas stove. The living area was defined by a large, very old Persian rug. On it were piles of cushions and their one big purchase, a vast L-shaped leather sofa imported from Italy. The rest of the space was reserved for Joe's studio, with paint-scattered tarpaulins on the floor and various bits of canvas and wood leaning against the walls.

Once they moved in, they discovered that the Jewish-owned factory beneath them didn't operate on the weekends and, when it stopped, so too did their only source of heat. Joe found an old potbellied wood-burning stove and paid two construction workers he found on Houston a small fortune to carry it up the two flights of stairs into the loft. Frankie liked the way it looked, but the only way anyone was able to enjoy its heat was by sitting right next to it. In the winter, dinner guests would sit at the long trestle table, eating bowls of Frankie's beef bourguignon or her bouillabaisse, still wearing their coats and scarves. In the summer, all the windows had to be left open and everything became covered in a thick layer of city dust.

Despite the various indignities of living in their new home, Frankie had to admit that she enjoyed it. It was fun having what amounted to an open house. They served cheap wine in paper cups so in the morning, bleary from the night before, the only clean-up involved wandering around tossing debris into a large garbage sack. They still saw their married couple friends, but Frankie noticed the crowd getting younger. Some nights there was less conversation and more of a lecture from Joe on the purpose of art or the role of the artist in modern society. The art scene in New York was moving and changing at such speed that, after only three or four years, Joseph Haffen was already seen as an establishment figure.

Ivan Karp, who had worked at the Castelli, tried to poach Joe for his new downtown gallery, but Joe stayed loyal to Leo. Castelli promised that he too would open a space in SoHo, which he did, but he also started to bring certain important collectors to Spring Street for studio visits. Peter and Irene Ludwig looked like affluent tourists who had taken a wrong turn as they sprawled uncomfortably on the low leather couch, but they bought the art. Around this time Leo Castelli had tried to convince Joe to try some commissioned portraits – 'People ask all the time.' Joe had been adamant: 'I don't paint people. I paint to get away from people.' Leo hadn't forced the issue. 'Well, if you're sure?' 'I'm sure.' The subject was closed.

Joe's prices and popularity were both growing at an extra-ordinary rate. None of it made any sense to Frankie, but she knew better than to question Joe. It was her job to be *his lovely Irish wife*. '*You know she has a restaurant?*' '*The one with the Haffen interior? Yes, I know.*' Artists had begun to gift them small sketches and prints to thank them for their hospitality and, alongside that art, Joe was buying pieces from almost every opening they attended. Soon the walls were crowded with all sorts of artworks, of which Frankie could only identify a few. She knew the rows of scribbles were by Cy Twombly, Lee Bontecou had done the big plastic flower, the coloured stripes were Frank Stella and the neon tubes had been put there by Keith someone. She didn't like all of them, but she enjoyed the overall effect on the loft. It could never be described as cosy, but at least it now looked totally lived in.

Of course, sometimes it was difficult to still have a job and be the hostess of the frequent gatherings at Spring Street. It wasn't ideal trying to sleep behind a thin partition while a party was going on, but earplugs helped. One night she came home from work to find the loft in darkness. She wasn't sure if Joe had gone to bed or if the party had moved on, but there was a man she didn't know asleep on a pile of cushions and he was wearing her dress, the bronze one she had worn to Joe's first opening. She took great pride in not being angry. This was the new bohemian Mrs Haffen, she told herself. She just checked to see if the man had ripped the dress – he hadn't – before kicking off her shoes and going to bed.

There were breaks in the hedonism when Joe had to travel. He had shows in Canada, Germany and Sweden, along with some group shows around America and in Europe. When Joe wasn't in residence it was as if a closed sign had been hung on their loft. Frankie found herself perched on the long couch all alone. It appeared that *their* friends were in fact Joe's. She didn't mind. If she wanted to see people she could head down to the new Spring Street bar, where she always knew somebody, but mostly she chose to stay in. It was nice to get a full night's sleep and spend enough time alone, so that she looked forward to the next round of parties. Two, almost three years passed this way in what felt like the blink of an eye.

IV

Two things happened at the same time, but it seemed more like one. Donna, Nor's old chalet girl, disappeared from Pomme and Gretchen arrived in Spring Street.

Nor was uncharacteristically quiet when Frankie asked her if she knew that Donna was going back to England.

'Is she? To be honest I've hardly seen her since she went to work for you.' Similarly, Donna said nothing about Nor when she broke the news of her leaving, just that she was tired of feeling like an alien, and felt her life couldn't start properly till she was back where she belonged. Apparently that place was Winchester.

Gretchen was just a name at first. Frankie only slowly became aware of how often she was hearing it.

'Gretchen needs to see me today.' 'Gretchen thinks I should do it.' 'I'll hear from Gretchen later.' Joe pronounced her name with a sudden frequency, as if Frankie should know all about this Gretchen.

She didn't, but she made it her business to find out. Gretchen Schmidt was in her late twenties and from Switzerland. She had been a personal assistant to the Ludwigs but was now working for the Castelli Gallery – though, judging from the way Joe spoke about her, *he* seemed to be her full-time job.

One afternoon, Frankie walked into the loft and sniffed the air. 'What's that lovely smell?'

'Do you like it?' Joe asked enthusiastically.

'Yes, it's gorgeous.'

'Peach oil. Gretchen smeared it on the lightbulbs.'

Frankie was no longer quite so sure how much she liked it.

At the time it felt as though Pomme had reclaimed Frankie, while back at Spring Street Gretchen had been recast in her role. Gretchen was now the one gliding around the loft offering people more wine; she was the one leading everyone down the stairs off to see a band at Max's, or some happening at Club 57. Frankie might have been uneasy about this arrangement but then she met Gretchen. She was tall, an inch or two taller than Joe, which

Frankie knew would be off-putting for him, and, in addition to that, her thin body was angular and awkward in a way that Joe would never be attracted to. Frankie of course noticed the way Gretchen tried to flirt with him, how she played with her long dark hair or stroked her neck as she listened intently to Joe's every word, but that sort of behaviour didn't bother Frankie. She'd seen it hundreds of times before with the long-haired waifs who seemed to flock around every artist in New York City. Never once had she suspected Joe of reciprocating any of their desires. There might have been times in their relationship when she had felt insecure, but that was years ago. Jealousy wasn't something Joe had ever given Frankie cause to feel. He was hers and she was his. They laughed when they heard stories of friends having affairs or dabbling in the notion of 'free love' with lovers and partners all living together. None of it held any allure for Joe and Frankie. Every night, no matter where they had been, they ended up falling into bed together. It was where they belonged.

It wasn't as if Frankie did nothing to try to lessen the demands of the restaurant. She had placed ads, various chefs had been given trial shifts, but no one had worked. They were either too old-school and formal, unable to accept Frankie's slightly eccentric menu, or they lacked the authority to run the kitchen and keep everyone in check. It was only in retrospect that Frankie understood how lucky she had been with Donna. Being the head chef at Pomme was not for everyone. At first, Joe didn't seem to mind that his wife had vanished from their social whirl, and when he did eventually realise what was going on he had a very simple solution.

'Sell it.'

'Are you serious?'

'Sure. We don't need the money and . . . well, it's just a pain in the ass.'

Frankie couldn't believe that Joe was talking about Pomme like this.

'But it's mine. Madame Barre gave it to me, and I, we, we, the two of us, have made it into something really special.'

'It's making you miserable. Just dump it. I mean, I've put lots of work into it too and I don't care. You're chained to the place, so let yourself go.'

The way Joe was talking made her sad. It was as if he was just casually suggesting they put a beloved pet dog to sleep.

'And what would I do?'

'I don't know. Cook for our friends more.' There was something in his tone of voice that for a moment made her think of Alan back at Castlekeen and how dismissive he had been. Joe had never spoken to her like that, not until now.

'I can't, Joe. Even if you don't want it any more, Pomme is mine. It'll sort itself out. I'll find another Donna and things will calm down.' Despite her uneasiness she kissed him as if to seal the deal, even though he hadn't made it.

Looking back. Oh, she saw so many things when she looked back. Had not giving up the restaurant been her big mistake? Would things have been different if she had been around more? She doubted it.

When had Frankie become fully aware of the affair? Her first suspicions had been raised by the way Joe had started making love to her. It was still frequent, perhaps even more so than it had been of late, but something had subtly altered. It was as if the act had become more performative for Joe. Frankie felt as if her husband was trying to convince her that he still found her attractive. He made strange grunts, or he might whisper, 'Oh yeah, baby.' It was as though a third party was now watching and judging him. She wondered why he might be trying so hard to make her believe he was still passionate about her and, as she thought about it, a small doubt sparked into life.

One night when it had been unusually quiet at Pomme, she had come home to find the loft in full swing. Joe had rushed up to her when she appeared in the doorway and made a great show of kissing her. At the time Frankie put it down to drunkenness. Later, when she came out of the bathroom, she found a young girl she hadn't seen before waiting to go in. She was swaying slightly but seemed to study Frankie in a disconcerting way.

'Are you Gretchen?'

It bothered Frankie how much this question unnerved her. Why would this random girl think she was Gretchen?

'No, I'm Frankie. What's your name?'

The young woman took a great gulp of air.

'Oh, you're the wife.' And without waiting for any response, she pushed past Frankie into the bathroom.

The wife? Why would someone refer to her in that way? The sparks of doubt began to burn brighter.

The truth was that Frankie had probably known all along, but hadn't wanted to know. Those occasional drunken mutterings of Nor's; looks exchanged at gatherings that now seemed more significant. If she didn't acknowledge that something was going on, then she didn't have to have a messy confrontation or decide on a course of action. Pretending that everything was fine was so very close to things actually being fine that it was hard to tell the difference. Months drifted by.

In the end, it wasn't Frankie who said something, it was Joe. One Sunday morning Frankie was curled in her robe on one end of the couch. Her cup of fresh coffee smelled strong and a blanket of sunshine from the wide windows fell across her lap. Lazy pigeons lined the windowsills, waiting for something to rouse them. Joe had gone out to get the Sunday papers, but she knew that he'd be back soon. They'd been invited for lunch with Donald and Julie down the street, and that night the philanthropist Barbara Tober was holding a dinner for a Colombian textile artist.

She heard voices on the stairs: Joe and a woman. She could tell they were trying to whisper but the echo in the stairwell made that impossible. She couldn't make out the words but was fairly certain the female's voice had an accent. Why would Gretchen be here? Without deciding to, Frankie stood, braced for what was about to enter.

The whispering continued for a few more minutes and then Joe's footsteps, unaccompanied, approached the door. Gretchen must be waiting in the stairwell. Waiting for what?

Joe looked flustered when he found Frankie already standing, her eyes immediately on him.

'No paper?' she asked. She was surprised by how calm she felt.

'What?' He didn't understand the question.

'You went out for the paper.'

'No. No, I didn't get the paper. Look, do you want to sit down? We need to talk.'

'No thanks. I'll stand. I've a feeling that *we* aren't going to talk. My guess is that you're just going to tell me something.'

He ran a hand through his hair. 'Please, Frankie. Please just sit.'

'Oh, I'm sorry. Should I be making this easier for you?' There was a steeliness to her tone now, her anger sharpening every word.

Joe bowed his head and took a few breaths. When he looked up, he met Frankie's eyes.

'No, I don't want you to make this easier, but it is fucking hard. Really hard.'

Frankie almost felt sorry for him. Almost. She chose to stay silent. Let him talk.

'OK, fuck it. I can't sugar-coat this so I'm just going to say it.'

Yet he continued to just stare at Frankie. Was he hoping she might read his mind, say it for him? Eventually he gave a furtive glance towards the windows and then back to Frankie.

'Gretchen,' his voice was quiet, as if the volume might make his news easier to accept, 'well, she's pregnant, so I'm going to, we're going to be together.' His shoulders slumped as if he had dropped a heavy weight.

Frankie could feel her body reacting even before her brain had time to process what she was hearing. Her limbs were quivering and her mouth was dry.

'Anything else?' she asked.

'I don't . . . what do you mean?' His body edged slightly towards the door, as if he couldn't wait to make his getaway now that his news was out.

'Don't you think you have something else to tell me?'

Joe threw his hands up. 'Jesus, Frankie, this isn't the time to play games. What do you want me to say?'

'I just wondered if you were ever going to tell me that you've been fucking Gretchen, fucking her for how long? A month? Six months? Or did you just think your baby news would do all that for you?' Despite her best efforts, she felt the tears fill her eyes and cascade down her face. She hated how pitiful she must look in this apartment where there was nowhere to hide. She pulled her cotton robe around herself and strode back towards the kitchen. 'Just get out,' she shouted as she walked away. No footsteps, no door slam, she knew he hadn't left, so she turned back to him. 'What?'

'The loft. You stay here. We're going to live uptown. Gretchen has a place near the gallery.'

Frankie froze, clueless as to how she was supposed to respond to this additional piece of news. Did Joe expect her to be grateful, touched by his kindness? She slumped into a chair at the long table, where she had fed so many of his friends.

'Just go.'

The door gave a mournful creak, then two sets of footsteps rapidly descended the stairs.

V

'Do you like living here?' Nor did little to disguise what she thought the correct answer to that question should be. She was sitting on the edge of the couch with her knees almost touching her chin. She hadn't taken off her dark fur coat and she was still wearing her sunglasses to protect her eyes from the sunlight streaming in from Spring Street.

'I'm not going to stay here, if that's what you mean.' Frankie was putting another garbage bag of Joe's clothes by the door. It had been a week since he had walked through it for the last time.

'I don't blame you. Rooms give your life a sense of purpose. I mean, I spend most of my time walking from one room into another, and I honestly feel as if I'm doing something. Here,' she looked around, 'I don't know, I'd just feel as if I were waiting for something to happen.'

Frankie sat beside her friend. 'Well, it did.' She gave a long sigh.

Nor embraced her. 'Oh darling, I'm so sorry.'

'I just keep thinking back to you talking about a baby. Is that really what went on here? He left me for a baby?'

Nor took off her sunglasses. 'He left you for a Swiss bitch, who, just like the cheese, has very attractive holes.' She gave a small pout, pleased with her joke. Frankie was surprised to find herself laughing.

'I mean, I do hate her, but I don't want to be one of those women who blames the mistress. I hate Joe more. He did this to me, not Gretchen.'

'Agreed. Absolutely. And . . . I'm only asking . . . do you think, is it possible he might come back?'

A look of mild horror came over Frankie's face. 'That hadn't even crossed my mind.' She thought for a moment. 'No. He's never coming back and, even if he did, I could never . . .' She shook her head, repulsed at the very idea.

'So,' Nor announced brightly. She was changing the subject. 'If you're not staying here, where will you go?'

Frankie shrugged. 'Back over to 8th Street? We never gave up the apartment. Leo had some idea of turning it into an installation, but the building wasn't keen. I thought Joe might go there but I can see why Gretchen wouldn't be so keen. Don't get me wrong, I won't want to live with all those memories forever, but it's closer to work and feels more like home than this place ever did.'

'Well, if you need help with the move or anything, just let me know. We leave for London on Wednesday but Teddy can organise people.'

'Thanks, but I've only a few bits and pieces I want to bring and some of the boys from the restaurant can always lend a hand.'

The two women sat in silence for a moment or two before Nor hauled herself up from the sofa.

'Let me take you out to lunch.'

'I can't. The clothes.' She indicated the garbage bags.

'Just leave them out on the landing. You don't want to see him.'

Frankie buried her head in her hands.

'I never thought of myself as childless.'

Nor sat down again.

'Sorry darling, what was that?'

Frankie looked up, her face now tear-stained.

'That time we spoke about Joe being a father. I never thought of myself as a childless woman, never considered myself *barren*.'

Nor stroked her arm. 'Of course not, darling.'

'To be honest, I always thought that it was Joe who couldn't have children. That was why he was so careless about protection. I thought he knew something about himself, but that wasn't it at all.' She wiped away tears. 'Since he left with his pregnant Gretchen, I've just sat here feeling like a shrivelled grape.'

'Stop it, Frankie. You're being ridiculous.'

'No. No I'm not, and everyone is going to be so understanding to Joe. Of course he left that husk of a woman who couldn't give him what he wanted. She just worked all the time, and who can blame him for wanting something more, something fertile . . .' She buried her head in Nor's shoulder before immediately pulling away. 'Your fur coat! I'll ruin it.'

Nor smiled and kissed her friend on the forehead. 'An awful thing has happened. Be sad. Cry. But do not let this make you feel like a failure, not for a second. Look at the life you've built. Little Frances Howe who was afraid of the whole world, I am so, so proud of you, and if Joe Haffen is too stupid to realise what he's walking away from, then so be it.' She wrapped her arms around Frankie and held her tight before putting her sunglasses back on. 'Would it be very insensitive of me to point out a certain irony in the fact that abortion is finally legal in this country, and yet you still find yourself with a baby you can't get rid of?'

'Nor!'

And the two women fell into each other's arms, their laughter echoing through the loft.

Wapping, 2024

Frankie was in the bathroom, while Nor and Damian sat together at the small kitchen table, the several coffee cups in front of them bearing witness to how long they had been there.

'She's going to miss you.'

'And I'm going to miss her. Mind, I wasn't sure I'd be saying that when I started.'

'And I was confident she was going to send you packing. The fuss when I suggested a carer, I can't tell you.'

The sound of flushing and the bathroom door opening ended their conversation. Frankie appeared in the doorway.

'Don't even pretend. I know you've been talking about me.'

Nor and Damian laughed. 'Only lovely things.'

'I was saying that you're going to miss having Damian.'

'Well, now, let's not get carried away. It's been nice having company, I grant you, but I won't miss the fussing. Did he tell you I did the stairs first thing this morning?'

'No, he didn't. How was it?' Nor asked Frankie but she in turn looked to Damian.

'Good like. A wobble or two but after another two or three days, I'd say you'll be back to full speed.'

Nor stood. 'Shouldn't you be off? Your shift ended ages ago.'

'Ah, I'm in no rush, and I've only got two more nights and then I'll be gone.' Damian didn't intend for this to sound as dramatic as it did. 'I mean, I'll pop back, have a cup of tea the odd time, if you'll have me?'

'Frankie would love that, I'm sure,' Nor declared and picked up her coat from the back of her chair. 'Well, I must away. I have to hand out cheques – RADA are having the Theodore Forrester awards this afternoon. Thank God I've had all this coffee to keep me awake.' She kissed Frankie's cheek. 'Don't keep this young man chatting for too long, and for God's sake try not to depress him too much.'

'Nor, how dare you? Enjoy giving away money.'

'You know I will.' And then she was gone.

Frankie sat at the table and Damian began to stack the various coffee cups in the sink.

'Have you ever had your heart broken?' Frankie asked. This had become the sort of question they asked each other now. Damian thought about it. A couple of faces drifted through his mind, but he quickly dismissed them. He pictured his mother. She had broken his heart when she chose his father over him, but he supposed Frankie was referring to the way her heart had been broken by Joe.

'No, not really. There was a boy in school all right, and I'd cry myself to sleep over him, but sure he didn't know I existed. I was just breaking my own heart, really. What do you call that? It has a name – loving someone who doesn't love you back.'

'Unrequited love?'

'That's it. Yeah, that. I've never had a Joe in my life.'

'Not yet – and maybe a Joe isn't exactly what you're after.' Frankie chuckled.

'What was it like? I mean, after Joe. Did you go on dates and stuff?'

'Dates? No, no I didn't. I mean, I say that as if I decided not to, but the truth is no one ever asked. I just gave myself to Pomme completely, I didn't even try to find a way out.' Frankie became still, remembering how difficult that time of her life had been.

'And what about Joe, did he keep in touch at all?'

Frankie let out one of her rare honks of laughter.

'He didn't need to. If someone leaves you, you always think that the worst thing will be never seeing them again. Well, let me tell you, there is something even worse and that's your ex being everywhere. Like, everywhere. You've no idea what it was like. Gretchen wasn't just good at getting herself pregnant – a boy by the way, Luca, very sweet, they never had another – she was a demon in the art world, too.'

'Like how?' Damian was leaning against the sink, drying the cups slowly, one by one.

'Luca was hardly born when she took Joe away from the Castelli; she became his manager, assistant, everything, and he blew up. I thought that he was successful already, but it was nothing compared with what Gretchen managed. She did all the things you'd expect – you know, the Guggenheim, a solo show at MoMA, one of the youngest artists ever I think, at the time, exhibitions all over the world – but then she came up with all these other things no one had really done before, not a serious artist anyway. He designed fabrics for a Kenzo collection, he had a range of crockery exclusive to Neiman Marcus, wallpaper, an album cover for Earth, Wind & Fire, you name it – and this was years before Keith Haring. Prints, they were different, prints had been big business for a while – they didn't call it the Factory for nothing – but this was insane. He was, what's the word? Omnipresent! I wasn't living in his shadow, I was living in his world. I can't believe you don't know his work. I still see it all over the place.'

Damian pulled a face. 'Oh, I forgot to tell you. I googled him. I did kind of recognise his stuff. A guy I knew had a shower curtain and I'm pretty sure it was Joe Haffen, or at least a knock-off.'

Frankie raised an eyebrow in disdain.

'Oh, there'll be no knock-offs on Gretchen's watch. She's notorious.'

'And were you still in the flat, the one with all his paintings?'

'God help me, I was.' The memory made her smile. 'I thought about painting over it all, but I was afraid they'd arrest me for vandalism or something. And the restaurant, you can't imagine what that was like. We had to bring in a minimum spend just to weed out all the tourists coming in for a glass of water or one tea, just to see the Joseph Haffen interiors.'

'Were you not tempted to sell then, start something new?'

'Isn't it mad, but no. I've often thought about it since. Why didn't I? But the truth is, it never crossed my mind at the time. I think it would have felt like throwing in the towel, letting Joe and Gretchen win, or something like that. I don't know. And besides, it was mine. That place was my home – my everything, really, after Joe left.'

Damian folded the tea towel he'd been using and hung it on the handle of the oven door.

'And were you not lonely like?'

'Not really, no. Pomme was like my family; we were all so close, bound together by the place until . . .' She looked at Damian. 'You said you googled Joe?'

'Yes,' he said sheepishly.

'So you know what happened?'

Damian hadn't wanted to say anything. Frankie enjoyed telling her story so much and he loved listening to her. 'I mean, sort of. But I just know the facts.'

'The facts,' Frankie repeated. 'I wonder if you do.'

New York, 1981

I

'What do you say?'

'Thank you,' the little boy said before hastily filling his mouth with the piece of caramel Frankie had handed him. She smiled at his greediness. She had grown used to the sight of Joe and his son Luca. It no longer made her feel like someone who had been banished from a kingdom of plenty. Joe brought Luca to the restaurant more often than Frankie felt was strictly necessary. It seemed that Joe was determined to remind Frankie of why he had left her as often as possible. Every time someone was writing an article about Joe, or a film crew from somewhere in the world was making another documentary about the New York art scene, Joe would have his replica by his side. Luca was six now, dark like Joe, and quietly confident without being overly precocious. He seemed reserved around Frankie, as if something in his growing brain sensed the history between his daddy and the lady who made sweet things. Joe's idea of getting him to refer to Frankie as his aunty had quickly been nipped in the bud. Frankie had asked him to stop, but she suspected that Gretchen had not been a fan of the notion either.

Joe looked older. Frankie liked to think it was being with Gretchen that had made him so drawn and tired-looking, but she accepted that it was probably just the toll of being a global art star. If she was being completely honest, Frankie had to admit a certain respect for Gretchen. Frankie had always believed in Joe's talent and supported him in pursuing his dream, but what Gretchen had done for him was unimaginable. Had it made Joe happy? Frankie thought it probably had. True, she had read sniping articles about him, the younger artists that were beginning to colonise the East Village dismissed him as an illustrator, not a *true* artist, but she knew how much money had always meant to Joe. Being rich suited him, and she imagined it provided a pleasant buffer between him and any of the barbs from people who were clearly just jealous of his success.

Being rich also meant he was free to indulge his guilt over how things had ended with Frankie. She had never asked him for anything but still Joe found generous ways to show her how sorry he was. Wendell called it 'the price of being a shit'. Joe gave her the Spring Street loft, which she didn't want – but then, she assumed, nor did Gretchen. After she sold it, he refused to take even half of the money. His studio had been moved to a new one in the Bowery, the Italian sofa had been given to the artist Joan Jonas, and most of the art was stored in what was still called Betty's bedroom in the 8th Street apartment.

Frankie had never brought up the subject of divorce, in part because she had no desire to make things easier for him. She wanted to force Joe to be the one who raised the subject, the one to squirm. Much to her surprise, as months and then years went by, he never did. Wendell and Nor both thought it must be something to do with Gretchen. A divorce settlement might cost the newer couple an eye-watering sum, given how well Joe was doing. Maybe Gretchen felt that being the mother of his child gave her all the security she needed. Whatever the reason, Frankie remained Mrs Haffen.

At the restaurant, Frankie found that she had slowly become more involved with the staff. She had always chatted with the married women in the kitchen who worked long, hard hours to help their families – Carla who had a sick son, Peggy who was about to become a grandmother, Anna whose husband had fallen from scaffolding – but now she found herself spending more time with the youngsters who worked front of house. Of course, Wendell had long been her rock. No matter what was going on in her life he had been there, calm and steady, offering her words of wisdom, and often a stiff drink. She wondered if she would have been able to keep going in those weeks after Joe left if it hadn't been for Wendell. He had made a point of picking her up from home so that she had no excuse not to show up for her shifts, and he stayed late, waving the others off, to sit and listen to her rant and cry about *that bastard Joe*.

After fourteen years of being with one person, it was clear Frankie was going to need a new social circle, and it was only natural that she turned to the fun young crowd that Wendell had assembled to wait tables. The only original member of the team, Wendell was now in his early forties and had accepted that working in a restaurant was what he did. He was no longer an aspiring actor, dancer or singer. In his heart he had never really decided which, or indeed really tried to succeed. Wendell appreciated all the responsibility that Frankie had given him, along with a significant pay-rise. They both knew how much she needed him. The rest of the team were all much younger and all still held on to their ragtag collection of dreams. Brady was in his early twenties and had come from Gary, Indiana, to study acting at NYU. Jeffrey wanted to be an actor too, or so he said, but with his punky haircut and earrings he seemed more interested in clubbing. His family in New Jersey were not fans of his new look, so he had felt his only option was to find his tribe in Manhattan. Frankie had questioned Wendell's decision when he hired him.

'Won't he scare off the customers?'

Wendell had laughed. 'Look around you. If they want to eat in here, Jeffrey isn't going to bother anyone.'

Patty was the only girl who worked in the dining room. When Frankie had seen her severe, scraped-back hair and learned that she was studying biological illustration, she wondered how well she would fit in, but it seemed she was able to let her hair down, because most nights at the end of her shift she emerged from the bathroom in eye-catching outfits, clearly destined for a dancefloor. Omar was the beauty of the group. His family were recent Persian émigrés who had settled in San Francisco. His perfect English coupled with his jawline and dark eyes gave him the air of someone who should not be in a position of servitude. Waiting tables seemed wrong for him. His stated plan was that he would become a photographer, but everyone at Pomme assumed he'd become a model first.

Frankie referred to them as 'the kids', and night after night they developed a social routine with her. She would happily sit and drink with them after work, but then she would wave them off to whichever bar or discotheque they were headed for and the next day she listened eagerly to all their stories. Each of them had their own specific roles to play. Obviously, Omar was the heart-breaker, with young men calling the restaurant and Wendell taking messages. Some would wait outside for him to finish his shift, while others would book tables in the restaurant just to spend more time with him. Omar seemed utterly unfazed by his effect on them, never cruel but also never willing to accept someone whom he felt was not worthy. Frankie sometimes wondered, as she watched Omar wave yet another man off in a cab, if he would ever meet someone he felt deserved his love. Young Brady couldn't have been more different. He was the romantic. Everyone he met was *the one* until they met someone else, or just stopped showing up for their dates. Happily, his heartbreaks seemed to mend almost instantly, and he would reapply his hair gel ready to head off to the bars to find the next *one*. Punky Jeffrey had no interest in finding a boyfriend. He was a young man who had just been let off his tight New Jersey Catholic leash, and the only thing he wanted was to have fun, all the fun. Frankie worried about him, but then consoled herself with the thought that if somebody was going to do drugs and have lots of sex, then better to do it when they were young. Besides, no matter how spaced out he might have been from the night before, when he showed up at the restaurant, it had never affected his actual work. Despite the blue streaks and gelled spikes on his head, he became a sweet, helpful boy the moment he approached a table. Patty, the studious one, seemed solely interested in music. Her cool demeanour only ever cracked when she was describing some group she had seen the night before, with names like Suicide, The Dictators, or Dead Boys. None of it sounded very appealing to Frankie, but Patty truly believed that, every night in sweaty basements, she was seeing the future of music.

In a strange way it was Wendell that Frankie knew the least about. When he was listening to her and giving advice, he would often use a phrase like 'I was dating this guy once and he . . .' but they never had names and no one seemed to be a current boyfriend. Frankie was certain he did very well on the dating scene. Tall and slim, a few years earlier he had decided to do away with his receding grey hair and now sported a bald head with a luxurious sheen. When the others urged him to come along to some special night at Danceteria or Flamingo, he would just laugh and say, 'No thanks – Daddy wants somewhere to sit and a barman who can hear me. Have fun, kids.'

Frankie heard the names of the various bars often enough to know most of them – Uncle Charlie's, Ty's, Ninth Circle, Mineshaft – but she'd never been to any of them. She imagined that a middle-aged woman who smelled like garlic and chicken would not be very welcome. Besides, she wouldn't have wanted to inhibit any of her waiters out trying to have a good time, especially Wendell.

One night at the end of the shift, after Patty and Jeffrey had run shrieking out the door trying to catch a cab they'd seen passing with its light on, Frankie and Wendell sat quietly. She imagined it was how parents must feel when their children have left home. The place was so quiet she could hear each sip of wine that Wendell took.

'You heading out tonight?' she asked.

'Not tonight. I can't keep up. This will do me.' He held up his glass.

'Do you . . .' Frankie began. 'No, of course you don't, you go out all the time, but I sometimes wonder if I missed out. I was never those kids out on the town.'

'Those kids? Our kids?'

'Yes.'

'Oh, we were never those kids. The world was so different back then. They don't know they're born. A little Irish girl wasn't running around the Village by herself back then. And me?' Wendell leaned back in his chair. 'I don't feel old but when I see Omar and Brady and all the bars they have to choose from, the clubs, the magazines, it makes me feel like I was born in the last century.'

'Really? I seem to remember you were always heading off somewhere.'

He laughed. 'I'll give you that, but, like, when you met me, did you know I was gay?'

Frankie tried to recall. 'I don't think so, but then I didn't know anything back then.'

Wendell leaned across the table. 'You didn't know, and I know that for a fact because no one knew. I wasn't going round telling people that I was a fruit or a pansy or whatever. My family still don't know. It's so easy for little Jeffrey and Brady and the rest of them.' He seemed irritated.

'But isn't that a good thing?' Frankie asked hesitantly. She didn't want to say the wrong thing.

'Yes, yes of course it is. I'm so glad. I just . . . I don't know, sometimes I wish the kids were more grateful. They just take it all for granted and . . .' He sat up in his chair. 'I remember the first bar I ever went to. I'd just arrived in New York. My momma only let me come because she was friendly with an aunt of Charlie Wise.' He pointed to where the jazz albums had hung behind the bar. 'I was staying with him and Madame Barre.'

'I know. I remember.'

'Of course you do, sorry. Well, I knew there was a bar, it was right over there past you on Eighth, opposite the Bon Soir – it was called Mary's, for Christ's sake.' He rolled his eyes and grinned. 'I was too scared to go in – didn't know what I would find, if I'd be welcome, if the police would raid the place and my momma would find out about me – but oh, I still really wanted to see what was in there. So, I figured if I went to the San Remo Café often enough, you know artist types went there, well, maybe one of them would take me to Mary's.'

'Did it work?'

'Well, I met someone and he took me somewhere but it wasn't Mary's!' Wendell slapped the table and laughed. 'And it was fun and dangerous and exciting and I don't know why I'm in this mood. But these days, all the go-go boys with their asses hanging out, the bathhouses, it's too much, or too easy or something. I don't know.' He drained his drink. 'I should get home to my knitting.'

'You sure? I can sit for a while yet.' Frankie wasn't used to seeing her friend like this.

'Yeah. I should sleep.'

'If you're sure. I guess I should go too. I'm working another double tomorrow.'

Wendell kissed her on the cheek. 'Good night, darling.'

'Be safe!' Frankie called as he walked out the door.

It was something Frankie often said to 'the kids' as they headed out into the night. She wasn't quite sure where it had come from. Had Betty said it to Joe when he was heading out to drive? Maybe. But what struck Frankie about the words that night was how she meant them, but at the same time had never really worried about Wendell and the others. She wondered why. All she heard in this city were horror stories. There had been that big fire in a bathhouse a few years earlier; Wendell had known someone who died. She remembered everyone talking about the murders in the Anvil, and then just last year there had been the shooting outside the Ramrod. And that was on top of all the stories of muggings and break-ins and rapes that were just a part of living in New York. Despite all of it, Frankie never seriously considered that anything bad would happen to the people she knew. When had she become this person?

She was thinking all of this as she made her way around the restaurant, turning off lights, returning stray glasses to the bar. At the door she looked back at the dining room, now bathed in shadows from the streetlight that fell through the windows. The strange fronds and tendrils of Joe's murals could have looked menacing, but they didn't. The dark curves seemed inviting, like the fold of a blanket thrown back, or a lover's arm waiting to embrace you.

II

Afterwards, people only remembered the deluge. When had they felt the first few drops of rain that gave no real hint of the storm that was on its way?

Frankie could remember: it had been a joke. Early summer of '82. Brady and Jeffrey laughing. A gravy stain on a white work shirt.

'You've got the gay cancer!'

Shrieks of laughter, Wendell telling them to be quiet, Frankie rolling her eyes. She had heard the words but at that time didn't know that it was anything more than a dark joke. She didn't understand that there really was a cancer.

Omar was the first person who knew somebody who died. An older man who had taken him to stay in his house on Fire Island. It unsettled everyone to see Omar crying. So young and beautiful, sadness had no business bothering him. It was unnatural. He'd come by the restaurant before the funeral and Wendell had laughed: 'Oh my God, going to a funeral and you still look hot!' Omar's face broke wide open with a huge grin. For a moment he was returned to normality and things didn't seem so bad.

Then a friend of Wendell's died, then another. One day he pulled Frankie to one side.

'I just heard that Sidney passed.'

It took Frankie a moment. 'Sidney? Went to Canada, that Sidney?'

Wendell just nodded, his eyes brimming with tears. Frankie, too, welled up. Lovely Sidney. She could see him behind the bar, the light reflected in his glasses. He had escaped Vietnam, but he hadn't survived this, whatever this was. She sent a sympathy card to the last address she had for him, but it was returned.

Frankie became Wendell's funeral date. He couldn't bear to go alone and, besides, she wouldn't have let him. She became used to sitting in Redden's Funeral Home on 14th Street, or at the back of the church on 16th, with Wendell and the other New York friends of the deceased, while family members sat at the front. Sometimes the two groups mixed, a mother might introduce herself to her dead son's friends, but that was rare. Usually, the family just looked back at the other mourners with, at best, blinking incomprehension or, at worst, open hostility. Who had their son been? Why was this random assortment of people, who weren't even dressed properly, at his funeral? These must be the ones responsible for the death of their baby. It broke Frankie's heart. All these people brought together in loss and love, unable to share their grief. At some memorials there were no family members at all. That was worse.

It all brought back memories of the funerals Frankie had been forced to attend years before in Ballytoor and Castlekeen. She had hated them at the time, all the hand-shaking and 'sorry for your loss' repeated like a spell, but now she understood the ways in which those services had given the mourners everything they needed. Of course, Frankie thought, the difference back then was that those deaths had made some sort of sense. These awkward New York affairs were attended by people who should never have met, mourning someone who shouldn't have died. No wonder they were awful.

One night, in the fall of '84, Frankie came out of the kitchen ready to phone in her orders. Patty was polishing glasses at the bar, while Brady put the chairs up on the tables. Wendell was hunched over the reservations book. Frankie assumed he was doing a table plan for the next day. It was only when she reached him that she saw he was weeping. Heavy tears were splashing down on the pages of the book, making the ink run.

'What is it?' Frankie asked, even though she knew it would be the death of yet another of his friends.

Wendell wiped his face and looked at her. He opened his mouth but then began to really sob, his shoulders almost in spasm. Frankie hugged him and kissed the top of his head.

'I'm so sorry.' She repeated this phrase a few more times, until Wendell seemed more in control.

'I just can't,' he said. 'I'm sorry, I—' but then his words were swept away by more sobs. He grabbed his jacket from the coat rack and almost ran out of the door before Frankie even had a chance to call after him.

When she got back to her apartment, she thought about trying to phone Wendell, but decided against it. She'd be able to talk to him the next day after he'd had a chance to compose himself. As she got ready for bed, she wondered who could have upset him quite so much. Was it a boyfriend or lover that he had never mentioned? Surely not.

The next day she got to the restaurant early and was busy in the kitchen. She could hear activity in the dining room and assumed that everything was as it should be. It was only shortly before opening when Brady appeared at the door to ask if she'd heard from Wendell that she realised something was amiss.

'He's not here?'

'No.' Brady sounded nervous.

'Have you tried calling?'

'No. I wanted to ask you first.'

Frankie wiped her hands on a dishcloth and walked out into the dining room. She had just picked up the receiver when Omar walked through the door. Frankie knew he wasn't on the rota, and there was something about his expression that made her hang up without dialling.

'What? What is it, Omar?'

He took a deep breath and then said, 'I need to talk to you, Frankie.'

Omar led her to a table in the corner and they sat. Frankie was aware that her heart was beating faster. 'Is it Wendell? What's happened?'

Omar looked almost relieved that Frankie had guessed the reason for his visit.

'Yes. He called me. I don't know why me. He said how sorry he was, but he couldn't talk to you.'

'What?' Frankie was dismayed.

'He said he tried to talk to you last night. He wanted to but he said he couldn't get through it.'

'Oh Christ. What is it?'

Omar paused for a moment before saying, 'He's gone home. Back to Augusta, I think he said.'

'Yes, that's where he's from. But why? Why has he gone?'

Omar's chin began to tremble.

'Oh Frankie, it's not good. He found a spot on his foot. He showed me. I told him to get it checked.' He exhaled, clearly not wanting to cry. 'It's KS.'

Frankie's hand flew to her mouth. 'No. But he should be getting treatment. Something. Not going home.'

'That's why he's there. His mother has insurance, he doesn't. She said she'd let him use hers but only if he came home . . .' Omar's voice cracked and he bowed his head. In Frankie's mind, the sentence carried on '. . . came home to die.'

A postcard arrived, an aerial view of Augusta at sunset. On the back all it said was, 'I'm alive! Feeling strong. Hope to see you soon. Love you and miss you. W x'. Frankie turned it over as if she expected to find more words. That was it? Of course she was happy to hear from him, but this was almost insulting. Did she mean so little to him that all she deserved was a scrawled postcard? Didn't he realise that she had been out of her mind with worry? Wendell hadn't left any way to contact him, so she had tried every number Information had for a Mrs Peters in Martinez, Augusta, but without success. Frankie suspected Wendell's mother must have gone back to her maiden name after her divorce, but she had no idea what that might be. Now, with this postcard in her hand, it felt like Wendell was teasing her. Unless it was true. Was it possible that he would be back soon?

A couple of months passed. Omar was promoted to take Wendell's place and a young music student named Vincent was hired to wait tables. Frankie knew it was irrational, but somehow she couldn't warm to him. How could he be a part of Pomme when he had never known Wendell, never even met him? She constantly found fault with Vincent's work and hated herself for it. She knew the others had noticed it, but she couldn't stop herself.

'What's the abbreviation for the chicken?' She was almost shouting.

'C, h , k,' Vincent replied, flustered to be questioned yet again.

'So, what's this?' She brandished the order that the waiter had just handed in.

'C, h, k?' he offered, knowing that it must be the wrong answer.

'Then why does it say C, i, k? How many times? You must write your orders clearly. Clearly!'

'Yes, chef,' he muttered as he walked back to the dining room. Omar passed him in the doorway.

'Frankie, come quick. It's Wendell. Wendell's on the phone.'

'Oh my God!' she exclaimed, following Omar back into the dining room.

'I think he's calling from a hospital,' he said, handing Frankie the receiver.

'Wendell? Is that you?'

'Frankie. Frankie, it's me. It's Wendell.' He sounded very far away, and his voice was slurred. Was he drunk? Maybe it was something to do with his medication?

'Where are you, Wendell? How are you?' Frankie had her hand pressed against her other ear, trying to block out the noise of the busy dining room.

'I love you, Frankie. I love you.'

She could tell that he was crying. 'I know you do, I know you do. I love you too. How are you doing?'

'I love you. I've got to go. It's a payphone and I don't—' The line went dead.

'Wendell? Wendell!' Frankie called into the phone, but she knew that it was too late. She put the receiver down without hanging up and wept. Sobs seemed to come from deep in her belly, and she howled, while a silenced room of diners looked on.

Christmas came and went. Frankie was happy to be busy. It gave her less time to worry, less time to dwell on the news she didn't want to hear.

The letter arrived at the restaurant on the first Friday in January. Frankie sat in the empty dining room and ripped it open. The writing paper was heavy and light blue, the handwriting neat. It was from Wendell's mother.

Dear Mrs Haffen,
I felt I should write to you as Wendell always spoke of you most highly.

I'm very sorry to tell you that my son Wendell passed away on the 18th of December. In the end it was peaceful, and I was with him, along with his sister Rochelle. It was the hardest Christmas of my life, but I suppose they will all be hard from now on.

I don't pretend to understand my son's life, but I do know that he did not deserve this end. Some people can be very cruel. This is not New York City and everyone is very frightened. We were not able to have a proper funeral for my son, but he has all my prayers.

I know many families are going through what we have. This disease is an awful thing, but in the end it was what brought my baby back to me, and for that I must be grateful.

Thank you for all the kindness you showed Wendell. You sound like a wonderful lady.

With kindest regards,
Bernice Lowell

The letter trembled in Frankie's hand. It wasn't a shock; it was what she had been expecting. In her mind's eye she could see herself: the woman with a bandana in her hair, sitting in the window of Pomme with tears streaming down her face. She thought of all the tears she had yet to weep. Where was this going to end? Would it take everyone? Bernice Lowell was grateful that it had brought her baby home. Frankie was just grateful that she would never have to be as strong as Wendell's mother. It horrified her when she thought about what that woman must have had to endure, was enduring. Not just the loss of her son, but the whispering neighbours, the casual cruelty of officials. She wiped her eyes. She had a restaurant to open.

III

'Teddy is completely terrified.' Nor took a long drag of her cigarette. 'I mean, I don't really know how frightened he should be. We don't discuss such things but I'm practically certain his sex life is . . . well, let's call it sparse.'

'Who can tell?' Frankie said with a sad shake of her head. 'I hear all sorts of stories. The guy who sleeps with everyone who hasn't got it. The kid who got to the city yesterday and is dying already. Nobody knows.'

They sat in the revolving bar of the newly opened Marriott high above Times Square. Nor looked around to see if she could catch the eye of a waiter. 'I thought this might be fun. Sorry. I'm going to squeeze in another if I manage to order. You?'

'Why not?' It was a phrase Frankie found herself saying more and more these days. Nor was off to see Andrew Lloyd Webber's new show and had suggested that her friend meet her for a cocktail beforehand. Frankie was quite enjoying the lights of Times Square as they drifted by. It was a part of the city she rarely came to. Feeling like a tourist was fun, or a distraction at least.

Nor managed to flag down a waiter, and relaxed. 'I think the thing that scares Teddy the most is that for the first time in his life there's a problem that money can't fix. Did you meet Clark Russell? Very handsome, enormous moustache? Maybe not. I'm sure we dragged him down to Pomme at some point. Well, anyway, he got sick. Private jet to France, bribed his way onto some experimental treatment, still died. Liver failure. I've never seen Teddy so shaken. I think it finally dawned on him that he couldn't just wrap himself up in his portfolio to ward off danger.'

'And how is he? Does he seem sick?'

'Teddy?' Nor almost spat some of her martini out. 'No, darling. Teddy is the very picture of health. He's the only grown man I've ever known that one could still describe as "bonny". I'm sorry you'll miss him, but tonight's not the night – lots of theatre types, big producers and he turns into a cross between Uriah Heep and Joyce Grenfell. Ghastly. Speaking of which, how's your husband? Any news, other than world domination?' The bar continued its slow revolve.

* * *

Riding the subway back downtown afterwards, Frankie found herself scanning the other passengers. Looking for the faces of young men who might be sick. That gauntness that went beyond thin, clothes too big, the sunken eyes that didn't know where to look. She did it in the restaurant too, glancing around the dining room, or sometimes one of the waiters would whisper their suspicions about the guy on table nine. It seemed to Frankie, though, that everyone was changed, not just the ill. She herself had begun to feel untethered, almost disposable. In an odd way, all the death and illness made her life seem less precious, not more. She noticed, too, how Patty, Brady and Jeffrey were altered, each of them dealing with the situation in their own way.

Jeffrey became politicised and angry, heading to demonstrations and meetings, lecturing anyone who would listen about what should be done and why it wasn't happening. Patty announced that she had applied for a transfer to a college in Minneapolis, closer to home. It seemed that life in Manhattan wasn't for her after all. Brady, sweet romantic Brady, had shut himself off. He was still charming to customers and worked hard, but there was no more talk of love or boyfriends. It was as if he no longer knew how to be young. Frankie worried about him more than the others. She could tell that he was just putting one foot in front of the other and managing to get through each day, but for how long? She wondered if he thought he might be sick too.

Omar was the strong one, the person Frankie relied on now that Wendell was gone. He impressed her by how organised he was and how he managed to motivate the others without ever being bossy. Then one day he pulled his hair back and showed Frankie a purple stain on the side of his forehead. His dark eyes were pools of terror, but he kept coming to work. Then another lesion appeared on the tip of his nose. He tried to hide it with make-up, but the startled knowing looks of customers told him he hadn't succeeded. When his hair began to fall out because of his chemotherapy, he apologised to Frankie, he wept, and then he went home to San Francisco. She couldn't blame him. All she had to offer him was a long, tight hug and her tears.

With Wendell, Patty and then Omar gone, the restaurant felt very different. Brady was now running the front of house, while Vincent and Jeffrey were joined by Dawn, an aspiring model from Texas, and Jason, a well-spoken English boy who was studying the cello at Juilliard.

Pomme wasn't as busy as it had once been. They still had their loyal locals and tourists coming to see the Haffen interior, but the world had changed. The restaurant was too small for the new crowd that wanted to see and be seen. They preferred Raoul's over on Prince; she heard people talking about 65 Irving, or the new hotspot The Odeon. It also didn't help that Frankie's heart was no longer in her work. Lunch was now just a light menu of salads, sandwiches and soup, and she hadn't changed the dinner menu in well over a year. She felt like she was just carrying on because she couldn't bear another ending in her life. Seven months later, Brady got a message. Omar was dead.

What made things harder for Frankie were the constant reminders that life was going on. Parties were bigger and better than ever. She saw pictures of Joe and Gretchen, faces dazzled by flashbulbs, leaving Café Luxembourg, or dancing at Area or The Palladium. Frankie would study their faces, their wide smiles. No hint of sadness, as if they had never heard the word AIDS, never even heard bad news.

Afterwards, Frankie wondered if it was these photographs that had made her dig her heels in quite so firmly. It wasn't like her, and she had surprised herself. It had been towards the end of '86, when Gretchen had called the apartment to ask about the paintings in Betty's bedroom. She explained that they were starting work on a *catalogue raisonné* of Joe's art and she just wondered, in the most casual of voices, if any of his paintings were in there. Frankie had been fairly brusque, not wanting to be rude, but she was busy. 'No, all of Joe's work was sent to the studio.'

'Are you sure?' Gretchen asked, as if trying to coax a confession from a child.

'Yes,' Frankie snapped. 'And I should know, because I had to pack it all up by myself.' She hung up.

A week went by, and then Gretchen came to the restaurant with Luca. This was very unusual. She stood at the bar wearing a dark, tight-waisted, wide-shouldered business suit. The boy by her side seemed like an incongruous accessory. Frankie offered them a drink; Gretchen asked for a coffee, Luca had an apple juice. Gretchen sat at the bar and made awkward small talk about business and how busy she and Joe were, planning for a major show in Tokyo. Frankie was about to make her excuses when Gretchen brought up Betty's bedroom again.

'I totally understand, I get that Joe has no paintings in there, but I just wondered what else *is* in there.' She paused. 'You know, from his collection.'

Frankie wasn't quite sure what Gretchen was up to, but she had no inclination to help her.

'It's all just stuff that Joe didn't want.' Frankie maintained eye contact with Gretchen. 'You know, stuff he left when he walked out.'

Gretchen immediately looked over at Luca to see if he was listening, but he was engrossed in a comic book.

'Of course, of course.' She gave Frankie a tight smile.

It was the end of January when Gretchen returned to Pomme. Everyone was getting ready for the evening shift when Brady came into the kitchen to tell Frankie who was waiting for her.

She wiped her hands on a cloth, silently cursing Gretchen and her obsession with Betty's bedroom. Frankie was not in the mood.

Gretchen was waiting at a table at the far end of the dining room. At least she didn't have Luca with her. Frankie sat down heavily and with a sigh asked, 'And how can I help you today, Gretchen?'

Frankie was slightly unsettled by Gretchen's demeanour. She seemed uncharacteristically timid. She ran her tongue around the inside of her mouth and glanced down at the table.

'This is delicate. It's why I didn't phone. We don't want people knowing.' She smiled. Frankie was struck by the use of the word *we* and wondered if Joe even knew Gretchen was here.

'Knowing what?'

Gretchen placed a strand of hair behind her ear. 'Joe is undergoing treatment for cancer.' Reacting to the shocked looked on Frankie's face, she added, 'Don't worry. The doctors are confident. I'm only here because Joe has asked to see you.'

'Why does he want to see me?' It didn't make sense. If the situation was as optimistic as Gretchen was saying, why would Joe be asking for her?

Gretchen stood, holding her handbag with both hands. 'I'm just the messenger. He's in Lenox Hill. Visiting any time after nine is fine.' Without waiting for a response, she left the restaurant. Had her face been creased by emotion? Is that why she was in such a rush? Frankie couldn't be sure.

The next morning was cold but bright, so Frankie decided to get the subway up to 72nd Street and walk across the park. Light flurries of snow swirled through the air. Frankie pulled her hat down over her ears and stepped carefully to avoid any ice. It felt good to be up so early and to see the rest of the city getting on with their lives. People walking their dogs, children trying not to be late for school, everyone leaving a trail of breath in the air.

As she walked, Frankie wasn't worrying about Joe. Her mind was on other things. On the small incline from Park Avenue towards the hospital, she found herself thinking about the fact that there was an actual hill. Lenox Hill wasn't just a name.

The security guard gave her a visitor's pass and directed her to the elevators. She pushed through a series of double doors until she came to the nurses' station. She was struck by all the red plastic bags. Even the chairs in the small waiting area were covered in them. A stocky nurse was arranging a large pile of papers into three smaller ones.

'Good morning,' she greeted Frankie, the only distinguishing feature on her face a ribbon of lipstick the pale pink of a baby's fingernail.

'Hello, I was hoping to see Joe, Joseph Haffen.'

The nurse glanced at a clipboard. 'I'm sorry,' she said, sounding anything but, 'it's family only.'

'I'm his wife.'

A look of confusion crossed the nurse's face.

'I'm Mrs Frances Haffen.'

The nurse hesitated and Frankie wondered if she was going to challenge her claims, but no.

'It's the last door on the right. We would ask you to wear these.'

The nurse handed Frankie a small pack containing a face mask and thin rubber gloves.

'Oh.' Now it was her turn to feel confused. 'Is this normal?'

'It's for his protection, not yours.' The nurse returned to her papers.

Masked and gloved, Frankie made her way down the corridor, her shoes squeaking on the glossy linoleum. At the last door on the right, she took off her hat and rearranged her hair into something she hoped was presentable. When she entered the room, however, she stopped abruptly. How embarrassing. On the other side of the room an emaciated old man lay on the bed with his back to her. His hospital gown was hanging open, revealing the bones of his spine, like rocks at low tide, and his skin was mottled with dark patches. Frankie hoped she hadn't woken him. She left the room, closing the door as quietly as possible. She squeaked her way back to the nurses' station.

'Excuse me.'

The same nurse looked up impatiently. 'Yes.'

'Sorry, I think there's been a mistake. I wanted to see Joseph Haffen, but he wasn't in that room.'

'Which room?'

'The one at the end, the one you sent me to.'

Both women were clearly as irritated as each other.

'Let me show you,' the nurse said, hurriedly putting on a face mask and marching down the corridor. She entered the room that Frankie had just vacated.

'Now, Mr Haffen,' the nurse announced loudly, 'we have someone here to see you.' She reached forward and turned the figure in the bed so that he faced the door. 'Do you know this lady?'

Frankie gasped in horror but mercifully managed to suppress a scream. It was Joe in the bed, but a nightmarish cartoon of the man she knew. His thick dark hair was now just tufts on his skull, and a wispy greying beard covered the bottom half of his gaunt face. Only the eyes were unmistakably Joe's. He smiled when he saw her, revealing brown teeth that seemed too big for his mouth.

'I'll leave you alone,' the nurse said curtly.

Frankie stood perfectly still and took in the scene. A tangle of IV drips and wires connected Joe to a bank of machines. Above the bedside locker were some photographs of him with his family. Had Luca seen his daddy like this? Frankie inched towards the bed and sat down. Joe's mouth was open and she could hear the air as it went in and out. What had Gretchen been thinking? Why on earth would she have sent Frankie into this room unprepared? Cancer? The doctors were confident? This wasn't cancer. Frankie knew what this was.

'Good to see you, Joe.' She swallowed hard, not wanting to cry.

'Frankie,' he whispered, a smile tugging weakly at his mouth.

'You wanted to see me.'

He blinked and his head bowed slightly. 'Yes.' The word sounded like air escaping from a puncture. He inched an arm towards her. It was thinner than a chair leg. She thought of the body she had washed in the tub, the muscles she had soaped. How was this the same man? His hand edged off the bed, so she held it. A twitch around Joe's eyes. What was it? Disappointment? Quickly, she reached forward and peeled off her rubber glove. When she put her hand back, his fingers curled around hers.

'Thank you,' he mouthed.

Had Joe planned the things he wanted to say to Frankie? Apologies? Confessions? Whatever they were, they went unsaid. The two of them just sat silently, hand in hand. Joe's eyes brimmed with tears but a smile played around his lips. The sounds of a busy city drifted up from the streets below. Through the window Frankie could see a plane crossing the winter sky, bringing people to somewhere they wanted to be. After twenty minutes or so, Joe's eyes started to close. Clearly, he needed to sleep. Frankie gently pulled her hand away. 'I'll go.'

Joe's eyes opened and he stared at her as if seeing her for the first time that day.

'Frankie,' he rasped.

'Yes, Joe. It's me.' Despite her best efforts, she couldn't stop her tears from falling.

Joe shook his head and his lips were moving but Frankie couldn't hear him. She put her face close to his mouth. She could smell his sweat mixed with a faint medicinal scent. He spoke again. She could barely make out the words.

'I don't mind being dead, Frankie.'

She squeezed his hand. 'Oh, Joe.'

'But I don't like this. I don't like dying.' Tears were running down his hollowed-out cheeks. Not knowing what to say, she pulled down her mask and kissed his forehead. She held him until he fell asleep.

Standing inside the door, she wiped her eyes roughly. That nurse would not see her weep. She rushed past the nurses' station with a hasty 'Goodbye' and pushed through the double doors until she reached the elevator. Alone, as the doors slid shut, she felt herself begin to tremble. She had to get out of this building.

The moment she was on the street, the cold air tightening her damp face, she let herself go. Frankie leaned against the wall of the hospital and howled into the hard brick wall. She pressed her face against it as firmly as she could. She needed to feel something solid, something that couldn't be ripped away without warning. She stumbled along just thinking about the park. Somehow things would be better when she was away from the buildings and the cars. Then, through her tear-blurred vision she became aware of where she was: Leo's first gallery, and across the way The Mark Hotel. She turned and turned again; she could still see the hospital, then the gallery, then the windows of the hospital reflecting the scene of Joe's first triumph. Frankie felt as if she was caught between the book-ends of Joe's life. She kept walking until she was back in the refuge of Central Park, but she found everything changed. Now the people making their way along the various paths weren't getting on with their lives, they were just ignorant of what was really going on. The man she had loved, the man she thought she had grown to hate, was dying. Up there. She looked back to the point in the sky that she imagined was over the hospital. She walked on until her sobs were under control, then made her way back to the subway.

In her apartment, she sat in a state of shock. Each time she looked at the walls and saw once more the world that Joe had created, she would start to cry. Frankie leaned across and traced one vine with her finger. Following it, she was drawn out of her chair and around the apartment till she was standing in her bedroom. Their bedroom. This wasn't an apartment, it was an archive of her and Joe. She phoned Gretchen but she and Joe had an answering machine.

'It's Frankie. Please call me as soon as you get this. I'm at home. I . . .' No, she had nothing else to say. She hung up. Twenty minutes later she called again. The tape started to play. She put down the phone.

A bath might help. She turned on the taps and waited. She was standing wrapped in a towel and about to step into the water when the phone rang.

'Hello.'

'Frankie. It's Gretchen. You called.'

'Yes, yes I did.' She wanted to reach through the phone line and crush this woman's throat. 'What . . . how did you not tell me how bad it was? What it is? How was I—'

Gretchen spoke across her. 'Sorry, sorry. It looks much worse than it is. He was like this before Christmas and then he was fine again. They just need to find the right meds, that's all.' She sounded brisk and detached. She might have been discussing a patch of damp. Frankie stared into the receiver. She couldn't quite believe what she was hearing.

'Gretchen, he has AIDS, why not tell me?'

'He has cancer. I will not have you saying anything other.'

'What? Oh Gretchen, I'm so sorry. I am. But, you need—' She stopped herself. Who was she to tell this woman what she needed? The father of her son was dying.

'He has cancer and he is going to get better.' Gretchen's voice was a restrained snarl, then the line went dead.

A secret was a burden that Frankie didn't want to carry, but what choice did she have? Gretchen was now the one to tell Joe's story, so Frankie said nothing. She tried calling the hospital over the next few days, but was told that Mr Haffen was resting. Phoning their house, she just got Gretchen's voice on the machine. It felt as if Joe was gone already. And then he was.

Carla, the woman who had worked at Pomme even longer than Frankie, in charge of salads and cold plates, came into the kitchen and gave Frankie a hug.

'I just heard. I'm sorry.'

'What? I don't understand.' Frankie stepped back. 'What is it?'

Carla's face changed as she realised that she was going to be the one to have to break the news. 'Oh no, I thought you'd . . . I just heard on the radio – no one told you? It's Mr Haffen. He's passed.'

Frankie stumbled backwards, catching herself against the counter. She couldn't be here, not in the kitchen. She wrenched opened the deliveries door and stepped out into the back alley. She bent forward and took some deep breaths. A grey cat sitting on the wall opposite eyed her suspiciously. Hearing the traffic, Frankie walked, as if in a trance, to Sixth Avenue and picked up copies of the *Post* and the *Daily News*. She half ran, half walked back to the restaurant. In the dining room, she tore through the papers. He hadn't made the *Daily News* but there he was in the *Post* on page three: ARTIST JOSEPH HAFFEN DEAD AT 56. There was a large picture of Joe taken in front of one of his collages, and then a smaller photo of him with Gretchen and Luca. The article detailed his meteoric rise to fame, his son, his partner Gretchen, his short battle with cancer and . . . that was it. No mention of Frankie, or how he'd really died.

Instantly Pomme became a shrine. Candles in jam jars, bunches of flowers, prints of his work surrounded the restaurant like a moat of grief. They had to close. Frankie didn't know how long for. She stood on the far side of the narrow street, observing the restaurant as if it had nothing to do with her, and maybe it didn't. Perhaps Pomme had been about Joe all along and she had been deluded in her belief that it was her creation. Nor, like a fairy godmother who manifested in times of need, was by her side. She had been visiting Teddy's family on Long Island when Teddy had phoned with the news about Joe. Nor had headed straight to Pomme.

'I don't understand it. By all means, like his work, be sad he's gone, but why put dead flowers on a pavement? There's a very thin line between a shrine and a garbage strike.'

Frankie didn't have the energy to respond, but she was grateful for her friend's chatter. She hooked her arm through Nor's and leaned against her shoulder. Apart from her breakdown outside the hospital, she hadn't really cried for Joe. Perhaps there was a limit to the tears one had available to shed. She had folded the newspapers, put them on the bar and then written out a sign for the door explaining their closure. Vincent had hugged her. Brady had sat with her while they cancelled the few reservations they had in the book. It had been eerily calm.

'Let me take you for dinner, darling. You need a big fat cocktail. I'm sure I can get us a booth at Indochine. Fancy it?'

Frankie just nodded. It was good to have someone to take care of her.

'Come on, I need you to tell me what the fuck happened.'

And as the two friends walked off through the group of mourning fans that is precisely what Frankie did.

Wapping, 2024

They sat in silence. Frankie dabbed her eyes with a tissue, while Damian, at the end of the bed, massaged her feet. It had been a long night.

'Well, you're not wrong. None of that was in Wikipedia.' His voice was hushed as if there was someone close by he didn't want to wake.

'I'm sure.'

'You were in it, though. The wife. You get a mention.'

Frankie smiled. 'Fame at last.'

'Should I put those away?' Damian indicated the old newspapers strewn across the bed. He had retrieved them earlier from the boxes next door.

'I suppose. I don't know why I keep them. For who?'

Damian began to fold the papers. 'For me. You kept them for me.' He touched her hand.

'Perhaps I did. It's funny. Less than a month later, Warhol died. He got the front page. I remember thinking at the time, well, at least Joe didn't live to see that.'

'Was he AIDS too?'

'Warhol? No, an operation I believe. It was a shock, I remember that.'

Damian was standing by the door. 'Why did Gretchen lie? Why didn't she want people to know about Joe's AIDS?'

Frankie shrugged. 'If I was being kind, I'd say it was to protect Luca. The world was very different and it would be a lot for a boy about to start high school, if their famous daddy had AIDS.'

'And if you were being unkind?'

'Money. I think she was protecting Joe's legacy, and maybe her own. I don't know. Who knows what she went through? I mean, she must have been worried she'd get it – Luca too, even.'

Damian hesitated. It wasn't an easy question, but he really wanted to know. 'And how, like, how do you think Joe, like how did he get it?'

A sigh. 'I don't know. Maybe he was caught up with drugs, shared a needle. That makes the most sense to me, but who knows what was going on? Some of the circles he mixed in were pretty wild. I mean, I had been clueless he was having an affair with a woman. It's possible . . . I can't imagine it, but the world is complicated, or at least it was back then.'

'Oh, it still is, it still is,' Damian said, stepping into the hallway. 'Now you should get some sleep.'

'Yes, nurse. And you too.' She reached to turn off her lamp as Damian closed the bedroom door.

Lying in the dark, Frankie tried to get comfortable. It felt good not wearing the cast any more, but it seemed she had forgotten how she liked to sleep. She lay on her side, facing away from the door, but her shoulder ached. Had it always done that? She wasn't sure. Turning to face the door, she felt a jabbing pain in her hip, so she abandoned that idea and lay on her back, staring up at the ceiling.

She was going to miss Damian – or was it that she was going to miss the way she'd used him to step back into the past? Maybe she really had been keeping all those boxes of photos, clippings and notebooks for precisely this moment. She doubted she would ever look at them again. Was she done? She could just throw it all away, make Nor take back the furniture she had forced her to store after Teddy died. She closed her eyes and imagined the flat as an oasis of calm. Empty rooms painted cream and nothing on the walls; well, maybe one painting. She smiled and fell asleep, thinking of the canvas rolled up beneath her bed.

The next morning Nor arrived with a large bouquet of flowers and a bottle of champagne wrapped in pink tissue.

'Last day!' she announced as she presented her gifts to Damian. Frankie, sitting at the kitchen table with her tea, gave a round of applause and a couple of whoops.

'Ah, that's lovely, lovely, but sure I'm only doing my job.'

'Above and beyond,' Nor said as she slipped her blanket of a coat onto a chair. 'We're going to miss Damian, aren't we, darling?'

'Nor, the boy is sick of hearing about how much we'll miss him. Let him get back to young people.' Frankie sat up straight and put down her cup. 'Damian, do not become me. Sat in this flat for twenty years with nothing but memories.'

'A little harsh, I feel,' Nor said under her breath.

'Still not deaf.' Frankie sounded irritated, but she was smiling.

Damian made the coffee the way that Frankie had taught him and brought it to the table.

'I made some chocolate Florentines. They're in that tin, next to the bread.'

'She's back!' Nor declared, clapping her hands.

Damian delivered the biscuits and sat down.

'A Florentine for farewell.' Frankie waved her biscuit at him.

Damian looked at the two old ladies. He felt a surge of affection for them.

'Ah, you haven't seen the last of me. I'm only up the road. I'll pop down for a cup of your fancy tea.'

'The only thing fancy in this flat is Nor Forrester.'

Nor patted her hair. 'Well, isn't that the truth.'

After coffee, Damian went and fetched his backpack and stood hesitantly in the hallway.

'Well, that's me away.'

Nor and Frankie appeared in the kitchen doorway.

'Would you not have another cup of something?' Frankie asked, trying and failing not to sound too eager.

Nor put a hand on her friend's arm.

'The boy has to go.'

'I know, I know.'

The trio stood awkwardly. Damian wasn't sure if he should hug the women, but, before he could decide, Frankie's face lit up.

'But you don't know how I ended up here.'

'That's true,' Damian said, looking at Nor, who stepped back from the kitchen door.

'It's quick,' Frankie assured him.

'Right.' Damian grinned as he put his backpack on the floor.

New York, 1987

Even by Nor's sartorial standards, she had outdone herself. A black and white polka-dot scarf was wrapped tightly around her head, jet black sunglasses remained firmly in place despite being in a church, and her shawl-collared black brocade coat was floor length. She looked as if she had just put down her cigarette holder in the other room. Frankie felt protected simply standing beside her. Teddy, in an expensive Italian black suit, flanked her on the other side.

Gretchen hadn't banned Frankie from attending Joe's funeral, but nor had there been an invitation. If it hadn't been for Teddy and Nor's encouragement, she might not have gone, but here she was sitting near the back of the Marble Collegiate Church on Fifth Avenue. It was packed with people she didn't recognise. She assumed all the big names were near the front somewhere.

'Frankie!' It was Betty, standing in the aisle with three young adults, who presumably were her children all grown up. Betty seemed strangely unmoved by the occasion, but then Frankie herself felt as if she had already shed her tears for Joe.

'Betty. Good to see you.' They embraced. 'You remember my friend Nor, and this is Teddy.'

'Nice to meet you.' Betty looked around conspiratorially. 'Is this a Protestant church?'

'I think it is, yes,' Nor replied.

'What was she thinking? I mean, Joe wasn't really anything, but Catholic would have made more sense. My mother would have a fit. I hope she never finds out.'

'She's not here?' Frankie asked.

'Too frail to travel. There's a private cremation back in Albany. She'll be at that, we hope. Oh Christ, Gretchen is glaring at us. We'd better get seated. We'll see you afterwards.' She blew a kiss and scurried down the aisle with her brood. Frankie just smiled and nodded. She knew nothing about afterwards.

The funeral felt oddly impersonal. The prayers, the hymns, nothing brought Joe to mind, but then Luca stepped up to the lectern to give a reading. Frankie raised a hand to her throat. At a glance, it was as if the ghost of Joe had appeared before the congregation, but then he spoke, and his light lilting voice broke the illusion. The young man almost managed to get to the end of the text, with its many repetitions of the phrase 'children of God', but on the final few words, his face became distorted, and the voice became the querulous cry of a child. Nor took Frankie's hand and squeezed it firmly.

After the service was over, milling with the congregation as they left the church, they discovered that there was a reception being held at the Union Square Café.

'What do you want to do? Are you bothered?' Nor asked.

Frankie thought for a moment. 'No. I've said my goodbye. And we've made it this far without having to talk to Gretchen. Let's get out of here.'

'Cocktails ahoy!' Teddy called as he led them around the corner to their waiting car, seemingly unaware that they had just been attending a funeral.

It was less than a week later when Gretchen began her campaign. A phone call came first.

'As executor of the will, I will need an inventory of the art and assets you've been holding on to. I mean, I'm happy to do it if you're busy.'

'Excuse me?' Frankie didn't understand. 'If I have anything it's because it's mine.'

'Of course, of course. It's just that because you were still married when Joe died, his share of everything, according to his will, should pass to myself and Luca. You understand?'

Frankie did not understand, but she knew that this didn't sound good.

'Let me think about it.' And she put the receiver down as if trying to put the stopper back in a bottle.

When the phone rang again the following day, Frankie didn't answer it. She knew she was being foolish, but she needed more time. She didn't want to deal with any of this now. How was Gretchen managing to be so focused and business-like? She had just lost her lover, the father of her son. Perhaps, Frankie reasoned, this was her way of coping.

Two days later, the first of the letters arrived.

It was from a firm of attorneys, acting on behalf of Gretchen Schmidt, executor of the will of Joseph Haffen. It was brief but packed with legal language Frankie didn't fully understand. She suspected that it didn't really say anything at all and was merely a tactic designed to frighten her into allowing Gretchen to rifle through her things. She filed it on the kitchen shelf, between the tea caddy and the honey. A week later, another one arrived. She barely glanced at it before filing it with the first one.

Gretchen's attentions did at least help to focus Frankie's mind. She needed to sort out her own life. She had decisions to make. What was she going to do with Pomme? It had remained shut since Joe's death and, whenever Frankie did go back in to clear out the fridges, cancel orders or open mail, she couldn't imagine ever opening it again. How could it be filled with noisy diners chatting and laughing, waiters sharing jokes and gossip? Even the murals seemed flat and faded in this new world without Joe in it. Frankie wasn't overly concerned about Brady and the others, they would all find jobs elsewhere, but she did feel guilty and anxious about the women who worked with her in the kitchen and of course Bruno, the long-suffering kitchen porter. Now the thought of Gretchen somehow getting her hands on the restaurant spurred her on to a decision. She'd have a closing party for the regulars and the staff and then split the money in the Pomme bank account with the kitchen staff. She still had most of the money from the sale of the loft sitting in the bank, so she could more than survive until she decided what to do next. For the first time in her life it felt as if she had choices. No one was telling her what to do.

The party was a mistake. Frankie wasn't exactly sure what she had hoped it would be, but at the very least she had imagined people might care. The regulars had just drunk their free red wine and thanked her for all the good times before stepping out into the night, smiling and laughing. It was as if they were more excited about what new restaurant might be opening in their neighbourhood than sad about losing this one. Bruno and Carla had shown a little emotion when Frankie had broken the news, but the others hardly displayed any reaction at all – well, until she had mentioned the money. Then they were so happy she felt as though their only regret was that she hadn't closed years before. The waiting staff were all so new, they barely remembered Wendell or Omar, never mind Joe. At the end of the night she saw them hiding glasses and silverware in their bags before they left. Frankie didn't care. Anything that was taken, all the wine that had been drunk, they were just things that Gretchen could never get her hands on.

Nor and Teddy were horrified when Frankie finally told them about the solicitor's letters, which by this point totalled five.

'You have to talk to someone,' Teddy insisted. 'I can set you up. Don't worry about the money, he's a friend. You just need to know if you should be concerned or not.'

They were sitting in the vast hushed living room of Teddy's family's apartment in the Beresford on Central Park West. A wiry woman in a maid's uniform was arranging snacks on the coffee table. Teddy suddenly looked stricken.

'Oh Ruby, do we not have any more of the little cheese straws? They're our favourite.' He gave her his best smile.

'They were on the order, I know that. I'll check for you, sir.' She scuttled from the room, her face the very picture of concern.

'I mean, why is she bothering?' Nor extinguished her cigarette violently. 'The woman owns all of Joseph Haffen Inc. Why is she bothered about some little restaurant? No offence, darling.'

'It's the apartment too.'

'What? But you don't even own that!'

'I told you before – she has a bee in her bonnet about Betty's bedroom.'

'Why? What on earth's in there?'

'It's stuff from the loft on Spring Street. Art, pictures mostly.'

Nor put down her lighter without lighting her fresh cigarette.

'The art from the loft?' she asked and glanced at Teddy.

'Not his – that all went to his studio. Just the stuff from the walls.'

'Well, Frankie darling, that's your problem right there. You had everybody on those walls; I remember at the time being impressed. Everyone – Johns, Stella, Bontecou pieces, Lichtenstein . . . imagine what that lot is worth now.'

Teddy gave a long, low whistle.

'No wonder little Miss Gretchen wants to get her hands on it,' Nor said, remembering about her cigarette and lighting it.

'But it's mine. He gave it all to me.'

Teddy grimaced. 'But did he? Very hard to prove and if it is jointly owned, well then, she may have a claim on half the value.'

'Really?' Frankie looked panic-stricken. Nor glared at Teddy.

'What do I know?' He raised his hands, hoping to reassure their friend. 'You'll have to speak to our man.'

Ruby reappeared at the door with a china bowl. 'Cheese straws,' she announced, and Teddy clapped his hands together, making himself look even more like a happy baby than usual.

The attorney's office was in a building opposite the library on Fifth Avenue. Frankie already felt as if she had lost. This was not her world. She belonged in the Village or SoHo, not these marble-lined corridors and ornate elevators. The attorney himself was pleasant enough: 'Call me Theo' with dark wavy hair and the broken red veins of a farmer or fisherman rather than someone who had devoted their life to the world of law. He fired off a list of questions.

'When were you married?'

'And the marriage, what year did it break down?'

'And have you children?'

He listened to her answers, making notes and strange clicking noises in his throat. Frankie had no idea if this was a good or a bad sign. After hearing everything, he put his pen down and thought for a moment.

'Mrs Haffen.' He leaned back in his chair and placed his soft hands on his tight little belly. 'I don't think you have too much to be concerned about. Miss Schmidt might have a case, *might*, but it would be so complicated and costly to pursue, with no guarantee of a successful outcome. I'm confident that no lawyer is going to advise her to risk it.

Frankie wished she shared Theo's confidence.

Days began to drift now that they were untethered from the routine of the restaurant. Not wanting to be in the apartment, Frankie found herself walking aimlessly, exploring areas of the city in a way she had never done before. She stood by the Hudson, a light drizzle being blown into her face. Her whole life seemed to stretch before her, as grey and nondescript as the distant shore. She walked south through Tribeca, into the unfamiliar sloping streets of the financial district. Some days, she headed north past the glittering shop windows of Fifth Avenue till she reached the park, and all the people busy getting fit for some unspecified challenge life was going to throw at them. She found she could easily spend an hour sitting on a bench just watching joggers or people walking by, listening to snatches of conversations. Other people's dramas, the lives of strangers. She found an odd comfort in them.

Six months slipped by, and then it was a new year. No more letters had arrived. Perhaps the lawyer had been right, and she could forget about Gretchen. Frankie had begun to consider her next steps. She felt like making a change in her life, something big. Could she move to the West Coast? She had read about the restaurant scenes in San Francisco and LA, or maybe somewhere like Portland might suit her better after New York? But then one more letter arrived.

This envelope looked innocent enough. It had none of the warning signs like the name of a law firm emblazoned on it, and her name and address were handwritten, rather than typed. Sitting at the kitchen table, she opened it with more curiosity than fear. The letter inside was headed 'The Haffen Foundation', whatever that might be, with an address in SoHo. It was from a man Frankie had never heard of called Scott Broder. He was writing on behalf of the foundation's president, Gretchen Schmidt. Frankie's heart began to pulse like that of a creature caught in a trap. The words tumbled in front of her eyes. A marriage certificate . . . Ireland . . . Canon Alan Frost . . . bigamist . . . illegal alien . . . authorities . . . the art collection of the late Joseph Haffen . . . by the end of the page, Frankie was gasping. This letter was like a punch in the stomach. Her life was over.

The question that Frankie kept repeating to herself was how had she been stupid enough to underestimate Gretchen? The woman who had turned Joe into a worldwide brand, the woman who had stolen her husband. Except, of course, he wasn't her husband – he never had been. It was all so long ago but Frankie honestly couldn't remember having worried for even a moment about her marriage to Alan. West Cork had seemed like a distant planet, of no relevance to Manhattan. She did recall a question on some form asking if she had been married before and she had happily answered no. Why look for problems? It had been a way of erasing her past, declaring that her life was just beginning. A clean sheet.

Frankie stared at the page with 'The Haffen Foundation' printed on it, her name or what had been her name until moments before. As terrified as she was, she had to marvel at Gretchen's tenacity. How had she found Frankie's ancient history? She couldn't possibly have known she had been Frances Howe or Mrs Frost. It was possible, just, that she might have known Frankie's birthday, but even then it would have been a huge undertaking to find everything else. Had Gretchen sent some minion to Ireland to sort through documents and parish registers? Frankie had a vision of a tanned man in polished shoes attracting attention as he made his way through the frayed streets of Ballytoor. She stood and began to pace the apartment. Should she just give in and allow Gretchen to take the paintings, in the hope that she would permit Frankie to get on with her life?

But no. Frankie could never relax now that someone had this knowledge and could use it against her at any time. She began to sort through the miscellaneous debris on her dressing table, looking for lawyer Theo's number.

This time Theo did not lean back in his chair. Frankie noticed his manicured nails as he turned the letter over. Then he leaned towards her across his desk.

'I mean, this is blackmail, short and simple. It might be all dressed up in a bow, but it is just common blackmail.'

Frankie felt a glimmer of hope.

'But,' Theo said sombrely, 'I'm not sure what choices are open to you. This' – he brandished the letter – 'may be nefarious, but the fact is you have broken the law. This Alan Frost may be dead, but he wasn't when you married Joseph Haffen. I'm afraid to say, you are a bigamist. You are in this country illegally.' He gave a long sigh. 'I'm very sorry.'

'So what do I do?' Frankie asked in a small voice.

Theo squeezed the bridge of his nose. 'I would say that you might be able to argue your case for becoming a naturalised citizen after all this time, but I'm afraid there is no getting around the bigamy.' He shrugged. 'It wasn't a mistake; you knowingly got married while still married to someone else.'

Frankie fought the urge to try to explain. What was the point? This was the law, it didn't make room for excuses.

'So, I . . . ?'

'Leave, and as soon as possible.'

'And the restaurant?'

'You could try and sell it, but it doesn't sound like you have time – and besides, they could seize your assets.'

Frankie felt her life slipping away. She had lost so many people already and now she was going to lose everything.

'The art? What about the art?'

Theo bared his teeth. 'Not really my area of expertise, but if the ownership is disputed no one will touch it, certainly not any sale room or auction house. Miss Schmidt might offer you some compensation but, on the basis of this letter, that seems unlikely.'

Frankie looked out of the window and then back to Theo.

'What if I took it with me?'

'Again, you should seek expert advice, but from what you've told me about the collection the taxes alone would make that prohibitive, even if you had the correct paperwork. You should also be aware that if you were to be caught smuggling that amount of art, of that value, I imagine there would be a custodial sentence. Jail.' Theo exhaled and pressed his lips together. 'I wish there was something better I could tell you, but . . .' His voice trailed away and he raised his hands like Christ summoning the Holy Spirit – who, Frankie assumed, was her only hope at this point.

She rode the subway downtown, her head bowed. Even the idea of making eye contact with someone alarmed her. She didn't want to be noticed by anyone. It felt as if the whole city was seeking her out, ready to catch her by the scruff of the neck and throw her out of the country. When she got back to the apartment, she sat silently on the bed. She felt nauseous. As it got dark, she didn't get up to switch on the lights. A knock on the door could come at any moment. She wondered how much time she had before Gretchen acted. Even if Frankie wanted to flee, she had no passport. How long would it take to get one of those issued?

She went to the door of Betty's old room and looked at the shape of the various canvases and sculptures waiting in the gloom. Could it really be as simple as giving these up and getting her life back? She leaned back against the chilled wall. She was just being foolish. Gretchen might have presented things as a choice but that was never how this was going to end.

Frankie's dark thoughts were interrupted by the shrill ringing of the phone. She froze. Who could be calling her? It must be nearly eight o'clock now. Offices would be closed and she couldn't imagine Gretchen getting personally involved at this grubby stage of the game. Frankie approached the phone and gingerly picked up the receiver.

'Hello.'

'Frankie? Is that you?' It was a breathless Nor.

'Yes, it's me.'

'Oh, thank God, I thought I might be too late.'

'Too late?'

'That you might be gone already. Theo called Teddy and told him what happened. Why didn't you call us?'

'What for? There's nothing to be done.'

'Frankie,' Nor snapped at her friend, 'there is always something to be done. Teddy is making calls. Can you put yourself in a cab and get up here pronto?'

Frankie glanced at the darkened apartment. 'Yes, yes of course. I'll see you soon.'

As she clattered down the stairs, the phrase *life or death situation* popped into her mind. That's what this felt like. She held her coat across her chest as she half walked, half ran to Sixth to hail a cab going uptown. Just the thought of being in the warm lamplit living room in the Beresford made her feel better. She wouldn't have said she was hopeful, but not being alone was at least some sort of an improvement.

Ruby answered the door and ushered Frankie in. Teddy was standing by a small table near the window, phone in hand. Nor saw her friend and put a finger up to indicate they should be quiet. She pointed at a green gin bottle and a clear one of vodka. Frankie indicated the vodka and Nor started putting handfuls of ice into a glass.

'Thanks, Harry. I'll be in touch with Jean and let you know.' Teddy ended his call and turned, smiling, to the women. 'It might work.'

Nor let out a little yelp of excitement and ushered a confused Frankie to the long couch. 'Tonic?' she asked, pressing a glass into Frankie's hand.

'Yes, thanks. Thank you so much. What is going on?'

Teddy sat with a contented sigh. 'Nor, do you want to do the honours?'

Nor took a preparatory sip of her drink and began.

'Well, you know Teddy has been working with another producer, Harry Rigby? But, wait — first things first. How are you, darling? I wish you would have called us. We are both livid — I mean with the Gretchen creature, not you.' She paused long enough for Frankie to respond.

'I don't know how I am. Awful, I suppose. I mean, I understand that she wants the art, but does she have to take everything away from me?'

'So, that's what I'm trying to tell you. There has been this tragic tour of *Sugar Babies*—'

'Nor!' Teddy objected.

'Sorry, darling, I know you like it. Well, anyway, Teddy is helping to bring it over to the West End.'

'Yes,' Frankie said, wondering where this was heading.

'Well, they're shipping a bunch of props and backcloths to save money with the London production and Teddy had the brainwave of putting all your things in the container too.'

Frankie knew that this sounded too easy. She looked at Teddy, but he was beaming.

'But what about customs? Surely the shipping company will have to know what they have?'

Nor smirked. 'Teddy's uncle owns the shipping company.'

Teddy raised an eyebrow. 'The less you know the better but, if I tell you that this sort of thing isn't that unusual, you understand my drift?'

'I think I do. But what about me?'

'She'll never find you in London,' Nor declared with a dismissive wave of her hand.

Frankie put down her drink. 'But how do I get there? I haven't got a passport. It'll take weeks.'

Nor's face became grim. 'Fuck. We didn't think of that. Teddy?'

Her husband just pulled a face.

Nor lit a cigarette and took a long drag. 'Tourists must lose passports all the time. How do they get home? You can say it's an emergency.'

Frankie shook her head. 'But those people will be in the system – there'll be a record of them entering the country. Otherwise anyone could just wander in asking for a passport.'

'I suppose so,' Nor reluctantly agreed.

The three of them became quiet as they tried to think of a solution. Frankie wondered if she could go into hiding while she was waiting for her passport, but no, they'd just catch her when she tried to go through security at the airport. She could sneak into Canada somehow? They weren't looking for her there, or maybe they would be by the time she got her hands on a passport?

Suddenly, Teddy broke the silence.

'Da!'

'What are you talking about?' Nor asked, a note of irritation in her voice.

'That Irish play *Da*, do you remember about ten years ago? They had trouble getting a work visa for one of the actors – Bryan Murray I think, terribly good – anyway, I gave them some contacts. On the Irish end of the thing, I dealt with a very nice woman in the embassy – name, gone, but Abby in the office will have her number, and she more or less said that, if I ever needed anything, I should get in touch.' His beam was back.

'More or less?' Frankie didn't want to get her hopes up.

'More! More! I mean, that's what she said.' Teddy was excited now that his plan was back on track.

'That's if she even still works there.' Nor tapped her cigarette against the ashtray.

Even Teddy was deflated by this thought. There followed another short silence and then he clapped his hands together. 'Well, we can't know that until tomorrow. Now what about I treat you ladies to some dinner?'

The next morning, numbers were found and calls made. An Angela Dunphy did indeed still work at the embassy and she remembered Teddy Forrester fondly. Nor called Frankie to tell her the good news. Did she still have her old passport?

'Oh God. Maybe, somewhere. Let me look.'

As if it had been waiting for her, she found the little green book in one of the silky pockets inside the case she had brought to New York almost thirty years before.

That night a nondescript van pulled up outside Frankie's building. It was nearly midnight, and she had spent the evening trying to save the parking space using a couple of her kitchen chairs. A few drivers had sworn at her and she was afraid she might attract attention, but now the wait was over. Frankie thought she might have preferred the waiting. It was really happening. She was leaving 8th Street and New York. Her chest felt tight as she showed the two men up to the apartment and into Betty's room. Without any fuss or preamble, they started ferrying everything downstairs. Soon a large black sedan pulled up alongside the van and Nor stumbled out of it wearing a gold sequinned jacket over a black blouse and trousers.

'Sorry I'm late, darling.'

Frankie pulled her into the doorway. 'Could you look any more conspicuous? I thought the plan was we didn't want anyone to notice us.'

'City Ballet gala. If I hadn't gone, people would have wondered why. Sorry, shall I take this off? How's it going?'

'Fine. I think they're nearly done.'

'All right. And you've packed?'

Frankie thought about the boxes upstairs.

'Yes. It's more than I thought.'

'Not to worry. Abby will take care of it all and if it gets searched, then you're squeaky clean.'

'What about Theo?' Frankie asked.

'Done. He's contacted the Haffen Foundation asking for their evidence, proof of their allegations, that sort of thing. I'd say that should buy us a couple of days at least. We're meant to get your temporary passport in the morning and, if that happens, we can fly tomorrow night.' Nor smiled and hugged her friend. Frankie found that she was trembling, and she didn't think it was because of the cold night air.

The next day nothing went wrong and yet, as the hours ticked down, Frankie found herself getting tenser and more anxious. It felt like she was being wrenched away from everything that had made her feel safe for so many years, but now holding on was the most dangerous thing she could do. She was never going to see the inside of the apartment again, the smells of paint and cooking that had merged to create something unique, the memories of all that had happened there, the love and the tears. It was all behind her now.

She thought she might black out as she finally took her place in line at security. Nor stroked her arm, whispering, 'Nearly there now,' and then they were walking through duty-free with Nor exclaiming over the new perfume from Boucheron. Once on the plane, Frankie sat with her teeth clenched. Her breathing was rapid and shallow. Every figure that appeared in the cabin, she expected to be someone who had come to manhandle her off the flight. Finally, the doors were closed but she still couldn't relax until the plane began to taxi, then she refused to stop worrying until the wheels were up and they were at last climbing through the air.

To her right, Nor smiled and patted her hand. Frankie smiled back and wanted to say something but couldn't find the words to express her gratitude. What had she done to deserve such a friend? What would her life have looked like without this unlikely guardian angel? Frankie found her breathing was finally becoming easier. She glanced out of the window and, through the patches in the cloud, saw the lights of New York. That glittering carpet which she had peered at with such wonder all those years before. She thought back to the young woman on the plane with a suitcase full of borrowed clothes. In the reflection of the dark-ened window she could see the face of the woman she had become. Almost fifty. Older than she thought she'd ever be, but other things too. Frankie Haffen had loved and been loved, seen things and met people that Frances Howe could never have imagined. All the mouths she had fed, the pay cheques she had signed. Frankie was reminded of the letter from Wendell's mother Bernice, her words of thanks. *You sound like a wonderful lady.* The woman in the window smiled. Wonderful was a bit strong, but maybe she had done some good. The clouds behind the glass became thicker, and she imagined all the ghosts she was leaving behind, all the gifts the Big Apple had given her. Silent tears began to roll down her cheeks. There was a ping. She could undo her seat belt.

London, 2024

The chirping of his phone on the chair by his bed woke Damian. It had been a long night shift in Holland Park with an elderly man who never seemed to sleep, so nor had Damian. He assumed the caller would be Nadine from the office.

'Hello.'

'Damian, is that you?' It took him a moment to place the familiar voice. It was Nor.

'Hello, yes, it's me. Is everything OK?'

There was a pause and a sort of rustle on the other end of the line.

'Oh God, Damian. So you don't know?'

'Know what?' Damian pulled himself up in the bed, trying to follow this call with his sleepy brain.

'I feel awful. I think someone contacted your agency to tell you, but, well . . . I'm afraid, darling, that our Frankie, she died.'

Damian was wide awake. 'What? When?'

'That's the awful thing. It happened a month ago. I thought you knew, but then weeks went by and I still hadn't heard – I'm so sorry. I should have called but with the arrangements and everything . . . God, I sound feeble.'

'But what happened? I feel like we texted each other just a few weeks ago.'

'A clot, they think. Into the heart. It would have been very quick. Oh Damian, I feel terrible you didn't know, just awful.'

As the meaning of Nor's words began to sink in, he allowed himself to cry. Slow, heavy tears dripped from his chin onto his chest.

'So, so have I missed the funeral?'

'There wasn't one. She didn't want a funeral. Typical Frankie. So, I've just got her ashes sitting here in my kitchen.'

'Right.' Damian was unsure of how to react to all this information. He wiped his tears away. How do you say goodbye without a funeral?

'I have something for you, something Frankie wanted you to have. Can we meet?'

'Of course, yes.' Despite his tears, he felt a jolt of excitement. What had Frankie left him?

Five days later, a smartly dressed Damian made his way to an address on Connaught Square, just north of Hyde Park. It seemed impossible that the tall building with its ornate entrance was a single house rather than flats but he could find only one bell. He was slightly taken aback when Nor herself was the one to answer the door. He had expected staff. She was wearing her usual uniform of high-collared white shirt and cascading dark beads.

'Damian! Sweet boy! Give me a hug.'

He allowed Nor to pull him into a fragrant embrace.

'Come through,' she said, making her way along a wide hallway that, in contrast to the outside of the building, was entirely modern. The floors were polished concrete, the art contemporary but discreet. Through a door on the left Damian found himself in a large, almost industrial kitchen with a dining area that ran the length of the building. On the table there was already a bowl of salad and some plates.

'How have you been? Busy?'

'Yes, you know, the usual.' He looked around. 'I like your house. It's not what I expected.'

Nor gave a short laugh. 'Ha. I had it redone after Teddy died. That's why all the furniture was in Frankie's flat. The family would never have forgiven me if I'd sold it all.'

Damian nodded. 'I wondered why it was all there.'

'Frankie complained about it endlessly but she had no furniture of her own, so . . .' She shrugged. 'Now, a glass of wine to toast our friend. White?'

'Please.'

Nor opened a large metal door and peered inside. Not finding what she was looking for, she opened a second wide door. Damian had never seen such a large fridge.

'Here it is!' Nor pulled out a bottle of wine and poured it into the glasses that were set on the table. She handed one to Damian and then walked over to the counter. She stood beside a plain pewter urn.

'To Frankie.'

'Frankie.'

They sat and Nor spooned chicken salad onto their plates.

'And there was no family in the end?' Damian asked.

'Not that we could think of. The Ropers are long gone and presumably had no children, so it was just Frankie. Perhaps that's why she didn't want a funeral?'

Damian poked at his salad, trying to avoid the olives. 'But she must have had friends. I mean, she was living here for years.'

Nor sighed and thought for a moment.

'You're young. Everything is ahead of you, but, when you get older, sometimes it can feel like it's all behind you. Does that make any sense?'

'Yes, Frankie said something like that to me. I remember her telling me that the happiest time of her life was running Pomme with Joe.'

Nor smiled. 'And that is a sort of gift, isn't it?'

Damian chewed and swallowed. 'Is it? It seems kind of sad.'

Nor touched his hand. 'No, I disagree. To know that you've known happiness, to know that you've been loved, there is a great comfort in that.'

The conversation seemed to be upsetting Nor. Damian could see the glitter of tears in her eyes. He tried to change the subject.

'But she was here for years. She must have done something? Did she not work?'

Nor grinned. 'Yes, yes she did. But it was never quite right. When she first got back, I thought I'd set her up catering for lazy rich people, but she was miserable.'

'Why?'

'Oh, honestly, I don't know. She claimed all anyone wanted was rack of lamb and dauphinoise potatoes, but I think she missed working with a team. She loved that little Pomme family.'

They paused for a moment, both of them remembering their friend sitting in her chair, coming alive as she relived her past. Nor took a sip of her wine.

'After that, she did a stint at a lovely restaurant called Café Pelican. Long gone. St Martin's Lane. But that didn't last.'

'How come?' Damian was wondering if he could just leave all the olives.

'It was ridiculous. They loved her. The owner, Karen something, was opening that chain Café Rouge – you know it?'

'I do.' Damian was relieved to find that he did know something. 'There's one by Tower Bridge, I think.'

'Yes, well they wanted our Frankie to help plan menus, train chefs, that sort of thing, but . . .' She waved one hand as if Damian knew the rest of the story.

'What? She never told me any of this.'

Nor looked to the ceiling and sighed.

'I suppose it was two things, really. She didn't like working for people, but who does?' Damian smiled in agreement. 'But I think the main problem was that she thought she was old. We all did – about ourselves, I mean. Then this happens.' She indicated herself.

Damian didn't follow. 'What?'

'You become *really* old!' Nor laughed and stood up. 'Now, unless you're desperate to eat all those olives, grab your drink and come upstairs. I've something to show you.'

Gratefully, Damian pushed himself away from the table and followed Nor into the hallway.

Upstairs, double doors led into a high-ceilinged room with tall windows overlooking the garden square. Everything seemed to be shades of white. Two low curved sofas sat on either side of a white marble coffee table, on which lay a large artist's folder covered in a red and black ikat design. Nor sat and pointed to the folder.

'For you, from Frankie.'

Damian hesitated, before sitting on the other sofa.

'Should I open it?'

'Of course. I'm curious.'

'You didn't look?'

'I swear.' Nor laughed. Damian wondered if she was telling the truth.

He untied the black ribbon and opened it. He pulled out a pile of glossy black and white photographs. He looked at the first one. It was Frankie and Joe with linked arms, mouths open in laughter, standing in front of City Hall on their wedding day. In another they were embracing, each of them with one leg kicked out behind them. The ground was covered in old confetti. Then a photograph of Joe lifting Frankie in the air. Her face was blurred in motion but her smile could still be seen.

Nor gasped. 'Oh, they look like children.' She reached across the coffee table and took the photograph. Peering closely at the faces, she said, 'If only . . . things could have been so different.'

While Nor was speaking, Damian had extracted another piece of paper. This was an original Pomme menu hand-drawn by Joe. The colours were faded but that only added to its beauty. Damian hated himself for immediately wondering how much it might be worth.

'That's gorgeous,' Nor said when she saw it. 'Just lovely. I mean you could probably sell that, but be sure to get it framed properly, use good glass. I can give you the name of a place in Islington I use.'

'Thank you.' Damian placed the menu at the far end of the table away from the wine glasses. There was something else in the portfolio. He took out a wide piece of tissue paper, behind which was a large sheet of thick drawing paper with writing on it. Damian held it up and read aloud, 'Dearest Frankie, a small token of . . .' He hesitated. 'I can't make that out, anyway . . . for all the wine and all the food. Love always . . .' He squinted. 'Cecil, maybe?' He looked over at Nor, who was sitting slack-jawed. Her eyes were wide with shock at the sight of whatever was on the other side of the paper. Damian turned it over to see a series of grey loops and scribbles.

'What is it? What's wrong?'

Nor composed herself.

'All right, Damian, this is what you must do – no, you're a grown man, you can do what you like, but this is what I strongly suggest. First, put it back in the portfolio with the tissue paper.' Damian did as he was told and Nor visibly relaxed. 'That drawing is by someone called Cy Twombly and it's worth – well,

I don't want to pluck a number out of the air, but it will be life-changing.'

'Really?' Damian was finding it hard to believe this. The drawing really did not seem special in any way.

'You may not like it, that's fine. But trust me, I suggest you go straight to Sotheby's on Bond Street after here and ask them to appraise it for you. I think it might be best to allow them to store it for you as well. I mean, I haven't seen your house, but I doubt you want something that valuable lying around.'

Damian just nodded. Nor's intensity was infectious and he now felt nervous just sitting beside the portfolio.

'I'm . . . I don't know what to say. It's mad. Why me?'

Nor smiled. 'She was very fond of you. Just you listening to her stories meant so much to her. I know it doesn't seem a great deal but letting her relive everything, well, you gave her her life back. This is her way of repaying you, I suppose. Good old Frankie. I'm so happy for you.' Nor raised her glass. 'To Frankie.'

'Frankie,' Damian repeated.

'But all the fuss about the rest of the art. Gretchen and who owned it and all of that. Can I sell this?' He touched the folder.

Nor drained her glass. 'Yes, the inscription makes it clear it was a gift to Frankie, so it's hers to give to you.'

'And what about everything else? What's going to happen to all of that?'

'Frankie did what she thought was right. She always did, rather like Pomme.'

Damian leaned forward. 'Oh yeah, what happened to the restaurant when she left?'

Nor gave a little smirk. 'Frankie donated it to the Whitney Museum. The whole thing. Little Miss Gretchen was probably livid but what could she do? It's The Haffen Café now. So strange to see it, all inside a glass box, full of tourists, milling around.'

'So has she left the art to a museum as well?'

'No.' Nor paused. 'She left it all to Luca Haffen.'

'So, Gretchen . . . ?'

'Might see some of the money – it all depends how close she is to her son. He's selling the lot. There's going to be a sale at Christie's this October. They might include your Twombly if you hurry. I think this calls for champagne, don't you?'

Damian did.

One bottle quickly disappeared, and a second was opened. Nor was now sitting beside Damian, her head on his shoulder.

'I'll have to phone the office. I can't go to work now.' Damian said what he had been thinking for almost an hour.

'Work? God, no.' Nor sounded appalled. 'You should go out, celebrate. Do you have a special someone yet?'

'Me? No, no I don't.'

They were silent for a moment and then, emboldened by the champagne, he asked Nor, 'What about you, do you have a girl-friend or a wife?'

For a moment Nor's expression made Damian fear he had said the wrong thing, but then a slow smile spread across her face.

'No. That was not the life I lived.' She wrapped an arm around his shoulder as if they were bonded by this, but Damian wanted to protest. That wasn't the life he saw for himself.

'Did you not want to meet someone?'

She curled her lip and shrugged. 'There was Teddy, of course. No!' She slapped Damian's arm playfully. 'Don't pull that face. We might not have been a conventional couple but we adored each other in our own way.'

She reached for the bottle and topped up their glasses unsteadily. She seemed quite drunk.

'But there were girlfriends too, right?'

'Oh, various lady friends over the years. I was no nun. I honestly think I was busier on that front than Teddy.'

'But no love of your life?'

It seemed like such an innocent question, but Nor's face crumpled and her hand covered her mouth. Tears trailed slowly down her cheeks.

'Oh, Nor. I'm so sorry. What is it? What did I say?'

Nor gasped and tried to control her tears. 'Oh, you silly, silly boy. Don't you know that I've just lost the love of my life.' She bowed her head and wiped the tears from her face.

And as the evening gloom enveloped the large white room, Damian held the grieving lover to his chest and let her sob.

Two months later, Damian got the bus into Piccadilly, walked along Jermyn Street and down into St James's Square, unaware that he was following Frankie's footsteps on her first night in London, heading to Van Everden's party. Leaving the square, he saw the large red flags of Christie's flapping outside the imposing building. As he drew closer, he could see posters in each window. There was a moody black and white photograph of Frankie, which Damian hadn't seen before, and, above it, lettering in the style of Joseph Haffen that announced 'The Collection of Frances Howe'.

Damian half expected to be stopped as he walked through the glass doors but the uniformed man just nodded. Following the signs, he headed up the wide staircase. It was so strange to see all the paintings that had hung in a dusty mosaic on the walls of the flat in Wapping. Here, they each had their own space and light. Damian wondered if it was just his imagination but some of them did look very special. He walked slowly, trying to look like an art lover, while surreptitiously checking the small cards on the wall to see the estimated value of each piece. He recalled burning toast while these objects were hanging on the walls next door. Damian felt slightly sick. Sotheby's had convinced him to allow them to sell his Cy Twombly drawing. He wouldn't know precisely how much he had till the sale next April, but he already found himself scrolling through flats on Zoopla and Rightmove.

He moved from room to room until he turned a corner, and there it was. The painting nobody knew Frankie had until she died. It had been rolled up under her bed, but now the large canvas was hanging alone in the centre of the end wall of the gallery. Damian wasn't sure if it was the way it was lit, but it seemed to glow. The little card explained that the painting was the only known portrait that Joseph Haffen had ever completed. It was entitled *Frankie, Spring Street*.

Damian stepped back to see the picture properly. A young Frankie was naked and leaning against a table. She was laughing. The red bandana in her hair seemed to be alive and trying to escape from her head. The loft window-frames behind her were strange bone shapes and the world beyond wasn't the industrial wasteland of reality but a fecund world of jungle greenery. Frankie's eyes stared from the picture, unembarrassed, just full of love as she watched Joe at work.

Small groups of people were dotted around the gallery. Some were muttering about Haffen's work, others were gazing at the painting. Damian's chin began to quiver. His friend was gone but here she was, young and happy forever. Damian wiped away a tear and smiled to himself. Frankie was finally the centre of attention.

Acknowledgements

I'm not sure this book qualifies as historical fiction, but it did require me to do some research. Unsure if I'd enjoy that aspect of the writing, I was a little hesitant, but it was in fact a huge pleasure. As well as my good friend Google, I also consulted a wide range of books, some of which I can heartily recommend.

David Higham's autobiography, *Literary Gent*, and *Home*, the first volume of Julie Andrews' memoirs, were both very helpful. Maeve Brennan's book of essays, *The Long-Winded Lady*, along with *The Bell Jar* by Sylvia Plath, provided a real sense of the New York that Frankie arrives in.

Sneden's Landing is an actual place and local resident Alice Gerard has written several wonderful histories of the area. I'd also like to thank Nick and Cass Luddington, surviving relatives of Gert Macy, who appears at the ill-fated party. Katherine Cornell was indeed a huge Broadway star, but some of the other attendees are fictitious.

Leo Castelli did exist and his gallery lives on, though it has since moved from its location on 77th Street. The gallery's website contains a wonderful archive of all the exhibitions that were held during the sixties and seventies. Calvin Tompkins' 1976 book *The Scene: Reports on Post-Modern Art* was also very useful, though you may have to search though second-hand book shops to find a copy.

So many wonderful and important books came out of the AIDS epidemic in the eighties, but *Ground Zero* – a book of essays by Andrew Holleran – and John Weir's sweet novel, *The Irreversible Decline of Eddie Socket*, were two of my favourites. The final words Joe whispers to Frankie are a version of something said by Gaëtan Dugas, the Canadian flight attendant erroneously identified as 'Patient Zero'.

I have tried to be accurate throughout, apart from the odd occasion when the facts didn't suit my fiction.

The good people at Coronet and Hodder continue to astound me with their enthusiasm and support. Top of the list has to be my editor Hannah Black, who always makes me feel like a novelist rather than a chat-show host with *notions*. Tom Atkins keeps everything running smoothly. Thanks go to Amber Burlinson and Jacqui Lewis for getting the text up to scratch. Anna Morrison and Saffron Stocker made this book a beautiful thing to behold, for which I'm very grateful. Claudette Morris miraculously turned it into a physical thing on shelves. Emma Knight and Rebecca Mundy, along with Vicky Palmer and Alice Morley, told the world about *Frankie*, while Jennifer Wilson and Richard Peters look after sales. Dominic Gribben created the audiobook with the wonderful team at Heavy Entertainment – apologies for the accents. Rebecca Folland sells the rights around the world, and of course I must thank head honcho Oli Malcolm. I'm also indebted to the Hachette teams in Australia, New Zealand, and especially Jim Binchy and Elaine Egan in Ireland. Without all of these people you would not be reading these words.

Many thanks to Anthony Butler, Gaby Jerrard and Ali Day for making the *Frankie* book tour so fun. Thanks also to all the audiences up and down the land.

The team at YMU who make sure I have the time to write, headed up by the GOAT, Melanie Rockcliffe, along with Rebekka

Frankie

Taylor and Charly Briscombe, and not forgetting Amanda Harris of the literary division.

Rebecca Nicholass keeps the wheels on the bus and everything else. Life would be chaotic without her diligence and never-failing good humour.

And finally, all the thank yous to Jono. Enjoy the brief interlude before I start wanging on about the next book.